# CHAINS OF DUTY

---

## SURVIVAL WARS BOOK 3

## ANTHONY JAMES

Cover Design by Dan Van Oss www.covermint.design

Follow Anthony James on Facebook at facebook.com/anthonyjamesauthor.

# THE BEGINNING

Halfway across the Garon sector from humanity's nearest populated world, the prospector *SC Lupus* emerged from lightspeed into a barely-charted solar system, which consisted of an average sun orbited by nine equally average planets.

"Captain Carlson? We're fifty minutes from the fourth planet," said 2$^{nd}$ Lieutenant John Houston.

Captain Eva Carlson nodded, though her expression of concentration didn't change. She continued to examine a series of data streams on her primary monitor. The ship's sensors fed through the results of their first scan and blue text flew across Carlson's screen at a speed which seemed far too quick for a human brain to comprehend.

"It's nice to know the mainframe on this old bucket can get it right once in a while," said Ensign Seb Lynch. "Last system we visited, it took us a day on the gravities to get where we should have been."

"It was only nineteen hours," said Carlson, finally dragging her attention away.

"Have you found anything, Captain?" asked Houston. "Want me to take a look?"

"I don't think there's any need just yet, Lieutenant. It's as I thought – we don't have enough data to make an informed decision. The last time a scout ship came here was thirty years ago and they didn't stay for long."

"We're going to go in close and do it by hand, huh?" asked Lynch. He knew absolutely nothing about geology and had no idea why they'd assigned him to a vessel designed for the specific purpose of discovering new and viable planets for the Confederation's mining operations.

"It looks that way, Ensign," said Carlson. She was usually happy to put up with Lynch's questions – he had the makings of a good officer once he decided where to specialise. For now, he was covering most of the comms and engines work, allowing the other two to focus on deciphering the reams of data they'd scooped up from the four solar systems they'd stopped at so far. Finding new resources wasn't quite needle in a haystack work, but Carlson would be first to admit there was an element of luck involved. A skilled crew could improve the odds, yet there were times when the *Lupus* had come home after six months of searching with nothing to show for it.

"Glantia-312 is what they've called the sun," said Lynch, repeating what they already knew. "I wonder how much they pay the guys who name all this stuff. Do you think the salary is good?"

Carlson gave a shrug. It was a gesture that said many things, depending on her mood. At the moment, it was saying *stop asking stupid questions.* She waved Houston over. The bridge on the prospector was large, well-lit and furnished with expensive, padded chairs – the Space Corps' scientists expected a little more comfort than soldiers and they usually got what they wanted. The reasoning behind it was fairly straightforward – a soldier who was kept in cramped quarters for weeks on end would be more inclined to fight than one who spent his or her life cosseted and happy. On the other hand, if you kept a scientist or researcher in those same conditions, they'd never work at peak efficiency. There was no proof behind any of this apparently smooth logic and the truth of it was rarely challenged.

"I've had a quick look already, Captain," said Houston. "We can discount six of the planets right off the bat. Two of them are too hot, two of them too cold and two of them just outright hostile."

"I agree," said Carlson. "The largest planet here might be viable for further checks, but I can see a storm over it that's almost fifteen thousand klicks across. I don't think the guys below would be too pleased if we dropped them off there."

"That leaves us with just the last two," said Houston, leaning over her shoulder for a better look at the sensor data. Images of both planets appeared on a screen, each as dull and featureless as the other. "This one's about Old Earth sized and this other one fifty percent larger. Which one takes your fancy?"

"Neither," replied Carlson truthfully. The Glantia-312 system was the last stop for the *Lupus* and after that, Carlson was due almost a month of leave. Nevertheless, she knew her duty and had no intention of leaving without checking out these two planets to see what metals were held in their crusts. They still had the Resource Base Establishment Dropship in the cargo bay – a kilometre worth of men and machinery ready to be deployed wherever there was enough metal to make it worthwhile. Carlson knew her superiors would be disappointed if she returned with the RBED still unused. She sighed. "We're closest to the largest planet. Let's get that one out of the way first. Ensign, can you give me a detailed sweep of the surface, please? I need a topographical and atmospheric scan."

"Yes sir!" Lynch replied. "Should be ready in a few minutes."

"I'm taking us towards the surface. Let's get this over and done with quickly and efficiently."

Carlson powered up the gravity engines. The prospector wasn't fast and didn't need to be. They weren't meant to face danger and their crews expected to be away from home for a long time. It was too expensive to fit bigger engines in spacecraft like this, especially with the current drain on Gallenium from the Space Corps' extensive ship-building programme. Besides, bigger engines would have needed an overhaul of the basic design and there wasn't much appetite for that.

"There's not much of an atmosphere to speak of," said Lynch. "Nitrogen at fifteen percent. Oxygen at zero-point-one percent. Inert gases at two percent. All the usual run-of-the-mill stuff. I'm sending the latest data to you."

The atmospheric data popped up on Carlson's screen and she scanned it idly. "It says oxygen at zero-point-two percent here," she said.

"It was definitely point-one," said Lynch. "See, look here." He went silent for a moment. "That's not right. I'll do a quick check on the sensor calibration."

Houston had taken an interest now. "What have we got?" he asked.

"The oxygen level is at point-two-two now," said Lynch. "It's climbing."

Carlson frowned. "Are you sure those sensors are reading right?"

"As sure as I can be. We have three independent front arrays, all of them reporting exactly the same thing into the mainframe. I don't know anything about rocks, but I'm sure this isn't meant to happen."

Carlson winced inwardly at Lynch's reduction of her entire profession to the word *rocks*. "Keep an eye on it and continue with your scan." She already knew they couldn't leave until they'd found out more about the anomalous oxygen readings and they certainly couldn't pretend they hadn't noticed, since there was a good chance the audit logs would betray them later.

After another twenty minutes, Lynch called out with an update on his progress. "I'm detecting metal on the surface."

"Just lying there, waiting to be picked up?" asked Houston. He realised he'd sounded a bit harsh. "Sorry."

"Not metal ore, sir," said Lynch. "A metal object of some type."

"Have there been reports of missing spacecraft in this area?" asked Carlson.

"None that I'm aware of," said Houston.

"We're definitely not at war with the Ghasts anymore, are we?" asked Lynch.

"Our instructions are to report any sightings, but hostilities are at a temporary end," said Carlson. "If those are Ghasts down there, we should take a look and confirm. What size is the object?" She'd also been given instructions to watch out for anything else unrecognized, Ghast or otherwise. Her superiors hadn't given specifics and had warned that the information was top-secret.

"I'd say it's more than kilometre to each side and nearly as much tall. The mainframe's estimation is that it's regular like a pyramid, rather than anything spacecraft-shaped. The oxygen's up to point-three. Do you want me to have a guess at something, Captain?" asked Lynch.

"Fire away, Ensign."

"The atmospheric levels of oxygen aren't uniform. In fact, they're at almost zero across much of the surface. They're at their greatest intensity within a few thousand klicks of the object. Like it's throwing out oxygen."

"Get on the comms," said Carlson at once. "Highest priority message to the base on Atlantis."

Lynch made a few gestures across his panel. An expression of worry appeared that he made no effort to disguise. "I'm getting nothing on the comms, sir," he said. "Not even static."

Carlson chewed her lip. Something was wrong and she knew she had to act quickly. "Take us to lightspeed," she said. "Immediately."

"Right you are, sir," said Lynch. "It's going to be a few minutes until we can launch."

With a feeling of dread, Carlson turned the nose of the *Lupus* away from the planet. She wanted to put some distance between her ship and the surface object while the deep fission engines got ready.

"There's something heading towards us," said Lynch. "It's coming directly from the planet's surface at about two thousand klicks per second. Our sensors are struggling to pick it up at that speed."

"What is it?" asked Carlson. "How did you miss it?"

"We're a prospector, sir, not a warship. Our equipment doesn't see everything," said Lynch. "It's over two klicks in length."

"How long until it can fire?" asked Carlson.

"If you're asking are we going to reach lightspeed before the inbound craft reaches likely weapons range, I'm going to have to disappoint you." Lynch sounded deadly calm and Carlson remembered that he'd served for a time on an Anderlecht cruiser. He sounded every bit like a military man now.

The SC *Lupus* was still more than five minutes from escape when it was destroyed. The approaching ship fired a powerful particle beam, which swept through the *Lupus'* engines and hull, melting a huge chunk of the vessel's structure. This first attack killed the eighty men and women who were stationed on the RBED in the hold, heating the air and burning them alive within moments. A warship would have had sufficient engine mass to disperse the first strike, while the *Lupus* was easy prey. The second beam strike followed soon after, killing the remaining crew. The last thing which went through Carlson's mind before she perished in the superheated air, was regret that she'd failed the people onboard. There was no way for her to know that their deaths had been inevitable as soon as they'd arrived in the Glantia-312 system.

# CHAPTER ONE

CAPTAIN JOHN NATHAN DUGGAN SHIVERED. It wasn't
the temperature in his office which made him do so – though it
was admittedly a couple of degrees colder on the *Juniper* than
he'd have liked. Rather, it was the words on his screen which
made him feel cold. *Fleet Admiral Slender confirmed dead,* was
the opening sentence on the file. Duggan stared at the details for
a few moments longer. He'd read the file a hundred times
without knowing if he felt relief or happiness. Deep down, he
couldn't bring himself to feel either – the most suitable description was that he felt nothing.

The file was top secret and he closed it off his screen. There
was nobody in his office, but he didn't want to leave it there for
everyone to see. At the moment, it was hush-hush, presumably
while the Space Corps frantically tried to come up with the best
story to explain what had happened. The Dreamers had killed
him, yet the news of this new alien threat was deemed too
dangerous to be given to all and sundry – at least while the business with the Ghasts was still to be concluded.

A message pinged into his inbox and he sighed when he read

the subject. It was another one of the countless humdrum memos which clogged up his mailbox day in and day out. The more such messages he received, the less time he had to deal with other issues. Before he could send a bluntly-worded reply, his communicator chimed softly to alert him to a priority voice call. Duggan saw who it was and accepted it immediately.

"Captain Duggan? I need you in my office at once." It was Admiral Teron, his tone of voice neutral.

"Yes, sir," Duggan replied and ended the call.

The conversation had been terse, since neither man liked to waste words on niceties. Duggan stood and headed towards the door, hardly noticing the utterly anonymous furnishings around the office he'd been assigned to for the last two months. The door slid open and he turned left along the metal-walled corridor. Men and women passed him by, one or two smiling absently as he made his way along. He had no idea what the Admiral wanted and he hadn't spoken to Teron directly in over a week. The familiar plasmetal door whisked aside once the *Juniper*'s AI had decided that Duggan was permitted to enter.

"Come in!" said Admiral Teron from the recesses of his office.

Duggan wasn't shy and had covered several paces within before the words reached him. He'd visited this room so often it felt like a home. The light in the office was average and amplified by the glow of a dozen status screens around the walls. Someone who was less familiar with Teron might have thought they were for show. Duggan knew they were not – the Admiral had an excellent eye for detail and liked to keep a watch on everything that was going on.

"Good morning, sir," said Duggan. Since the death of Fleet Admiral Slender in the Dreamer attack at the Helius Blackstar, life had become a bit more straightforward and Duggan found he wasn't looking over his shoulder all the time. He'd almost got to the stage where he'd forgiven Teron for tricking him into flying the *Crimson* on its mission to destroy the Ghast planet Lioxi. Teron had always been a man who liked to find order amid chaos and Duggan was willing to accept the Admiral had been acting in what he thought were the best interests of the Confederation.

"Have a seat, please," said Teron, gesturing with one thick-fingered hand. The plasma scars on his neck burned more vividly than usual today.

Duggan sat and met the Admiral's gaze. "I'm going somewhere?"

Teron grunted. "Never one to mince your words, were you?" Then, he laughed gruffly. "I swear that ninety percent of the people I deal with spend their lives making unimportant comments about unimportant things. I don't have the time for it. You *are* going somewhere and we'll get to that in just a moment."

Duggan's skin prickled with rising excitement. He'd been posted on the *Juniper* as part of an extensive debriefing ever since the vast Dreamer mothership had destroyed much of the human and Ghast fleet at the Helius Blackstar. The Space Corps wanted him to be available at all times to speak to representatives of its many divisions about the coming threat. If they'd put him on a warship and sent him on a mission somewhere, he would be incommunicado when travelling at lightspeed. Even worse, he might end up getting killed and his store of knowledge lost with him. Duggan didn't especially enjoy being confined to the *Juniper*, but he accepted the necessity. As it happened, he was kept constantly busy and he found it refreshing that he could provide input and be listened to. *How one man's death has changed things,* he thought.

"The Space Corps believes my fonts of intel have been emptied, sir?" he asked.

"I'm sure you've had enough of being grilled, Captain Duggan. I've decided it's time to move you on to something else."

Duggan raised a mental eyebrow at Teron's choice of words – the suggestion that it was the Admiral's choice to do this, rather than having to wait for confirmation elsewhere. "Is it to do with the Dreamers, sir? Do we have something new on them?"

A brief look of irritation came over Teron's face - he didn't like to be second-guessed. "We don't know what it's about, Captain Duggan, that's what you're here for. One of our prospectors has gone missing out in the Garon sector – the SC *Lupus*, though I doubt you've heard the name. It's just one ship amongst many."

"It didn't send out a distress signal, I assume?"

"No, we've heard nothing from it. They were due to dock at the Atlantis main spaceport a few days ago. They stopped broadcasting over a week back."

"Could they have landed in a place with so much ore the planet's density has prevented them sending their status reports?" Duggan was clutching at straws, more in desperation than anything else. If a spacecraft had gone missing, it was hard to avoid concluding the unthinkable.

"It's not very likely. We believe something has happened to the *Lupus*. I'm sure you know what that means."

"Do we trust the Ghasts?" he asked. "Or do the stats teams say it's Dreamer?"

Teron sighed and took a piece of paper from his desk. "If you want the exact breakdown, the Projections Team has provided a weighting of five percent for accidental ship destruction, thirty-five percent for a rogue or planned Ghast attack, with the remaining sixty percent attributed to *an unknown alien threat*. You can draw your own conclusions. Furthermore, we've asked the Ghasts to stay away from the Garon sector while negotiations take place, so they shouldn't be anywhere near. From what I've heard, our former enemies take pride in their trustworthiness."

There were few people better-placed than Teron to hear how

the peace negotiations were proceeding. In fact, Duggan wouldn't have been surprised if the Admiral had a part in directing them. The death of Admiral Slender had opened doors for more than just Duggan.

"I hope that's the case, sir, I truly do."

"The Ghasts are never going to be liked after what they've done, but we can at least hope they have enough redeeming qualities that we never need to face war with them again." Teron's face twisted in anger. "Not that we'd give them another chance at it." The expression vanished as quickly as it had arrived. "Have you heard of the ES *Terminus*?"

Duggan racked his brains. The Space Corps was producing new ships at such a rate it was difficult to keep track of them and the impending peace with the Ghasts hadn't slowed the building programme one bit. Suddenly, the name prompted his memory. "The first of our new heavy cruisers," intoned Duggan. "Designed to fill in the operational requirements for a vessel larger than an Anderlecht, yet smaller than a Hadron. A direct rival to the Ghast Cadaverons."

"Indeed," said Teron. "We laid down three such hulls a number of years ago. The work was mothballed during the cuts, but luckily, they weren't dismantled. As a consequence, we were able to proceed with the work on these vessels once our funding levels were increased. The ES *Terminus* is the first of its kind to reach completion." Teron leaned forward. "Captain Duggan, you will be the first person to captain it."

For once, Duggan was lost for words. "Sir?"

"You're a good man, Duggan and one of our best officers. Your treatment has been tantamount to criminal and I include myself as party to it. Things have changed now." He let those last words hang in the air.

"Where am I taking the *Terminus*, sir?"

Teron laughed for the second time. "Don't be too happy,

Captain Duggan. We wouldn't be the Space Corps if everything was easy. The *Terminus* is going to look for the *Lupus*. At least that's what your order sheet says - in reality, you're searching for our enemy."

It was Duggan's turn to laugh this time, a mixture of giddy excitement and cynicism. "You weren't joking, were you? It's a suicide mission to go looking for the Dreamers. How many did they destroy from our combined fleets? Ten? Twelve?"

"Fourteen warships lost, as it happens. That was the mother-ship. You managed to bring down one of their smaller fighters."

"It was a close-run thing!" said Duggan. "Without the *Ghotesh-Q* to launch its Shatterers, we'd have been destroyed. Wouldn't it be better to send out the *Crimson* again?"

"From a purely martial standpoint, I'm sure you're right. However, this time the *Crimson* is going nowhere. We've made strides in copying certain parts of the processing core– it's really quite advanced and much of it is still beyond us. We've learned a great deal from the disruptors and the engine design, but again it's nothing we can fully replicate – at least not on the scale neces-sary to place on a warship."

"You mean we can partially copy this stuff?"

Teron's face went blank as he considered his words. "In bits and pieces. We can recreate the core design at a molecular level, we simply can't scale it up yet. The lab could make you an *outstandingly* fast wristwatch if you wanted one. Otherwise, we're not quite there when it comes to making something that could run a fleet warship. On the plus side, our next generation beam weapons will be smaller and with a longer range. We esti-mate we'll be on a par with what the Ghasts have been producing for the last year or two. It's a start."

Duggan got the impression Teron was hiding something. He knew the Admiral well enough to pick up the nuances in his behaviour. "There's something else, isn't there?" he asked.

Teron didn't have the good grace to look guilty. "There's always something else, Captain Duggan," he said dismissively. "I thought you'd have learned that by now. In this case, you'll be accompanied by a second warship. A Ghast vessel – the Oblivion class *Dretisear*."

Duggan was too much an old hand at these games to be surprised. "I think it's a good idea, sir."

Teron had clearly expected to deal with objections, so he launched into his speech anyway. "The Dreamers are an enemy to both sides. After much deliberation, we considered it for the best that we undertake this as a joint exercise. It will demonstrate to the Ghasts that we are willing to trust them and to work with them."

"And we need their Shatterer missiles to do the business for us if we come across any more Dreamers."

"Maybe and maybe not," said Teron cryptically. "There is more to this exercise than you might think, Captain Duggan. On the one hand, we have the Dreamers to contend with, but we would be fools to discount the Ghasts as an ongoing danger. We're sending our newest ship along with one of our best captains as a show of force. The *Terminus* punches above its weight as it was always intended to. Why make a new ship that's the equal of what the enemy has? This is why we insisted they send an Oblivion, rather than a Cadaveron. We want them to see what our heavy cruisers are capable of."

"The Space Corps must really be confident," said Duggan.

Teron smiled a grim smile. "We are," he said. "The hull of the *Terminus* was ready and we've had ample time to fit in the latest and best we've got. Humanity never moves faster than when its existence is threatened and we've had enough development money to make a few leaps of our own in the last year and a half."

"I'll need my crew," said Duggan.

"Take whoever you need, as long as they're already here on

the *Juniper*. The *Terminus* has been stationed in near space outside the orbital for two hours. For once you've been given a warship that won't fit inside one of the hangars."

"We're to find out what happened to the *Lupus*, flex our muscles at the Ghasts and destroy any hostile aliens we meet?"

"That sums it up nicely," said Teron. "The *Lupus* was assigned to an area of space that is almost mid-way between the Helius Blackstar and Atlantis. We have more than ten billion people living on Atlantis. I don't need to remind you we're getting ever nearer to Hyptron. We have eight of our populated planets in that sector. It's the second-most populated area of Confederation Space, with over one hundred billion people living across those eight worlds."

"If the Dreamers get there, all our recent successes against the Ghasts will have been for nothing," said Duggan.

"Exactly. There's a lot riding on this, Captain Duggan. We have additional ships searching the other solar systems on the *Lupus'* logs, but you're going the furthest out. If you discover anything, let us know as soon as possible."

"Will do, sir," said Duggan. "Permission to find my crew and board a shuttle to the *ES Terminus*?"

"Granted."

# CHAPTER TWO

THE *JUNIPER* WAS immense – easily the largest object mankind had ever sent into space. Fortunately for Duggan, the orbital's internal communications systems were excellent and it didn't take long to locate the people he needed to speak to. He had to countermand one or two orders in order to get things moving and in the end, he got what he wanted. The report sheets for the *Terminus* told him there was already a full complement of troops onboard, but there was always room to squeeze in a few more.

The *Juniper* had a number of small, personnel transport shuttle docks, to avoid the intrusive procedures necessary to open the gargantuan doors to the main hangar bays. By the time Duggan reached the transport, there was already a familiar face onboard. The vessel was faithful to its type, being little more than a brightly-lit metal box, with a number of worn seats and a single viewscreen. There were plenty of luxury models available, but the Space Corps tried not to be overtly wasteful in its usage of taxpayer funds.

"We're moving out?" asked Lieutenant Frank Chainer from his seat. "Why all this cloak and dagger stuff, sir?"

"What cloak and dagger, Lieutenant?" asked Duggan, slightly bemused at the accusation.

"It feels like we're sneaking off the *Juniper*. Don't we normally climb into whatever Gunner is waiting in the hangar bays?"

"Not this time," said Duggan.

Commander Lucy McGlashan and Lieutenant Bill Breeze arrived on the shuttle and he greeted them. Seniority allowed Duggan his choice of officers and these were the three he wanted. In other circumstances, they might have already been assigned to a new ship. As it was, they'd been subjected to the same extensive debriefing as Duggan, which had kept them here on the orbital.

"Sir," said Breeze, nodding his head and smiling. Then, he remembered procedure and offered a salute. His eyes were sharp and he looked eager to be on his way.

"Good morning, sir," said McGlashan. "Many more to come?"

"Just a few," said Duggan. "I doubt they'll be long."

"There were some proper miserable bastards getting off this shuttle when it docked," said Chainer. "It looked like they'd been dismissed from the Corps or something. There were a couple of officers amongst them."

Duggan guessed who they were – the officers from the *ES Terminus* who had been taken off the ship in order to make room for Duggan's own crew. He didn't worry about it too much – if you couldn't accept your toes being trodden on every so often, you weren't tough enough to make the really hard decisions.

The sound of footsteps made Duggan turn. A small complement of soldiers had arrived, dressed in smart blue uniforms. They weren't allowed to carry their gauss rifles around the orbital without specific clearance and they looked lost without them.

"Sir!" said Sergeant Ortiz. "Corporal Bryant is with me, along with infantrymen Flores, Butler, Dorsey and Morgan."

The men and women stood smartly to attention in the enclosed interior of the shuttle. "What about Santos?" asked Duggan.

"I have no idea where he's gone to, sir," said Ortiz. "I thought we'd all been ordered to stay on the *Juniper*."

"You had," said Duggan. "Never mind, there's always someone who slips through the net. He's probably safer wherever he is."

"Will there be action, sir?" asked Ortiz. Her expression and words were full of longing. The obvious yearning might have worried Duggan if he hadn't seen Ortiz in action. She could be gung-ho, but never suicidal.

"There's always that chance, Sergeant. Assuming we don't get blown up before we can disembark."

"When one threat recedes, another rises to take its place," she said, revealing her thoughts about the nature of the mission.

Duggan didn't confirm or deny anything. "Take a seat please. We need to be on our way."

The shuttle had no pilot and remained under the direct control of the *Juniper*'s AIs. The outer door whirred closed, sealing them inside. There was a clunk and a shuddering scrape to indicate the shuttle had detached from its moorings. The feeling of acceleration which followed was so slight it was easy to miss. The *Juniper* did everything by the book and the shuttle's exit from its launch bay was perfect. The internal viewscreen remained stubbornly blank, depriving them of what would be a magnificent sight as the orbital receded slowly away behind them.

"So, where *are* we going, sir?" asked Chainer, struggling to contain his curiosity.

Duggan didn't like to keep secrets just for the sake of it and they'd find out soon enough. "I've been given command of the *ES Terminus*. It's the Space Corps' first Galactic class heavy cruiser."

"A heavy cruiser? Wow, sir!" said Chainer. "They've finally seen sense and put you in charge of something decent?"

"I've not had time to study the spec sheets yet," said Duggan, smiling at Chainer's enthusiasm. "Admiral Teron assures me it's special. Let's wait till we get there."

As if prompted by his words the transport's internal screen flickered, before the picture settled on a distant object. The shuttle's sensors zoomed in once and then twice more, until the object filled the display. The image appeared grainy and blurred at first. Then, the sensors resolved the details and snapped them into focus. Without anything for comparison, it was difficult to judge exactly how big the spacecraft was, but when you'd seen enough of them it became easy to make a good guess.

"That's it?" asked Breeze, his mouth half-open.

Duggan stood from his seat in order to get a closer view of the warship. After he'd left Teron's office earlier he'd called up computer-generated image of the *Terminus* to study. It hadn't been enough to properly convey the menace possessed by the spacecraft.

"Even if none of the weapons were functioning, I wouldn't want to face it," said Chainer, his eyes fixed on the screen.

Like a dying man reaching for salvation, Duggan lifted his arm and traced a finger along the outline of the ship. It was clearly a Space Corps design, yet took cues from some of the older Ghast Oblivions. The result was a ship which could have looked like a patchwork of ideas, yet instead fitted together into something that was entirely new. The front third was a wedge, with a dome beneath. The centre third was sleek and flat, while the aft was thicker, with rounded edges. There was at least one more particle beam housing mounted there. The *Terminus* looked mean and fast.

"The Space Corps must be expecting trouble if they're sending that?" said McGlashan.

"You've seen what we're facing," said Duggan. "We've got nothing that will last against the Dreamers' technology. The Admiral told me the engineers have done what they can, but I doubt it's going to be enough. We're going to need brains for this one, as well as whatever weaponry the *Terminus* is carrying." He took a deep breath. "We won't be alone, either."

"What else are they sending with us?" asked McGlashan. "Another couple of Galactics?"

"The others aren't due to enter service for a few weeks, Commander. Our companions for this particular mission will be familiar to all of you. They're sending an Oblivion with us - the *Dretisear*. This isn't just about the Dreamers, it's about showing the Ghasts what exactly the human race is capable of."

He caught Ortiz grinning as she heard the words. "Maybe we'll get to fight next to them, sir. Show them what a real soldier can do."

"Maybe," said Duggan, unwilling to be drawn into a discussion on it. "Anyway, folks, there's our home for the next few weeks. At least this time we can't complain they haven't given us the tools to do our jobs properly."

"I only wish that for once we could be facing an inferior enemy, rather than a vastly superior one," said Chainer.

"Where would be the fun in that?" asked McGlashan.

"I'd settle for a bit less fun and a higher chance of survival," grumbled Chainer.

The transport came ever closer to the *ES Terminus*. The image of the warship remained a constant size on the viewscreen, as the sensors adjusted the scale. It made it impossible to judge how far away they were, but a countdown appeared in one corner of the monitor to let them know how long until they docked. Duggan regretted he'd not brought a hand-held tablet with him, since he dearly wanted to start checking the technical capabilities of the warship. He'd been so focused on other things when he'd packed his few belongings into a kitbag that he'd forgotten to do so.

The external image of the ES *Terminus* changed. The warship no longer remained static on the screen – it came closer and closer. The docking countdown indicated there were only a few minutes to go and the people in the passenger bay started to shift impatiently with the imminence of their arrival. A port opened towards the rear of the *Terminus*, appearing as an area of image-intensified darkness against the grey alloy.

"Even got our own shuttle bay," said Flores nervously.

"How else did you think we were going to get onboard?" asked Dorsey. "Put on a suit and float over the gap?"

Flores didn't rise to the bait. "Yeah, maybe I didn't think it through."

The unlit dock filled most of the screen and Duggan admitted to himself he wouldn't have enjoyed trying to fit into the bay with the transport under manual control. There were some things you just had to trust to the computers. There was no sensation of deceleration, though the view from outside indicated they'd slowed to a crawl. A gentle thump was followed by the clunking sounds of magnetic clamps latching onto the transporter's hull. A green light appeared over the door, to let them know it was unlocked and safe to open. Duggan didn't wait. He stabbed at the release button with his forefinger and tapped his foot for the few seconds it took for the door to open outwards and form a ramp.

The compact docking bay was bathed in deep red light, with a single exit behind a sealed airlock door. Duggan marched across the solid metal floor, the sound of his footsteps muffled by the thickness of the metal. While the others scrambled to gather their belongings and follow, Duggan disengaged the door locks and watched as the square of metal sank away into the aperture and then slid to one side on heavy-duty runners. The walls were about three metres thick here and the door itself almost as deep. He paused on the threshold and closed his eyes, as he always did before he stepped onto a new warship. A faint draught washed over him, bringing tepid air and the sharp-edged scent of metal. It was the impersonal disdain of a killer.

The others gathered behind him and Duggan wondered if they experienced the same feelings he did. McGlashan's expression gave nothing away and she craned to see into the room beyond the door.

"Come on," said Duggan. "Let's see what the Space Corps has given us to defend against our enemies." With that, he walked ahead and onto the ES *Terminus*.

# CHAPTER THREE

DUGGAN REALISED how ill-prepared he was, since he didn't even know how to reach the bridge. Whilst McGlashan grinned, he called up the ship's plans on a wall screen in the room beyond the airlock. The bridge was located slightly in front of the ship's mid-point, which he knew was statistically the safest place for it. The infantry men and women were a few hundred metres away towards the aft, which was statistically the second-safest zone of the ship. On a small fighter like a Vincent class, it often didn't matter that much – a single missile strike could easily engulf two or three of these safe zones, while a couple of missiles could destroy the entire vessel. On a larger warship, it could make the difference between a quick death and the opportunity to escape.

"Sergeant Ortiz, lead the men to their quarters. You're to take charge. If there are any complaints, tell them to message the bridge and speak to me about it."

"Yes, sir," she said, saluting.

"We're a warship, not a troop carrier, but there are still almost one hundred fighting men and women on board. I'm sure you can handle it."

Her face hardened and her dark eyes gleamed. "Of course, sir."

Duggan dismissed her and she headed off through the left-hand doorway with the other five men and women behind.

"We're this way," he said, pointing straight ahead. The corridor ahead was illuminated in the Space Corps' standard blueish-white artificial daylight. There was room for two people to walk abreast, albeit with little spare. Duggan went first, followed by the other three. The faint humming of the gravity drives told him the engines extended along much of the vessel, though that was normal on a fleet warship. So far, there'd been no surprises.

"You've seen one ship, you've seen them all," said Breeze.

"I always feel as if I'm walking inside an enormous metal cube," said Chainer. "With an unimaginable weight pressing down on me from above."

"Why a cube?" asked Breeze.

"I don't know. Maybe it's the shape my brain attributes to the experience."

Duggan listened to the conversation, without joining in. Some of the Space Corps' vessels were incomprehensibly large and even the smaller ones contained an enormous amount of the dense metals needed for lightspeed travel. Being on a spacecraft made Duggan feel many things, but he rarely spoke about it.

The bridge was behind a square blast-proof door at the end of another grey-walled corridor. The *Terminus* evidently had an automatic recognition programme that detected the approach of officers. There was a warning chime and a red light glowed from a beacon set in the ceiling. With barely a sound, the thick slab of a door slid away into a recess in the wall, revealing the bridge.

"A bit bigger than I'm used to," said Breeze, following Duggan inside.

The bridge was six metres square and well-lit – almost too

bright compared to that in the corridor outside. The air was chill and curiously free of odour. The captain's chair was in the centre, surrounded by consoles and screens. There was a place for the second-in-command nearby, along with seats and consoles for comms and weapons to the left and right. There were four people already here. They'd clearly been expecting visitors since they were stood to attention and faced straight ahead with the neutral, steely gaze of those who didn't know what to expect from their new captain.

"I'm sure you've been told who I am," said Duggan, looking at them in turn. "I'm Captain John Duggan, in charge of the *ES Terminus*. I've brought some of my own crew with me, who you will work alongside. They will introduce themselves in due course, but please be aware that Commander McGlashan here is the next in charge." He walked over and stood in front of the nearest officer. "Who are you?"

"Lieutenant Alice Massey, sir. Comms."

Duggan looked into her blue eyes. Massey was young and ambitious – he'd seen the type before and was suspicious. To Massey's credit, she didn't flinch under his gaze.

"Name?" he asked, speaking to a slim man, who hardly looked old enough to vote.

"Ensign Mick Perry, sir. I'll be helping out with the comms as well."

The next man was broad and with a lined face. It was clear he'd once been a soldier before he trained as an officer. "Lieutenant Gabriel Reyes," he rumbled. "Weapons. Pleased to meet you, sir."

The final officer was in his mid-thirties, below average height and with an expressionless face. His eyes, however, were bright and intelligent. There was something dislikeable in the set of his features. "Lieutenant Herbert Nichols, sir. Military Asset Management."

Duggan frowned. "What do mean by *military asset management?*"

"The *Terminus* is a valuable ship, Captain Duggan and it carries with it several items of non-disposable heavy armour. I've been assigned to ensure the Space Corps' equipment is treated with the respect it deserves."

"I've never heard of your department."

"We're recently formed, sir. We sit somewhere between the Space Corps and the people who approve the funding for all of these new warships."

"You've been set up by the Confederation Council?"

"There must be oversight to ensure the Confederation's taxpayers are getting value for their money," said Nichols.

Duggan stepped forward and looked closely at Nichols. "And what exactly do you propose to do if I treat the ship with what you believe to be a lack of respect?"

Nichols didn't recoil at the scrutiny. "I'm here on an advisory basis, sir. To watch and monitor."

"And to report anything you don't like the look of?"

"I'm sure I'll be thoroughly debriefed at the end of our current duties, sir."

This wasn't a pleasant surprise and Duggan had no idea if Nichols was here owing to new impositions on the Space Corps, or if he'd been assigned to the *Terminus* because Duggan himself wasn't fully trusted. "Have you been in action before, Lieutenant Nichols?"

"I'm a time-served officer, sir. You don't need to worry about me hiding under a table when the firing begins."

"Assuming I'm permitted to let the *Terminus* take fire?"

"You're the captain, sir," said Nichols, looking completely unruffled.

"I *am* the captain." Duggan lowered his voice. "If I catch you trying to undermine me, I'll lock you in the brig. If I'm feeling particularly annoyed, I might just fire you into space. Am I clear?"

"Very clear."

"Good."

Duggan turned so he could address everyone. "We're looking for a missing prospector, the SC *Lupus*. You don't need to be an expert to know that spacecraft don't usually go missing without external interference, so there's the possibility we'll be called upon to take direct action against threats currently unknown."

"Is it these Dreamers I've been hearing about, sir?" asked Perry.

In spite of efforts to keep a lid on things, most people in the Corps had heard at least a rumour about this new threat. It was as if the Ghasts were already a thing of the past. "We don't know, Ensign, that's why we're going to have a look. All I'm allowed to say is that there is evidence of a credible threat. The source is known to be hostile to the Confederation."

"Are they as advanced as people are saying?" asked Reyes.

Duggan sighed. There was no way he was going to be able to partake in the attempted cover-up – not unless he wanted to spend the whole journey speaking in half-truths and riddles. "I don't know how advanced these *people* are speculating the Dreamers to be, Lieutenant. Suffice to say I have encountered them once and it was enough to scare me. Their technology isn't within touching distance like that of the Ghasts – this new foe destroyed a number of our most powerful warships without effort or hesitation. If we encounter them, it will take every ounce of ingenuity, skill and luck we possess to defeat them or escape."

"If we're going to die, why are they sending us, sir?" asked Massey.

Duggan couldn't tell if she was attempting insolence or was genuinely concerned they were being sent on a suicide mission. He gave her the benefit of the doubt. "Death is never certain. I've fought against them once, as have my crew. We're still here to tell of it. We needed help and we will have the same assistance again. We'll rendezvous with a Ghast Oblivion in two days from now. Their weapons complement our own and together we stand a chance."

He let that sink in for a few moments. The expressions of his new crew told a variety of tales, none of them happy ones. Someone gave a deep chuckle – it was Reyes.

"I've spent years fighting the Ghasts and now I'll be fighting alongside them." He laughed again. "It's going to take some getting used to."

"Believe it or not, we had the Ghasts beaten, Lieutenant," said Duggan. "That's why we can make peace with them. The Dreamers are something else entirely and as things stand, we have no chance of winning. They may have a weakness to exploit and we need to find it." He took a deep breath before he spoke again. "We also need to find out what they want. They came through a wormhole and this was not their first attempt to do so. We believe they've tried it three times and succeeded twice. It's almost certain they'll keep coming. If their current incursion fails, there'll be another after that and then another."

The four new officers still had questions and they tumbled forth, voices speaking over each other. Duggan asked them to be quiet. "We're wasting time. We need to reach the meeting place with the Ghasts as soon as possible and then we can begin our search. Lieutenant Breeze, prepare us for lightspeed. As soon as we're underway, I'll convene a meeting for everyone onboard and I'll tell you what I can. If it comes to fighting, I want you to know what you're facing and what's at stake."

Everyone took their stations, with Duggan too much on edge to take his seat. He stood at Lieutenant Breeze's shoulder, watching him call up the engine data.

"I'm impressed," Breeze conceded. "There's a lot of power at high density and we've got a powerful core to use it properly. I'll bet we're as fast as the *Archimedes*."

"A true evolution," said Duggan.

"You can control evolution," said Breeze. "It's the revolution you need to worry about."

There was an underlying message that Duggan didn't quite agree with. He craved advancement – the fight to control technology and see what became of it.

"Anything you don't understand about these consoles?" he asked.

"It's standard stuff in a new suit," said Breeze. "Nothing unexpected, just everything's a little better and a little more efficient. I've got the coordinates from the *Juniper* for the first stop off. Then there's another, longer trip to follow. I'll not be able to provide an exact time until I've had a chance to dig around a bit more." He pressed an area of his screen and an orange circle appeared. "That's our fifty second warning to lightspeed. Not bad, I suppose. Nothing like the *Crimson*, but you can't have everything, eh?"

"Fifty seconds until we're gone!" announced Duggan. He guessed the transition to lightspeed would be a smooth one, given this was the Space Corps' newest vessel. Nevertheless, he decided it was time for him to sit in his cloth-covered chair, absently wondering if they'd stopped making the fake leather ones.

A low rumbling heralded the catapult into lightspeed, accompanied by a featherlight sensation of spacial uncertainty. Then, it was done and the *ES Terminus* ripped its way through the fabric of the universe in a way which nature had never intended. Ahead lay undetermined hints of death and conflict.

# CHAPTER FOUR

"LIGHT-M ACHIEVED, sir. She's got a lot of muscle," said Breeze.

"I could walk faster," said Chainer provocatively.

Duggan heard Lieutenant Massey snort. "This is the quickest ship in the fleet," she said. "I've run a few sims on the theoretical output and we're almost one percent faster than the *Archimedes*."

"In that case, we're the *second* fastest ship in the fleet," said Chainer, struggling to withhold his glee.

"Lieutenant," warned Duggan.

"What's faster?" asked Perry, not taking the hint.

"The *Crimson*'s much faster," said Breeze. "We recorded her at Light-V."

"Enough!" said Duggan, more forcefully. "We can't make another *Crimson*, so for all intents and purposes the *Terminus* may as well be the fastest thing we've got."

The conversation ended and the background noises of the bridge came to the fore – a mixture of electrical humming and a peculiar high-pitched whine at the extents of hearing. Duggan checked the arrangement of his consoles and found them more or less to his liking. He could access the ship's many systems and subsystems quickly and easily. The ergonomics department had put in a lot of effort. A series of control bars were positioned either side of his chair and within easy reach. Duggan rested his hands on them, letting the coldness seep into his skin. The manual controls weren't active and wouldn't work at lightspeed anyway, so he moved them carefully, testing the weight. There was much he needed to learn and he was desperate to get on with it. However, there was something he felt duty-bound to get out of the way first.

"Ensign Perry, please let the troops know there'll be a briefing in fifteen minutes."

"Where at, sir?"

"I have no idea," said Duggan. "This is the first time I've been onboard. You pick somewhere and we'll go there. I assume there's a mess hall or similar?"

"I'll tell them it's in the mess hall," said Perry, taking the easy way out.

Duggan set off with the crew, leaving McGlashan behind. The chances of anything going wrong were remote, and she'd be up to the task of keeping an eye on things for thirty or forty minutes. He located the mess hall with a minimum of deviation on the way - Breeze had been right in more ways than one when he said all ships were the same.

"Longer, wider passages, yet each going to the places you'd expect," said Chainer. "I'm not complaining by the way."

"Yeah, who wants to spend time learning the layout each time you come some place new?" asked Breeze.

The mess hall was the same as mess halls on every other ship Duggan had served on – bigger than some, smaller than others. There were long metal tables, firmly attached to the floor, along with a series of benches which were carefully designed so you wouldn't want to sit on them for a moment longer than necessary.

There were four food replicators visible – there could have been more, hidden behind the men and women streaming in from the far doorway. There was a low chatter amongst them – it was always the same on new ships with new people.

Sergeant Ortiz was already there, standing to one side. Duggan caught her eye and she gave him a nod to indicate she was in control. This was about the largest number of troops she could be given charge of without having a higher rank.

After a time, everyone was present bar the usual stragglers with their array of excuses. Duggan studied them, looking at the grim faces and hard eyes. These weren't fresh recruits - these were battle-hardened troops who'd seen their share of combat. It was logical for the Space Corps to handpick who it wanted on its latest warship. There'd be the wise guys and the loudmouths in amongst them, but for now they showed impeccable discipline with their blue uniforms clean and pressed.

Duggan spoke and they listened. "We're out looking for a lost prospector. You may be asking yourselves why the Space Corps has decided to send its first Galactic class heavy cruiser on a search and rescue. In reality, this mission may put each one of us in danger. The rumours you've heard – the Dreamers – they're real. The details you've been told may be lacking, but I can assure you this is a new threat and potentially a far greater one than posed by the Ghasts." There was some muttering at this. Rumours were easily believed, yet there were times when it needed a senior officer to drive home the truth. "We don't know what these aliens look like and we don't know the extent of their capabilities. In fact, we don't even know if they're responsible for the loss of the prospector. I'm a man who expects the worst in the hope that I won't find it. Therefore, I'm assuming we're going to run into a few of these bastards."

A woman raised her hand. Her face was fine-boned and she had her dark hair tied back "Sir?"

"Name?" asked Duggan.

"Sergeant Carpenter, sir. If we end up in a firefight with these aliens, how do we respond appropriately if we don't know their capabilities? Is there no intel at all?"

Duggan swept his gaze across the troops. "I can see from your faces that you're the best and that means you've been given the crappiest job. I can only reiterate that we know nothing about the Dreamer's ground capabilities. We don't know what they look like or how they deal with threats. The best advice I have at the moment is to try and put a slug in them from as far away as possible."

A man raised his hand this time. "Sir, Corporal Wong here. Are we definitely going to see some fighting?"

"There are no certainties. The SC *Lupus* might well have broken up owing to a fault onboard. I'm sure there's more to it. There are other Space Corps vessels searching as well, but we're the people who're going to the highest risk zone. If there's anything to find, I'm determined to find it. If there's anything to kill, we're going to be the ones to do it."

"Damn, I'll get a medal for this," said a man a couple of rows back.

Duggan raised his voice, to ensure they heard his next words clearly. "This is to be a joint mission. We'll have the Ghasts with us – an Oblivion battleship is coming. If the fighting starts, you can be sure they'll want to join in. Does anyone have a problem with that?"

It seemed like everyone started talking at once. Questions came and the volume rose to an uncomfortable level. Duggan stood impassively for a few minutes until it settled. When things had quietened, he spoke.

"Most of us have fought the Ghasts for as long as we can remember. I've lost more friends than I can put a number to. The thing is, I've seen what's coming and I know the Confederation isn't going to come out of this one – not without help. I don't know if the Ghasts hate us as much as we hate them and in truth I don't really care. We've beaten them and now we need them. What the future holds, I can't tell you."

"We've got to keep fighting, man," said a voice in the ranks.

"Yeah, it's not about the Ghasts anymore. We beat those, now we've got something else to beat."

"Nothing ever changes," said Duggan. "You know that more than anyone. When we beat the Dreamers, there'll be something else, and again after that. You might not have known it when you signed up, but you sure as hell must know it now."

"Alvarez here doesn't know shit, sir. He still can't tell the business end of a rifle without guidance."

"Hey, shut up, Hammond you Ghast lover," came the response, presumably from Alvarez.

There were a number of boisterous exchanges from the troops. Duggan smiled and waved them to silence, since he didn't want the meeting to get out of hand. "Anyone got a problem if it comes to fighting with the Ghasts?" he repeated. This time no one spoke and Duggan nodded. He had one last thing to deal with. "I'm sure you've met Sergeant Ortiz by now." There was more muttering, not entirely friendly. "Sergeant Ortiz has seen more action than almost anyone I know. She'll be in charge from now on. As of this moment, she'll also be Acting Lieutenant Ortiz. Anything you need, it comes through her."

Ortiz' expression didn't change. "Thank you, sir," she said.

"I have matters to attend to," said Duggan. "I know I can rely on the men and women in this room to do what's necessary. Lieutenant Ortiz may want to speak to you after I've left."

With that, he took the corridor which led back to the bridge. He'd hardly covered ten metres when he heard Lieutenant Ortiz raise her voice to a bellow. He smiled to himself – it had been a long time since he'd needed to promote anyone. Ortiz would have had a hard time of it if he'd left her at sergeant.

"Do you think they'll fight willingly with the Ghasts if it's required?" asked Breeze, falling into step.

"Absolutely," said Duggan. "They look the part and I'm sure the skills are there. They're soldiers and fighting is what they do."

"I'm not sure what I think about our situation."

Duggan laughed. "You've got to take the rough with the rough sometimes. As far as I'm aware, this is the first time we've done anything like it."

"Since Prot-7," said Breeze.

"That was through necessity," said Duggan. "There is also necessity here yet there's a lot more to it, bubbling under the surface. We're the lab rats, being tested to see what happens and how we react."

"You don't get an easy ride, sir."

"None of us do, Lieutenant. Anyone who's with me has to put up with the same."

"You live for it," said Breeze. It was a statement and not a question.

It wasn't a conversation Duggan would have permitted except amongst a few people he trusted most, and Breeze was one of those people. "I wouldn't have it any other way," he replied. "It's the only way I can make a difference."

They reached the bridge, to find McGlashan absorbed in an array of the ship's specification documents. She looked up at the sound of the returning crew and her eyes found Duggan.

"Sir, you need to see this. The Admiral wasn't wrong when he said the *Terminus* was designed to show off."

McGlashan was excited, like a child with a dozen new toys. Some of it rubbed off on Duggan and he crossed over to take a look. Before he'd covered the few paces to her station, another excited voice reached him. This time, it was Chainer, holding a metal tray in front of him. There were several items resting on it.

"They've got the same food replicators as they installed on the *Crimson!*" he said breathlessly. "Hi-stim, coffee and a couple of hamburgers. If I die, at least I'll die happy."

Duggan shook his head. "Try not to spill it over your console, Lieutenant."

# CHAPTER FIVE

"WHAT HAVE YOU FOUND?" asked Duggan. He waved Lieutenant Reyes over at the same time, in case he had any input.

"There are seventeen Bulwarks. *Seventeen* of them, sir. They've got a higher rate of fire than anything I've seen before."

"New heat dissipation modules," said Reyes. "They've figured out how to channel it out across the hull and into the engines. We could punch a hole through a twenty-metre steel plate with a single round."

"There are three beam weapons with overlapping fields of fire," continued McGlashan. "The range is still poor compared to the Ghast stuff."

"They have no travel time," said Reyes. He smiled. "If you can get in close enough to use them. These ones can draw from the main engines to increase their intensity and they have a firing interval of thirty seconds. I've heard they're putting eight of them on the *Maximilian*."

"Why not the *Devastator* as well?" asked McGlashan. The Hadron *Devastator* had been sent to the Helius Blackstar with the *Lancer*. The *Lancer* had been destroyed and the *Devastator* had taken six weeks to limp home on its scrambled engines.

"I've been told the *Maximilian* doesn't need extensive redesign to fit the modules in its hull. It's the only Hadron with a beam weapon."

"The *Devastator* won't be ready to resume service for a while," said Duggan. "They're trying to find out how the Dreamers managed to shut its engines down."

"So it's true?" asked Reyes.

"Yes, Lieutenant, I'm afraid it's true. Whatever they used, our sensors can detect it, but we had no way of stopping it happening."

"We've got thirty-six Lambda clusters," continued McGlashan. "Each with ten tubes, and get this – an eight second reload."

"They'll burn out if you use the rapid reload more than three times in succession," said Reyes. "After that, it's an expensive strip-down and repair on the damaged parts. We've been warned not to use it more than twice in a row – just in case."

"The range on these is good," said McGlashan. "Another change for the better."

"How far?" asked Duggan.

"They'll target at a hundred and fifty thousand klicks," said Reyes. "They've got new boosters as well, taking them up to almost three thousand klicks per second."

"Everything's new and improved," said Duggan. "Even so, there's nothing here that'll beat a Ghast Shatterer."

"There are two more options," said McGlashan. "Locked down, so I guess we've got some nukes with us."

"Lieutenant Reyes?" asked Duggan.

"I'd guess the same, sir. I've been told we have extras that are usable at the captain's discretion."

"I'll have a look," said Duggan. He sat at his chair and called up the weapons consoles. Sure enough, there were two options with a block on them. He enabled both, with the second option needing several layers of confirmation. "Can you see them now?" he asked.

"Yes, sir. The first one is definitely nukes." She gave a low whistle. "Someone in the Space Corps has taken a shine to the idea of radiation weapons."

"How so?" asked Duggan, standing again.

"There is a grand total of thirty-two nuclear weapon launchers on the ES *Terminus*. Not only that, but the payload is massive. Two gigatons per warhead from the looks of it and we're carrying eight missiles for each tube."

"They've had people working on this for a lot longer than the two months since we returned from the Blackstar," Duggan said, referencing the fact that the Dreamer energy shields were vulnerable to heavy bursts of gamma rays.

"It's been closer to two years since we brought the *Crimson* home," said McGlashan. "If you remember, we used nukes to pretty good effect against the Ghasts. Maybe this is just luck and they were developing these things to be used in a war we're no longer fighting."

"Whatever the reason, I'm glad," said Duggan. He leaned closer to one of the screens next to McGlashan. "Look at the propulsion section," he said. "That's something new, isn't it?"

"Lambda based, I reckon," she said, peering at the specification diagrams. "Should be a lot more useful than what we had before."

"A *lot* better," said Duggan. "I'm beginning to feel a little more relaxed about this whole trip. A few Shatterer launchers wouldn't go amiss, but I can't have everything." He frowned. "This final weapon isn't a weapon after all."

"What is it?" asked Reyes.

"Something I've not seen in a long time," said Duggan. "It's an option to simultaneously detonate every single warhead we're carrying. From the dates on these files, it's been cobbled in at the last minute."

"Why would you want to blow everything up at once?" said Reyes.

"Self-destruction, Lieutenant. To destroy the ship."

Reyes scratched his head. "I could understand how you might want the ability to do that if you were expecting the enemy to board and take a vessel by force. That's never going to happen these days."

Duggan guessed why the facility was available and he didn't like it. "It's to make us into a weapon - not to deny the vessel to the enemy. If our engines get scrambled or we're otherwise incapacitated, it's to give us one last throw of the dice."

McGlashan looked troubled. "Sir? What if the same happens to us again? Like what happened when we were sent to Lioxi on the *Crimson*."

"Betrayal?" asked Duggan sharply, not caring if Reyes heard the exchange.

"I don't know," said McGlashan. "What if they waited until we were close to a high priority target and someone decided remotely it was time to activate the self-destruct? We could be sacrificed in the name of the greater good. There are enough explosives to take a big chunk out of an entire planet."

"The Space Corps' new Planet Breaker," said Duggan with a humourless laugh. The idea left him uneasy and he returned to his station in order to disable the facility from Lieutenant Reyes' console. Experience had told him to be wary with whom he trusted. If there was to be a double-cross it didn't seem likely Reyes would be the source. Even so, access to the self-destruct facility was above the man's grade. It was above McGlashan's too, though she'd earned enough respect that Duggan was confident she could handle the responsibility.

When Duggan finished speaking to McGlashan and Reyes, he saw Lieutenant Breeze waving him over. The man looked to be in his element, with multi-coloured gauges and power bars covering three of his display screens.

"This ship is a marvel, sir. It just goes to show how things might have been if the Confederation Council hadn't cut our spending to the bone. If we'd had half a dozen of these on the frontline five or six years ago, the Ghasts wouldn't have come close to Charistos or Angax." He fell silent for a moment, wondering if he'd said too much.

"I understand," said Duggan. "If they'd poured in enough money back then, we'd have developed our technology faster and been better prepared. The Ghasts might not have had enough ships remaining to install their Shatterers." He didn't say that billions of lives – both human and Ghast – could have been saved.

"They've made some updates to the engines," said Breeze, changing the subject. "It would appear those debriefing meetings had some use after all."

"What sort of updates?"

"It's more to the core than anything else. The brain of this vessel is fast – from the model designation, we're carrying a pared-back version of the AIs they have on the *Juniper*. They have three full-fat models, of course, but there's a lot more stuff to control on the orbital. If you see here, our AI has been optimised – they've added some extra hardware to it. Without knowing the specifics, I'd say it's been designed to subdivide the engines into a series of linked units."

"Meaning what, exactly?"

"If the Dreamers try to scramble us, the AI will pretend we're only equipped with five hundred tonnes of engine, instead of nearly six billion tonnes."

"That must mean the lab guys are sure the Dreamer weapon instructs the ship's own AI to do the scrambling."

"Not necessarily," said Breeze. "Last I heard, they still didn't have a clue, if you can excuse the technical term for it. They're trying something, and that's better than nothing."

"Of course," said Duggan.

Duggan spent the remainder of the following two days familiarising himself with all aspects of the *ES Terminus*. The ship had a lot of firepower and the Space Corps engineers were clearly proud of what they'd designed and built. In other circumstances, a new captain would have been given weeks of trials and training before he was permitted to take a warship like this one on active duty. It was a sign of the Space Corps' concern that they'd sent Duggan out with this one immediately. In reality, there was nothing that would take an experienced captain unawares. There was always change and the best officers adapted to it.

So, the *ES Terminus* had newer and better weapons. Her rooms and corridors were kept at a constant temperature which never fluctuated more than a single degree in normal operation. There was a large gym and a small cinema room. The captain's quarters consisted of two rooms – one for sleeping and another for study and contemplation. The bunks for the soldiers were marginally more opulent than normal. Everything was just a little bit better than it needed to be and Duggan couldn't decide if he liked it or not.

"It's got no soul, has it?" said McGlashan, as they sat opposite each other in the mess. It was breakfast time and the room was lively.

"How did you know what I was thinking?" he asked.

"Your face always tells a picture," she said, laughing. "I've worked with you long enough that it's easy to read."

"I didn't know I was so obvious," he said gruffly. "You're right, though. I think I miss the *Detriment* most of all. Even more so than the *Crimson*."

"There's something about living on the edge, isn't there? We've had too much luck, sir. Maybe it was time to move on."

"Maybe," he hedged.

"And this is something you've deserved. Not just you – Frank, Bill and me too. You can achieve anything you want now there's nobody to hold you back." She winked. "I hear there's an opening within the admiralty. You should apply."

He laughed in genuine delight. "I'd love to see their faces when they opened that letter."

"Definitely," she said. "One day, though. You deserve a chance at it, sir."

"If the past had treated me differently, I think it may have been a path to follow," he said. "I don't know if it's something I want. I'm institutionalised – without a ship I feel lost."

"You need to change, sir. Fill the void with something else." Her eyes glittered – mischief tinged with sadness. "You should look up Captain Jonas when we get back."

He laughed again, causing heads nearby to turn - Duggan wasn't known for outward displays of humour, something the men and women on the *Terminus* had picked up on quickly. "Perhaps I'll do that, Commander. Perhaps I will."

The following morning, the *ES Terminus* exited lightspeed, ten minutes earlier than projected. The designated meeting place was located on the fringes of the Garon sector and close to nothing of interest.

"Anything here?" asked Duggan. He looked across in time to see Chainer giving Ensign Perry a nudge.

"Sir, just doing a sweep now," said Perry. He looked relieved to have delivered this tiny snippet of information. If he lacked confidence he'd need to get over quickly.

"Let me know soon," said Duggan, meaning *I need to know at once.*

The *Terminus* was bedecked in sensors and the comms team worked fast in order to collate the data.

"I've detected a single object, sir," said Massey. "Four-point-five kilometres in length, with a volume almost twice our own. They're twenty minutes away on full gravity drive."

"They're turning, sir," said Chainer. "Swinging about and coming to greet us."

"Send a message to the *Juniper* to let them know we've arrived and then hail the Oblivion," said Duggan.

"They are responding," said Chainer. "The captain wants to speak to you."

"Good, put him through to my earpiece," said Duggan.

A voice, startling in its clarity, came through. Duggan had been informed that the Space Corps had made rapid strides in the language modules in the last two months and it was apparent by the subtleties in inflection, where there had previously been only a monotone.

"Captain John Duggan. I am Nil-Far, and I command the battleship *Dretisear.*"

# CHAPTER SIX

"AT LEAST WE know who we're dealing with," said Duggan, when his brief conversation was over. Nil-Far was about as talkative as Duggan.

"You know their captain?" asked Massey.

"We've met once or twice," said Duggan drily. "If the other Ghasts are as trustworthy as Nil-Far, we can be sure they will stick to the letter of our peace treaty."

"When we sign one," said Massey.

"Precisely. The *Dretisear* has been kept in the dark as to our final destination. It seems as if the Space Corps wasn't ready to trust them with advance information about the *SC Lupus'* travels until we were available to provide an escort. Lieutenant Chainer, please send the necessary information to the Ghast ship. We'll be leaving at once."

"I've sent them the data," said Chainer.

"Deep fission drives warming up," said Breeze. "They're doing likewise."

"They don't stick around," said Reyes.

"If there's one thing I've learned, it's that the Ghasts are efficient," said Duggan. "Nil-Far is definitely not alone amongst them in having that trait."

"You sound as if you like them, sir," said Massey. There was a hint of triumph in her features and Duggan realised she'd been waiting for a chance to accuse him. It was widely-known he'd dealt with the Ghasts and that he'd brought one of their senior officers to the *Juniper*. Somehow it appeared as if this made him look like a sympathiser – at least in Massey's eyes.

"What do you mean, Lieutenant?" he asked, his voice neutral.

Massey opened her mouth and then closed it, knowing she'd started along a path without taking precautions against the dangers ahead. Her mouth opened again and she forged on regardless. "It's just the way you talk about them. Never a bad word to say. It sounds to me as if you like them. Sir."

Duggan stalked over to her seat. "Stand up!" he said. She stood and looked at him. Massey was a tall woman, but her eyes weren't level. Even so, she met Duggan's stare evenly and this time the insolence was clear.

"What do you recall of my address to the troops in the mess room two days ago?" he asked calmly.

"Not much," she said.

"Not much, *sir*."

"I don't remember very much of what you said, sir."

"You won't remember me saying how much I liked them, because I have fought against them for my entire adult life, Lieutenant Massey. I have nothing to prove to you or anyone."

"They're bastards, sir. Each and every one of them. You shouldn't call them trustworthy. They've killed billions of people!"

At once, Duggan knew. "Who have you lost?" he asked.

Her face wilted and her eyes glistened. "It feels like everyone, sir."

"You need to put it to one side, Lieutenant, before it breaks you. The Ghasts are not our friends, but we need them. The Dreamers will kill us all if we stand alone. We have no choice. Take your seat again."

She nodded and the hostility in her face was gone. Duggan was glad to get this over with so soon, rather than have Massey fester about it until she did something really stupid. The rest of the crew were sitting and watching their screens intently, pretending nothing had happened.

"Are we at lightspeed, yet?" Duggan asked.

"A couple of minutes ago, sir," said Breeze. "The Oblivion beat us to it by two seconds."

"Want me to keep a score?" asked Chainer. "One-nil to them in the pissing competition, with everything still to play for."

"That won't be necessary, Lieutenant," said Duggan, pleased to feel the air clear with Chainer's light-hearted remarks. "We're meant to be a Cadaveron-beater, remember? Not an Oblivion-beater."

"I don't believe that for one moment," said McGlashan. "The Space Corps engineers are dying to see how we compare."

"Yes, I bet they are," said Duggan. "One-nil, it is."

"I'll settle for a draw," said Breeze. "That would be effectively a victory, considering how much smaller we are."

"We can judge it at the end," said Duggan, his tone making it clear the conversation was over. "Now – what do we know of where we're going?"

"Glantia-312," said Breeze. "There's nothing remarkable about it from what I can see on the charts. There are two or three planets where you might expect to find metal ore and minerals."

"This was the last scheduled stop for the *Lupus*, wasn't it?" asked McGlashan. "The audit reports show they'd visited several solar systems beforehand and they checked in with base each time."

"So I see," replied Duggan.

"Why aren't they sending all the search and rescue vessels to Glantia-312, instead of spreading them thinly?" she asked.

Duggan shrugged. "The mission briefing documents give details of the Projections Team's findings. There are several places between Glantia-312 and the *Lupus'* previous stop-off. It's not entirely unknown for an experienced prospector captain to make a diversion if they come across data to suggest there's a greater chance of success elsewhere. Besides, if the Dreamers are responsible for the loss of this ship, having greater numbers might not be to our advantage."

"More valuable warships to get scrambled, jammed and shot down," said Chainer helpfully.

"The *Terminus* is the only vessel to be accompanied by the Ghasts," said Duggan. "This tells you where the Space Corps believes the largest risks are. If anything goes wrong, both the Confederation and the Ghasts will be equally weakened."

"I suppose," said McGlashan. "I can't help but feel like we're the stick they're poking into the viper's nest."

"We're definitely that, Commander. I thought you'd have learned by now – if you lift your head above the parapet in the Space Corps, you'd better be wearing a helmet. The more noticed you are, the more crap you get thrown your way."

Chainer gave Ensign Perry a gentle elbow in the arm. "You should listen to this. You might learn something about how the world works." Perry smiled nervously and said nothing.

"We've got five more days until we arrive," said Duggan. "As ever, we will expect the worst. I need the comms team to provide detailed early scans of the vicinity. The last time we encountered a Dreamer vessel it was difficult to get a sensor lock on it. Lieutenant Chainer has learned from this and he'll bring

ANTHONY JAMES

you up to speed on what to look for. We can't afford to get it wrong."

"We'll exit lightspeed approximately an hour out from the fourth and fifth planets – equidistant between the two," said Breeze.

"Why did you pick that location?" asked Massey curiously.

"I spent time on a prospector, many years ago. It's quite interesting what they do and I picked up a few bits and pieces. Generally, you'd choose the centre planets if you're after quick results. The inner ones are too hot and the outer ones too cold."

"We can mine at really low temperatures, can't we?" asked Perry.

"Yes, we can. It's not always feasible to do so and the furthest planets are usually small and therefore have less potential for holding big deposits. Hence we aim for the middle and see what happens."

"Oh," said Perry. He sounded disappointed somehow, as if he thought there should have been a far greater amount of scientific decision making involved in the process.

With a few days to fill, Duggan looked for activities to occupy his time. He wasn't a big sleeper, since his brain was always more active than was good for him. There was much to learn about the ES Terminus and he threw himself into the task, studying data sheets and specification documents. On the final morning, he took himself off to examine the hardware they carried in the hold. McGlashan came along, also looking for something to do. The cargo area was accessed by a lift or steps. It was big and it needed to be, in order to contain the firepower which had been packed inside.

"You could assault a major city with this lot," said McGlashan. "Assuming you didn't decide to destroy your target from orbit instead," she added.

"The needs of war change constantly," said Duggan. "I

42

imagine when they made the plans for the Galactic class, they foresaw a need for big guns on the ground. We must have been taking a few hits on our mining outposts at the time."

"These tanks look a bit more dangerous than the little ones on a Gunner," she said.

Four of the Space Corps' heavy tanks sat upon their launch hatches. The vehicles were held in place with gravity clamps powered by the ship's engines. The tanks were twenty-five metres long, ten wide and six tall. Their fronts were angular to help them deflect incoming rounds. The rear was ugly and squared off. There was a single turret on each, with a wide-bore muzzle that could unleash a projectile the size of a man's head. They could rip a hole in a mountain, or flatten dozens of buildings in a short space of time. In spite of their size, they were mostly armour and weapons, with little room for troops inside. Deeper in the cargo bay loomed two dark shapes, much bigger and far more intimidating.

"Colossus tanks," said McGlashan. "I thought they'd stopped making these."

"They did for a while," said Duggan. "The money it costs to make each one would shock you. These look pristine – the Corps must have started up production again once they got the funding."

Each Colossus tank was more than forty metres in length. They were a similar shape to most Corps tanks, but they carried a single, huge, slow-firing turret-mounted gun that was designed to knock out Ghast transporters on the ground – or anything else stupid enough to come into its sights. It also had two guided plasma launchers mounted on its shoulders.

"I once saw one of these get hit by two Ghast missiles launched from orbit and it still kept going," said Duggan. "It's almost solid alloy."

"What happened to that tank?"

"The next six missiles took it out," said Duggan. "What's on the ground can never beat what's in the sky." It was an old mantra and belief in it was why the Space Corps had subsumed the other branches of the military more than a hundred years ago.

They finished up their exploration of the *Terminus'* hold. There was a pair of slow-moving depleted uranium repeaters and two micro-batteries that could launch adapted versions of the Lambda missiles. *Micro* in this instance was something of a misnomer and the batteries weren't much smaller than one of the heavy tanks.

On the far wall were lockers which contained over two hundred spacesuits, along with rifles, grenades and a variety of hand-held launchers. All-in-all, there was a devastating array of weaponry, should it ever be needed.

"I've seen enough," said Duggan.

"Impressed?"

"I wouldn't have expected anything less on a top-of-the-line fleet heavy cruiser. They made sure the *Terminus* was ready for anything."

Duggan's earpiece buzzed and Lieutenant Breeze spoke to him briefly.

"We'll be arriving soon?" asked McGlashan, when the exchange or words was over.

"Thirty minutes. We'd best get back to the bridge and prepare."

They hurried away, through the wide corridors of the *Terminus*. As they ran, McGlashan asked something which had been on her mind. "You threatened to throw Lieutenant Nichols in the brig if he interfered. Do we even have a brig?"

"I have no idea, Commander. If we don't, I'll just have to proceed with my second threat and launch him into space." He felt his mood turning sour. "Damn the man, I won't have him interfering with anything aboard this ship!"

"He's just doing his job, sir."

"He likes putting his oar in - I can see it in his face. He'll cause trouble if he's given the chance."

The bridge lay ahead. The blast door slid open and they went inside.

# CHAPTER SEVEN

THE *ES TERMINUS* emerged into near space. Within five seconds, the *Dretisear* did likewise, a few thousand klicks off to one side. Given the distances involved, it was remarkably well done. The crew on the *Terminus* launched into a well-rehearsed drill, scanning the close, medium and far distances.

"Got nothing close, except the Oblivion," said Perry.

"Continuing with medium-range scan," said Massey.

"Working the super-fars," added Chainer, his face a picture of concentration. He'd given himself the most difficult task. "I'll shout when I've got something to tell."

"Ensign Perry, hail the *Dretisear* and enquire as to their wellbeing."

"Hailing them now, sir. Their comms uhm *man* is responding. They have nothing to report and are scanning the area. He reports them to be on full alert."

"Good," said Duggan. He'd spoken to Nil-Far enough to know the Ghasts worked in a surprisingly similar manner to humans. "Report that we are doing likewise. Afterwards, repeat your close-in scans and don't stop until Lieutenant Chainer or I tell you to do so."

"Sir."

Duggan sat down, sinking into the thick padding of his seat. He waved Breeze over and showed him a computer-generated view of the orbiting planets.

"We've got three in the middle of the nine. Which one do we check out first?"

Breeze furrowed his brow. "Planet six isn't a good bet. I reckon the *Lupus* would have been interested in four and five."

"One small, one larger," said Duggan. "It feels like picking a bottle of wine by the label and hoping it's a good one."

Breeze chuckled. "I don't see much to distinguish them. Two cold, grey balls of rock which may or may not be riddled with veins of precious metal. Choose whichever one you wish, sir."

Duggan stared at his screen, with the two planets side-by-side, as if he could somehow get a clue about which alternative the captain of the *Lupus* would have chosen. "Anything on the fars?" he asked.

"Medium range scan almost done, sir. No sign of anything untoward."

"Short range still clear," said Perry.

"We're going for the larger planet," said Duggan at last. "Please communicate our movements to the *Dretisear*. What's the planet called, anyway?"

"It doesn't have a name yet," said Breeze. "I can make the ship assign one automatically and have it pinged back to base for the records. Want me to do it?"

"May as well," said Duggan.

"According to this, we're going to Trasgor," Breeze said. "And the fifth planet has been named Virtus, should we need to search that one as well."

"Send a message to the *Juniper* and let them know we're safe and well," said Duggan, aware that the *Terminus'* AI would likely have already done so. "We're going to perform a slow orbit of Trasgor until the comms team are certain the missing ship isn't here."

"I've finished the first far scan, sir," said Chainer. He looked perplexed.

"I don't like it when you get that expression, Lieutenant."

"Something doesn't feel right. I've run a quick pass over the area of the planet's surface we can see and everything looks fine, except that the oxygen levels look abnormally high. It's not something I'd normally notice."

"What do you mean *abnormally high*?" asked Duggan. "One or two percent?"

"Closer to ten percent and it's not evenly distributed – the quantity increases towards the dark side to the west."

"I've got metal, sir," said Massey, urgency in her voice. "A couple of hundred thousand klicks away."

"Is it the *Lupus*?" asked Duggan, crossing for a look. "Keep the *Dretisear* informed," he told Ensign Perry.

"They're telling *me* about it," said Perry. "They must have seen it at the same time as we did."

"I can't confirm the origins, sir," said Massey. "I'm sure it's wreckage of some type."

"It's not going to be anything other than the *Lupus*, is it?" said Duggan, not really looking for a response.

"There's more metal on the surface," said Chainer. "On object of some sort."

"Parts of the wreckage?" asked Duggan.

"I don't think so, sir. This is big and it's not moving. I need more time or we need to be nearer."

Duggan didn't like what he was hearing. "I want you all looking out for an enemy vessel. Ignore the wreckage for the moment. I'm going to bring us closer."

He took manual control of the *Terminus* and it surged forward on its gravity drive. It was testament to the design improvements that there was no sensation of movement. The only way Duggan knew they were at fourteen hundred klicks per second was the reading on his display.

"Be prepared," he said to McGlashan.

"As ever."

"I've got something, sir," said Chainer, his voice louder than usual. "It's emerging from the planet's shadow and coming towards us. Half of our sensors are skating off it, like it doesn't want to be seen. It's making two thousand klicks per second – whatever it is, it's a lot faster than we are."

"Message the *Dretisear*. We're assuming the approaching vessel is hostile and we'll take appropriate action."

"I'm getting the same message from them," said Perry.

"Don't sound so surprised, Ensign. The Ghasts know how to deal with threats."

"The Ghasts have launched six Shatterers, sir," said McGlashan. Her expression was one of utter shock. "We're a million and a half klicks away."

"Ten times the range of our Lambdas," said Breeze with a shake of his head. "Who is showing off to who?"

"Our comms have just gone dead, sir," said Chainer. "No warning, nothing. They've fitted some ancient backup circuits, presumably in the event of this happening. I'm going to try and get a message off to the *Juniper*."

"Hold!" said Duggan. "We don't know if the enemy can trace our comms to their destination. The Space Corps knows where we are if anything goes wrong."

"Six minutes till the Shatterers reach their target," said McGlashan.

"What do we have on the approaching ship?" asked Duggan.

"It's smaller than we are," said Chainer. "Between two and

three klicks in length. It's got the same energy output as the one we fought on Prot-7, so it's got shields. Definitely a Dreamer ship – what the hell is it waiting around here for?"

"If it's more than two klicks long, this ship is bigger than the one on Prot-7," said Breeze grimly. "It might have a lot more juice to maintain its shields."

"Good job we've got a hold full of nukes," said McGlashan.

"They're definitely going to work?" asked Reyes.

"They did last time, Lieutenant. Who knows what they'll do against this particular warship? Just keep your fingers crossed it's only the mothership which has the engine scramblers," said Duggan. "Otherwise it's going to get really messy for us."

Reyes crossed himself, a gesture Duggan hadn't seen in a long while. "I'm praying, sir," he said.

"Captain Duggan, if the probabilities show the incoming vessel to have superior capabilities to the *Terminus*, I recommend you commence the transition to lightspeed," said Nichols. "They've already disabled our comms."

"Your advice is noted, Lieutenant Nichols," said Duggan, struggling to keep his voice calm. "My mission is to learn about our enemy, not to run away as soon as they appear in the distance. Nor can we abandon our allies to face this threat alone."

"They're not our allies yet, sir," said Nichols smoothly. "Negotiations aren't complete."

"We're staying," snapped Duggan. "This discussion is over."

"Yes, sir," said Nichols. There was the faintest hint of something in his voice, which bordered on mockery.

"The Dreamer vessel has launched something, sir," said Chainer. "Twelve objects, moving fast."

"Missiles?" asked Duggan. This was the first time he was aware they'd used ballistics.

"I'd guess so. Our AI has plotted their trajectory. They're

trying to shoot down the Ghast missiles. Damn those things are even quicker than the Shatterers."

"I'm detecting another six launches from the *Dretisear*," said McGlashan. "I hope they've got plenty of ammunition."

The distance between the three ships steadily closed. Duggan ground his teeth in impotent anger, unable to do anything more than watch. None of the *Terminus'* weapons would target an object from so far and he knew from experience they couldn't lock onto the Dreamer ships anyway. Range and targeting had become the most important factors in ship-to-ship combat, rather than the ability to launch hundreds of missiles simultaneously. The Space Corps needed to catch up and soon.

"Four of the Ghast missiles have been destroyed," said Chainer. "The remaining two from that wave will impact shortly. Maybe the Dreamer technology isn't so infallible after all."

It wasn't the best time to take comfort from the possibility and Duggan watched his tactical display like a hawk. "Commander McGlashan, as soon as we're in range I want to see thirty-two nuclear missiles heading for that Ghast ship and I want three hundred Lambdas following right behind."

"We can only launch ten nukes directly forward."

"Fine, launch ten."

"There's been another launch from the enemy vessel," said Chainer. "Shit – dozens of them this time."

"They're not all targeting the Shatterers," said Massey. "I'd estimate we've got twenty aimed at us and another twenty at the *Dretisear*. The rest of them are on an intercept course with the Ghast missiles."

"Another six Shatterers have just left the Oblivion," said Reyes. "This is going to be intense."

"You'd better get used to it," muttered Chainer, his eyes flicking between three different screens at once.

"We won't be within firing range until after their missiles reach us," said McGlashan.

"Here come some more," said Massey. "Another fifty."

"Two more of the Ghast Shatterers have been intercepted," said Chainer.

"Get our countermeasures ready," said Duggan.

"We're not lacking in those," said McGlashan. "Shame they're untested against the Dreamer missiles."

"It's going to be a very brief fight if our countermeasures are ineffective," said Duggan.

Through the void outside, dozens of missiles raced towards the *Terminus* and the *Dretisear* with combined velocities of over six thousand kilometres per second. At his station, Duggan hunched over the controls of the warship, his jaw set and his eyes hard. The thrill of the unknown electrified his mind and body and his eyes never left the incoming swarm of red dots on his tactical display. He tried through the power of his will to force the Bulwark cannons to target, not knowing if they'd fire or not. The seconds counted down and the crew waited to see how this first round of battle would conclude.

# CHAPTER EIGHT

AT INTERVALS along the front and top of the *Terminus*, hatches opened. Bulwark cannons tore along reinforced alloy runners in a fraction of a second, emerging into their exterior positions. Stubby muzzles rotated at terrifying speed as their tracking modules sought a target. In-built sensors sent out pings, detecting the inbound Dreamer missiles. The targets were travelling at a speed in excess of the design capabilities of the Bulwarks. Nevertheless, nine of the seventeen cannons locked on and sprayed thousands upon thousands of their projectiles into space, while the ship's AI tried to predict the future position of the missiles.

At almost the same time, other hatches opened in hundreds of places about the hull of the *ES Terminus*. Dense, metal globes shot away into the darkness, their transmitters spewing out interference to confuse the enemy missiles. There were other openings – a series of tubes ran along the back of the *Terminus*, protruding like the spine of an enormous, metal creature. Spheres of glowing white were hurled outwards, to explode in a blinding cloud that hid everything with its intensity.

Thousands of kilometres away – a tiny distance in the context of such engagements - the *Dretisear* lit up the darkness with its own ceaseless expulsions of superhot plasma. A dozen Vule cannons unleashed a barrage of projectiles, their trajectories converging, changing and converging once more, as their tracking systems switched from one target to the next.

"Countermeasures away," said McGlashan. "The Bulwarks are targeting." Her relief was palpable.

"I believe the Oblivion has launched six more missiles," said Chainer. "It's hard to read through their flares."

"We'll be able to launch our own missiles in a few seconds," said McGlashan.

"They won't target," said Duggan. "Make sure you've disabled their guidance systems and fire them in a straight line. I want the nuclear warheads to detonate automatically when they come into range of those bastards."

"Aye, sir. On with it now," she replied.

"Quickly," said Duggan, gritting his teeth.

"The Dreamer ship has launched another fifty missiles," said Massy.

A series of status warning lights appeared on one of Duggan's screens. The background hum of the *Terminus* became a rumbling.

"Two impacts aft," said Breeze. "Shit, and a beam strike in the same place."

"The Dreamer ship has been hit by four Shatterers, sir," said Chainer. "Their energy output went up by four hundred percent."

"Ten of our nukes are on their way," said McGlashan. "Flying straight outwards."

"Two hundred Lambdas hot on their heels," added Reyes. "It's the most we could launch, since half of the clusters are pointing the wrong way."

"Come on," said Nichols to himself. It was cool, but the man had a sheen of sweat across his forehead – the first sign he was affected by events around him.

"The Ghasts are launching too. Almost five hundred missiles!" said McGlashan. "They couldn't even launch their conventional plasma warheads at the Dreamers back on Prot-7. Seems as if they've done some work to sort it out."

There wasn't time to dwell on it – the *Dretisear* outgunned the *Terminus* by a wide margin. The Space Corps' newest heavy cruiser wasn't a match for the Ghasts' most recent battleship. *Foolish to think that it was,* thought Duggan. "What's our damage?" he asked.

"Two big holes out the back," said Breeze. "And it's pretty hot in there, too. We've lost some of our engine output."

"The enemy have fired more missiles," said Massey. "Another fifty. From their trajectories, these are intended to intercept our nukes."

"We've been hit by their particle beam again," said Breeze. "The *Dretisear* has taken at least two hits as well. She's spilling positrons from four places – a few of the enemy missiles got through the Ghast countermeasures."

"Our beam weapons aren't in range," said Reyes. "Not by a long shot."

"Give them another ten nukes," said Duggan. "Follow up with Lambdas."

"The nukes aren't ready to launch, sir," said McGlashan.

"Fire the Lambdas. Everything we've got."

"They're on their way. Our Bulwarks are going again," she said.

"Most of our first wave of nukes was successfully intercepted, sir," said Reyes. "Three have detonated."

"Another one of their missiles got through," said Breeze. "That's a third hit."

The light on the bridge changed abruptly, to the rich, deep red of danger. Warnings and alerts rolled over Duggan's screen in an unending wave.

"Some of our weapons have been disabled by the strikes," said McGlashan.

"That last one came close to the life support modules," said Breeze.

Duggan wasn't paying attention to the damage reports. He saw three growing circles bloom over his tactical display as the gamma rays from the nuclear warheads expanded from the centre. The Dreamer warship appeared as a red dot, moving at an incredible speed through the fringes of one of the circles. Hundreds of smaller dots converged on it, the human and Ghost missiles launched with their homing capabilities disabled.

"The *Dretisear* is changing course," said Massey.

"Running?" asked Duggan sharply.

"Damaged, I think," she replied.

"What about the enemy shields, damnit?" he asked.

"Another two jumps in their output, sir," said Chainer. "We got a couple of lucky hits, but their shields are still functioning."

Duggan swore – the nuclear detonations mustn't have been close enough to disable the enemy shields. "Are we ready to launch again?" he asked.

"Only Lambdas. The nukes have a different reload mechanism, which is taking a whole lot longer."

"Fire the Lambdas then," he said.

"Away they go."

"They haven't fired the particle beam for a while," said Breeze. "I wonder if they're unable to use it when their energy shield is under heavy bombardment."

"We'll think about it later, Lieutenant," said Duggan.

"Another missile launch from the enemy, sir. Divided

between us and the Ghasts," said Massey. "Their ship is coming in real close to us."

"The Ghasts have fired their disruptor, and launched another four Shatterers." said McGlashan. "They've lost two of their launch tubes."

"The Dreamer energy shield has gone, sir!" said Chainer excitedly. "The disruptor must have knocked it out."

Duggan gripped the control bars tightly. Experience suggested the enemy shields wouldn't stay down for long. In fact, he was surprised the disruptor had disabled them at all. On his tactical screen, the Lambdas and the inbound Dreamer missiles crossed over. Two of the Lambdas connected with the larger dot of the Dreamer warship, while the remainder flew onwards. The Shatterers appeared at the extremes of his display, their trajectory changing as they homed in on their target.

"We got a missile hit!" said Chainer. "Two hits!"

"Fire the Lambdas again!" said Duggan. He saw how close the enemy had come. "And get our particle beams on them. See how much they like it."

"I can only give you sixty Lambdas, sir. Half of our port tubes are jammed."

"Do it!"

A distant whining sound rose to accompany the rumbling of the damaged warship. "I got a beam weapon hit on them," said Reyes.

"Don't fire them again!" shouted Breeze urgently. "That last one pulled too much from our engines and they're already dispersing a lot of heat close to the infantry quarters."

Reyes jumped as if he'd stuck his finger in an electrical socket. "Sorry," he mumbled, even though there was no way he could have been aware.

"Their shields are back!" said Chainer in dismay.

A faint thrumming came through the floor and the walls as

the Bulwark cannons discharged once more. McGlashan activated the countermeasures again and the shock drones flew in all directions. Duggan watched the tactical screen from the corner of his eye as one-by-one, the Dreamer missiles winked out of existence. One final missile remained, having evaded a torrent of Bulwark fire and it plunged into the side of the ES *Terminus*, midway between the bridge and the troops' quarters. The shockwave of it coursed through the metal walls.

"We got another three Lambda hits on their shield," said Chainer. "Their energy output went up sixty percent. I think they're struggling to hold it, sir."

"Fire whatever we've got," said Duggan. It seemed like it would be too little, too late. The next wave of Dreamer missiles would destroy both the *Terminus* and the *Dretisear*.

"The Oblivion's fired its disruptor again," said McGlashan, an edge to her voice that could have been fear or excitement.

"Their shields are gone," said Chainer, with the same unidentifiable quality to his words.

Duggan didn't say anything. Aside from the three spacecraft, there were only four objects on his tactical screen. The four Shatterers reached their target, flickered and then disappeared. The red dot of the enemy vessel remained in place for a further two seconds then it too, disappeared.

# CHAPTER NINE

"YES!" said Chainer, jumping from his seat. "That's taught those bastards!" He sat down quickly when he realised their situation was still far from ideal.

"I need updates and I need them fast," said Duggan. "What's our damage? How is the Ghast battleship? And get me confirmation of the kill. I want to know for certain we've got them."

The details spilled out from his crew.

"The kill is definite, sir," said Massey. "There's a cloud of white-hot debris spread across a few thousand klicks. We've already passed a few of the bigger pieces."

"What's our status? I need someone to speak to the guys below and find out if they've had any casualties. Lieutenant Chainer, I want you to use the backup comms circuit – try and talk to the Ghasts. We can't be certain there aren't any more Dreamer ships in the locality."

"We'd be dead if there were," said McGlashan.

"Our status is that we're full of holes," said Breeze with concern. "Our engines have suffered a near-critical failure. Luckily, there's no sign of a breach into the life support modules."

"What about our weapons?"

"Not looking great," said McGlashan. "We've got multiple failures across offensive and defensive systems. I'm completely locked out of the nukes and we've lost twenty-two of our Lambda clusters."

"Is the loss permanent?" asked Duggan.

"Too early to say. The AI's looking to repair or reroute where it can. If it's heat damage, there's a chance we'll be able to recover some of our capabilities. I really don't know what's up with the nukes – they have their own reload and launch instruction set. It's different to what I'm used to."

Duggan swore under his breath. A single Dreamer spacecraft had nearly managed to destroy two of the most powerful warships in the human and Ghast navies. He didn't know what capabilities the *Terminus* had remaining now it was over – certainly they couldn't put up much of a fight if any other hostiles showed up. The most sensible course of action for the safety of the ship and its crew would be to leave the area immediately – assuming that was an option. Unfortunately, they'd been sent here to gather intel and there was something unexplained that needed to be investigated.

"I want details on the object you detected on the surface," he said to Chainer. "Lieutenant Breeze – I need to know if we can go to lightspeed and if not, when we *will* be able to." He turned to McGlashan and Reyes. "Get those weapons back online. We're a sitting duck without them."

There was a chorus of acknowledgements and Duggan dropped into his seat to do some testing of his own. He discovered there was some output from the gravity engines, but they were at a fraction of their maximum. The status of the deep fission drives was buried beneath layers of alerts and errors. He ignored them for the moment – that was something for Breeze to explore.

"Sir? I'm getting a response from the *Dretisear*," said Chainer. "They must have installed additional comms systems as well."

"What do they say?"

"It's difficult to understand and I keep losing the signal," said Chainer. "I think a summary is that they're pretty beat up."

"Tell me something I didn't know," said Duggan.

"Their fission engines are offline and their gravity drives nearly at zero. They won't be going anywhere until they cool down."

"I appreciate their honesty," said Duggan. "Update them with our status and ask if they have sufficient power to maintain an orbit over the planet – tell them it's called Trasgor."

"It's going to take them four or five hours to get there," said Chainer.

"I doubt we'll be going very much faster," replied Duggan. "We're going to see what it is the Dreamers left on the ground."

"Is that wise, sir?" asked McGlashan. "What if it's a weapon?"

Duggan acknowledged the comment with a nod. "We need to find out, whatever it takes. The Dreamers aren't our friends and I don't imagine their activity on the planet is benign."

"We should try and contact the Space Corps," said McGlashan.

"Yes, we should, Commander. Lieutenant Chainer? Can you get a message to the *Juniper*?"

"I think so. The signal will be slow and I thought you were concerned it might be tracked."

"What's our closest monitoring station?"

"Gamma – it's the only one in the Garon sector."

"Good, route the signal through Monitoring Station Gamma. Make the guys there aware of the risks we'll have subjected them to. They may want to abandon it for a while and I don't want any more blood on my hands."

"Preparing the communication," said Chainer. "What do you want me to tell them?"

"Tell them what's happened. We'll update when we can."

"Okay, I'm sending it. The signal won't get there for another couple of days. This backup equipment we're using is old and slow compared to the new stuff. Luckily for us it's a bit more robust."

"I'm taking us towards Trasgor. Send a recommendation to the *Dretisear* to remain at a distance. Nil-Far's no fool, so I'm sure he'll do so anyway."

The *Terminus* swung around smoothly. To an observer, the warship might have seemed graceful, even with its exterior charred and damaged. To Duggan, everything felt cumbersome and heavy. A vibration grated through the control bars and something creaked behind the bulkhead wall. The recent combat, combined with the planet's rotation had taken the surface object away from sensor sight.

"If we can't see them, they can't see us," said Chainer, trying to put a positive spin on their situation. "As soon as they come into view, I'll let you know. I'd estimate it'll be at least an hour at the speed we're going."

"Understood," said Duggan.

The updates kept coming, piling on top of each other and reminding Duggan how much more there was to consider on a warship as big as this one. It had been a long time since he'd captained anything larger than the *Crimson* and he didn't like the idea that he'd become rusty.

"Bad news from the troops below," said Perry. "Five confirmed dead and another six out of action. Lieutenant Ortiz apologises for the delay in updating you – there's been a lot going on."

"Patch her through, Ensign."

Ortiz spoke through the bridge speakers. There was an absence of background noise at her end and her voice was loud and clear. "Sir, we're all suited up. The temperatures aren't too good here."

"We took a beating, Lieutenant."

"I saw it on the update feeds in the barracks, sir. Some of the guys weren't where they should have been – they were practising laps in the aft corridors. They ignored the internal alarms telling them to get the hell away."

Duggan breathed out noisily. The soldiers who'd been killed had chosen to disregard procedure by remaining in a high-risk area of the ship. Even the experienced guys could become cocky once they'd survived a few engagements. "I'll get their details when things have calmed down. Is there anything left to give them a send-off?"

"There's enough, sir," said Ortiz. Her anger and frustration were easy to hear.

"Very well. We'll deal with it when we're able."

Duggan closed the line, shut his eyes for a moment and sat with his fists tightly clenched. He pushed aside the emotions. "What else has gone wrong?"

"Sir, the lightspeed engines aren't coming back anytime soon," said Breeze. "We've got some big areas completely burned out and the rest is going to stay hot for days. The gravity drives should improve slowly – you might have another jump in output within the hour."

"We'll die of old age trying to get home on the gravity drive," said Duggan.

"That we will. I can't tell you when we'll have lightspeed available. I'm certain we'll get them back eventually."

Another hour passed, without significant improvement in the ship's damage status. The *Dretisear* stayed within range, though the Ghosts didn't let on if they could go any faster. The emergency lighting on the bridge remained in place and every one of the displays was a sea of red. Aside from the extensive damage, Duggan was relieved the life support was fully operational and ninety percent of the sensor arrays were undamaged. Most of all, he was happy that the Dreamer warship hadn't been equipped with an engine scrambler – he assumed they'd have used it if it was available. If the scrambler was something only the mothership carried, it was significant news.

"The surface object is coming into view, sir," said Chainer.

"Are we close enough for you to see what you want to see?"

"The closer the better," Chainer replied. "It'll take longer to get specifics from here."

"Fine," said Duggan, leaving the ship on the same course.

"It hasn't moved from the place I saw it last time. Whatever it is – it's big. One-point-five klicks to each side and in the shape of a pyramid."

"I've checked out the wreckage we noted earlier, sir," said Massey. "It's the SC *Lupus* – it's in one piece, but all out of shape."

"They got taken out by the same particle beam that almost finished us," said Breeze. "They're nothing but a lump of ruined metal now. Poor bastards onboard must have been killed in seconds."

"Yeah," said Chainer. "At least we got some payback for them."

"They kicked us in the balls for our trouble," said Perry.

"It's rarely clean, Ensign," said McGlashan. "They might tell you about quick and easy kills in the classroom. The reality is, we've taken half a trillion dollars' worth of damage and we've lost some of our men and women. I'm sure Lieutenant Nichols will have plenty to include in his report."

Nichols said nothing, but he smiled thinly.

"I'm getting a transmission from the *Dretisear*, sir," said Perry. "They've detected an energy shield around the object on Trasgor, with a diameter of eight klicks. Their AI has calculated the chances of it being a Dreamer artefact at one hundred percent."

"Did they specify what precisely they mean by an *artefact*?" asked Duggan.

"I'm querying the word with them," said Perry. He looked up. "They didn't mean anything specific, if I interpret their response correctly."

"Beaten by a damned Ghost comms man," said Chainer angrily.

"Competition is a wonderful thing," said Duggan mildly. "See what else you can find."

"What the hell do they need an energy shield for?" asked McGlashan.

"It's got to be something important," said Duggan. "I'm afraid we can't go anywhere until we find some more information about what's going on."

"I think I might know what it is," said Massey, with a look of nervous pride. "The oxygen levels have climbed since Lieutenant Chainer first detected the unusually high quantity. The closer to the object you look, the higher the oxygen. I believe the artefact is generating it and pumping it out in order to create an atmosphere."

"What the hell would they be doing that for?" asked Perry.

"To make the planet habitable," said Duggan. The hairs on his neck prickled at the thought. "The Dreamers could have come through the wormhole specifically to expand into this area of the universe. If they're making habitable planets, that means they plan to keep coming."

"There's hardly room for us and the Ghasts," said Chainer. "Let alone a third race of murderous aliens."

"How big was that mothership when we saw it?" asked Duggan, with worry in his voice.

"Huge," said Breeze. "Twenty klicks to a side, approximately the same shape as a cube."

"You could fit hundreds of these artefacts inside that one mothership," said Duggan. "If they're dropping them around this sector – or beyond – humanity could be in even deeper crap than we thought. This means our enemy is here to stay, rather than simply have a look around and then leave."

"What should we do?" asked McGlashan.

"The first thing we're going to do is destroy whatever it is they've left behind on Trasgor. Then, we're going to return to the *Juniper* and leave the decision about what to do next in the hands of Admiral Teron and his superiors. This mission is shaping up to be a bad one."

# CHAPTER TEN

"HOW ARE we going to destroy it, sir?" asked McGlashan. "We can't launch the nukes and I don't know if I can get them working again."

"We'll have to launch conventional missiles at them and see if they run out of power," said Duggan. "It's crude and it's all we have at the moment."

"Sir, I've got the *Dretisear* on the comms. Captain Nil-Far wishes to speak with you privately."

"Very well," said Duggan in puzzlement.

His earpiece squealed with interference and there was an irritating buzzing sound which came and went. "Captain John Duggan, what are your intentions towards the alien artefact?" asked Nil-Far, eschewing the niceties of human conversation.

"We have made the decision to destroy it. It is our belief the Dreamers intend to create a breathable atmosphere on Trasgor in order to populate it later."

"That is also our conclusion. I would ask that you do not go ahead with your plans."

"Why not?" asked Duggan, doing his best to conceal his surprise. He wasn't sure if the language modules could convey emotion clearly, but he didn't want the Ghost to know he'd been caught unawares by the request.

"I lack the authority to provide that information. We have sent a signal to Vempor. Alas, our backup comms do not travel quickly and we do not anticipate a response soon."

"Do you have knowledge of this artefact that we should be aware of?"

"I lack the authority to provide that information," repeated the Ghost.

"It is my belief we should take this opportunity to disrupt the Dreamer plans," said Duggan. "What action will you take if we proceed with the destruction?"

There was a pause this time – a long one. "I also lack the authority to break the truce between our two races, John Duggan. Therefore, I will not intervene should you proceed with your stated action. I must warn you that the response from Vempor might give me a different instruction."

"You might fire on us?"

"If I am asked to do so, I will attempt to destroy your vessel."

Duggan's surprise had turned to shock and his brain fought desperately for an appropriate response. "There is no time for these games, Nil-Far! If you do not give me a good reason why I should leave this Dreamer artefact, I will proceed with its destruction."

"It is not a game, John Duggan. I cannot give you the information you request."

"We will speak again soon," said Duggan, cutting off the Ghost captain. He looked around at the others on the bridge. The conversation hadn't been entirely private and the crew had clearly heard Duggan's side of it. "What the hell am I missing?"

he asked in frustration. "Our supposed ally has come near-as-damnit to saying he'd break our truce on the basis of this unknown object."

"The Ghasts know more about it than we do," said McGlashan. "That's a certainty."

"Could they have found something like it in the past?" asked Breeze. "There was Dreamer wreckage all around the Helius Blackstar. Perhaps there was something like this which they recovered and it provided them with valuable technology."

Breeze's suggestion seemed reasonable, even if it didn't add up entirely. "We're sure they used alien technology to bolster their own research in order to try and defeat the Confederation," said Duggan. "We have a truce now and we've demonstrated our ability to destroy their populated worlds if we choose to do so. Surely the only benefit they could get from recovering this *thing* on Trasgor would be to increase their military capabilities to destroy humanity."

"And since we're at peace, their actions are unusual," said McGlashan.

"Unusual at the very least," said Massey. "Sir, something about this stinks to high heaven."

"I agree," said Chainer.

Duggan felt as if he'd been skewered on a spike, leaving his arms and legs free to thrash but with no way to escape. He wasn't expecting a response from the Space Corps for days, in the same way the Ghasts weren't able to reach their own superiors. The Dreamers would have certainly sent a warning to their mothership – it would be a stupid man who hoped otherwise. There was no way the *Terminus* could wait around to see what came back from Admiral Teron. Furthermore, the *Dretisear* might well receive an instruction to launch a surprise attack. There was little chance of a good outcome from this situation.

"Could the Ghasts make good on their threats to destroy us?" he asked.

"They've taken a lot of damage," said McGlashan. "Some of their weapons have been disabled, but they're a big ship and I'll bet they can still pack a punch. There again, so can we."

"If we destroy each other, nothing will be gained and peace will be lost," said Duggan. "That's not an option."

"I reckon I can get the ship to lightspeed in twenty-four hours," said Breeze. "It might be enough to get us away before the Dreamers come looking for their missing spacecraft."

"If we leave, the Ghasts might attempt to recover the object," said Massey.

"The Oblivion isn't a heavy lifter," said Duggan. "All they can do is fly overhead and look at it."

"What if the Dreamers don't come back?" she asked. "What if the Ghasts have requested a spaceship to recover the object and they get away with it before the Space Corps sends another ship here? The most charitable reason I can think of for the Ghasts behaving like this is because they're idiots."

"They're many things, but they're not stupid," said Duggan.

"At the very least, this system could become a flashpoint, sir," said McGlashan. "If the Space Corps sends ships, the Ghasts send ships and then the Dreamers show up."

With each word uttered, Duggan became more certain as to the best course of action. He raised a hand to stem the flow of suggestions. "It seems to me the best way to proceed is to remove the entire reason for any of us to be here. We'll go ahead with the plan and destroy the object. Ensign Perry, please communicate our intentions to the Ghasts. Advise that we do *not* expect any interference from them in what is now a Space Corps affair."

"I've let them know, sir," said Perry. "They've acknowledged receipt, with no return message."

Duggan hadn't expected one. He'd never seen Nil-Far lie

outright and assumed this was inherent to the Ghast species. However, there were plenty of ways to avoid giving anything away and whenever he didn't want to answer a question, Nil-Far would say that he couldn't provide the information or any one of countless variations on the same response.

"They're still following, sir," said Chainer. "Want me to warn them off?"

"I'd prefer them to stay close, Lieutenant. They have Shatterers that can target from at least ten times further away than our Lambdas. If there's a betrayal, we can fire back at this range."

"Sorry sir, I should have realised."

Duggan waved it away. "Keep monitoring the area, Lieutenant. We need to keep our eyes and ears wide open."

Another voice spoke up, this one unwelcome. "I disagree with your chosen course," said Lieutenant Nichols. "In its current state, the *Terminus* could be repaired and returned to action within months. You're taking an unnecessary risk in approaching the planet. If we made distance on our gravity drive until the fission engines were ready, we could return to a shipyard. I'm sure the Space Corps will happily send other ships this way and in greater numbers."

"You can't fight a damned war if you're checking the cost of every bullet!" said Duggan. "I've told you what we're going to do, Lieutenant. You don't have the authority to cross-examine my every decision."

"I assure you I do, sir," said Nichols. He had a look of self-satisfaction that infuriated Duggan.

"We're going to Trasgor," said Duggan with finality.

The *ES Terminus* drew steadily closer to the site of the alien artefact, travelling at twenty percent of its usual maximum speed. The Oblivion shadowed them at a range of a hundred thousand kilometres – comfortably within Lambda targeting range. Duggan was glad - the *Dretisear*'s proximity suggested there was no current intent to begin hostilities. If the battleship drifted another fifty thousand kilometres distant, then it would likely be time to prepare for an unwanted conflict.

"The artefact is on fairly flat ground, sir," said Chainer. "There are a few undulations within the eight-klick perimeter of the shield and a couple of valleys. Other than that, you know the score – rock, rock and more rock."

"Anything else of note?" asked Duggan. "Signs of life or activity?"

Chainer hesitated. "I can't tell you for certain. The shield distorts our sensors on the way through, which is why it takes a few seconds to get a lock on their spaceships. A spaceship tends to be a lot bigger than ground artillery."

"You mean you can't tell me what else might be down there?" asked Duggan.

"I can't," said Chainer, with a defensive tone to his voice. "I thought we were going to blow them away from high orbit?"

"We don't know if that's going to work," said McGlashan. "Another couple of minutes and we'll be close enough to give it a go."

"How many Lambda clusters can we bring to bear?"

"We've got sixteen operational, of which two I wouldn't want to chance using. Of the fourteen, we can use them all if they'll successfully target the object. If we need to launch in a straight line, we'll only be able to bring seven to bear at one time. The nukes are still showing a total malfunction."

"Be prepared with the countermeasures if they launch anything from below," said Duggan. A distance countdown on his screen showed how close they were to lock-on range.

"Our missile targeting is fully functional," said McGlashan. "Whatever it is on the ground it's not carrying the same tech as their warships."

"Let the *Dretisear* know we're about to commence bombardment."

"They've acknowledged, sir. Nothing more," said Perry.

"Fire when ready, Commander. Fourteen full clusters."

"Aye, sir, missile launch complete. One hundred and forty on their way."

"That should be enough to give them a fright," said Breeze.

From their furthest range, it took the Lambdas a full minute to reach a stationary target. The crew of the *Terminus* remained silent while the guided plasma warheads closed in on the artefact far below. Chainer diverted one of the sensor feeds onto the bulkhead screen. From this distance the image was grainy, but clear enough that the target was visible as a large near-black pyramid with blurred edges. Suddenly, the image became entirely white as the missiles detonated with an intensity of light far in excess of what the screen could replicate. Even so, it was bright and Duggan had to squint his eyes against the glare. The plasma fire dissipated within seconds.

"Still there," said Reyes.

"There was an immense power reading when we hit the shield, sir," said Chainer. "It only lasted a couple of seconds and could have powered a dozen big cities for the same amount of time."

"Fire again," said Duggan. "Every tube, and utilise the rapid reload for three waves."

"Roger," said McGlashan.

More Lambdas raced away, followed eight seconds later by another wave and finally by a third.

"If four hundred don't do the business, I don't know what will," said Chainer. "Apart from the nukes, that is."

The bulkhead screen lit up again and again. Each time the light faded, the artefact remained untouched, stubbornly defiant against the firepower directed against it. When the final wave of

Lambdas had exploded fruitlessly against the energy shield, Duggan slumped into his seat.

"Have we got anything else?" he asked. "Will the beam weapons penetrate?"

"In truth, I don't know," said Breeze. "I don't think it's safe to use them yet. If they burn out more of our engines, we could be stranded here for weeks."

It wasn't something Duggan wanted to contemplate – he wanted to destroy the object and get away from this forsaken place as soon as possible. He could continue to expend missiles against the shield, yet was convinced there was little hope it would succeed.

"The peak energy readings didn't drop," said Chainer. "Whatever they have powering the shield, it wasn't weakened."

"Sir? Maybe we should turn around and put some distance between us and the planet," said McGlashan.

"That choice does not sit well with me, Commander. It will resolve nothing." He had a thought. "Lieutenant Breeze, you mentioned that you'd contributed to the Space Corps' research into our own version of an energy shield."

"Just peripheral input, sir."

"You said you'd picked up a few things – like the shields' vulnerability to gamma rays. Do you think the energy shield below is a complete sphere, encompassing the artefact entirely?"

"I'm not sure what you mean, sir."

"Can you project an energy shield through rock, for instance?"

"I see," said Breeze, nodding his head. "Well, the Space Corps' research wasn't too far along and we couldn't do anything like the Dreamers have done. However, it needs exponentially greater power to maintain the shield through the resistance of other atoms – hence the power spikes we see when our missiles impact against them. You want to know if the surface energy shield goes into the surface of the rock and I would give you an educated response that it does not. It's probably something like an umbrella that comes very close to the surface, without penetrating beneath."

Duggan gave a humourless smile. "In that case, it's time for us to go down for a closer look."

# CHAPTER ELEVEN

IT WAS McGlashan's duty to suggest alternatives. On this occasion, she saw the set of Duggan's face and kept her own counsel on the matter.

"A full deployment, sir?" she asked.

"We don't know what's waiting for us, so we're going down there with everything we've got," he said. "The worst that can happen is we arrive and there's nothing to oppose us."

"We don't have a heavy-lift transporter with us," said Lieutenant Nichols. A ship like the *Terminus* had the ability to deploy troops and hardware. What it didn't have was any way to recover that hardware once it was dropped – there were dedicated pickup vessels for that work, none of which were within a weeks' travel.

"I'm aware of that, Lieutenant," said Duggan. "This mission is already an expensive one, but we aren't going to worry about the money." He smiled challengingly.

"Let's look after the guys and gals by giving them our full support, rather than sending them out with a dozen rifles to share," said McGlashan.

"Captain Duggan," said Nichols, ignoring McGlashan's words. "I am not convinced that a deployment of the hardware we're carrying is the best course. We are throwing good money after bad."

Duggan shook his head. "Didn't you hear what Commander McGlashan said? We support our troops with everything we've got."

"If you're set on this course, a scouting party would be the best way to determine what proportion of the ship's equipment you need to utilise," said Nichols.

"You're overstepping, Lieutenant," said Duggan with a dangerous edge to his voice.

"Not at all, sir. I'm merely performing the duties given to me by my department."

"You're interfering with the appointed captain of the ES *Terminus*. We're deploying everything, unless you're telling me the Military Asset Management people have assigned a greater value on their tanks than they have on the Space Corps' soldiers?"

"Everything has a price, sir. I am formally advising you that Military Asset Management disagrees with this release of hardware."

"Disagrees?" shouted Duggan. "We're at war, man! Where's your authority to tell me how to act in a hostile situation?"

"My superiors will confirm my authority."

"We have no comms, Lieutenant. All I can hear at the moment is hot air."

Nichols smiled knowingly. "As you wish, Captain. The resolution of this matter will happen later."

"Shut up and get out of my sight, Lieutenant Nichols! Your organisation is a disgrace."

Nichols didn't answer. He simply nodded his head once and returned to his seat. The confrontation had interrupted preparations for the troop deployment and left the others quiet with shock. It was Chainer who spoke first.

"Can we fit a hundred into the transport shuttle to bring everyone back?" he asked. "It's going to be a tight squeeze."

"We've got a shuttle on each side," said Duggan. "There's plenty of room." He didn't mention that it would be tough if they came back with a few injured – it felt like it would bring bad luck if he talked about casualties before they happened.

"Not so much room if one of those enemy missiles had impacted next to one of our shuttles," said Massey.

Duggan didn't respond. As it happened, one of the Dreamer missiles had come perilously close to destroying both the life support system and the port-side shuttle. In the end, both had survived the blast. He opened a channel to Lieutenant Ortiz.

"Get the troops ready - load them up into the tanks. We have a target object protected by a shield generator and we're going to see what we can see – it's Dreamer tech. We're taking everything in the hold and I'll be in command."

"Roger that, sir. It'll be nice to give our own input, if you know what I mean? Some of the boys here have got itchy trigger fingers."

"I'm sure they have," said Duggan, ending the communication. He found McGlashan staring at him.

"You don't need to go, sir. Lieutenant Ortiz is more than capable. You'd be better off on the bridge."

"You're right, Commander, I *would* be better on the bridge. However, I am giving you this opportunity to show what you can do. A commander does not become a captain without showing her worth."

"I don't care about perception of worth, sir. I care about the success of this mission," she said.

"We'll succeed with you or I in charge," he said. "I won't be swayed on this, Commander. It's vital I take a look at what's down there, rather than leaving it to others. I have a feeling that what happens on Trasgor will have repercussions and I can't deal with them if I haven't been fully involved in the actions I order."

McGlashan didn't look happy, but she wasn't one to shy away from responsibility. "Very well, sir. I'll look after the *Terminus* while you're gone." Her expression cleared like a cloud moving away from the sun. "Just don't try and blame me for those holes in our side. They can go on the list of Captain John Duggan's misdemeanours."

"Agreed," he said. He turned his attention to other matters. "Lieutenant Chainer, I assume you'll be able to keep in close touch using the backup comms systems?"

"Yes, sir. It's not as if they're prehistoric or anything. They were made when we couldn't travel the distances we can go on a modern spaceship. Messages will reach the planet's surface in less than a second and come back at the same speed."

"Good. I may well need you." He walked to McGlashan and spoke to her quietly so he wouldn't be overheard. "Keep an eye on Lieutenant Nichols. I have no idea why he's here, but I'm convinced there's more to him than meets the eye."

"You got it, sir. I can handle him."

"Make sure you can and don't put up with any insubordination. If tries anything, lock him up under my authority."

"Will do."

Duggan left the bridge and broke into a run towards the hold. There was noise and activity, with soldiers breaking out rifles and bandoliers of plasma grenades. It was warmer than it should be, though not so bad that there was any immediate risk of injury from it. He pulled a spare suit down from a wall locker and struggled his way into it, cursing under his breath as he did so.

"Need a hand, sir?" It was Lieutenant Ortiz.

"I think I'll manage," he said with a grimace. Something

caught his eye on the shoulder of Ortiz' suit. The word *Jess* had been written in black ink.

"Thought you deserved your own private suit?" he asked.

"I didn't want one of these sweaty bastards putting it on later, sir," she said. "We've got plenty of spares onboard so there's no need to share."

Duggan chuckled. "We need to tie the repeaters and launchers onto the backs of the heavy tanks," he said, bringing the subject on to the matters at hand.

"I've given instructions to hook them up," she said. "We'll be ready to go in less than fifteen minutes. There's ninety of us left, including you. A few of the guys suffered minor burns on top of the more serious injuries. I decided they should stay behind."

"That's fine, Lieutenant. It makes an even fifteen in each tank on the way down and a bit more breathing room on the way up," said Duggan. "I have no idea what we're facing. From what I've seen so far, it's not likely to be friendly."

"Maybe one day we'll meet a bunch of aliens who aren't determined to wipe us out."

"I'm not expecting to see them any time soon," said Duggan.

"What sort of gear do you think they'll have, sir?"

"Your guess is as good as mine, Lieutenant. I wish I had a better answer for you."

"Sometimes this job sucks," she said, the look on her face suggesting that now definitely *wasn't* one of those times.

Ortiz moved away, shouting orders at the men and women in the hold. The urgency increased noticeably wherever her finger pointed. Duggan finished putting his suit on and picked up the helmet. The nearest weapons locker was hanging open and he grabbed a rifle. He chose one of the two Colossus tanks at random. A set of eight steep steps went upwards through the outer armour, ending at a heavy servo-powered door that led into the tank's interior. There was a man stationed within, counting

80

off the numbers who came inside. Duggan assumed the soldiers
been given squad numbers and assigned their own vehicles.

"Welcome aboard, Captain," said Butler.

"Thank you, soldier," said Duggan, squeezing through.

"I thought these tanks were all in museums now."

You'll be glad they aren't when the shooting starts," replied
Duggan, moving away.

Duggan hadn't been inside a Colossus tank for years and
nothing much had changed. There were three rooms – one for
command and control, the other two for carrying troops in a
certain amount of discomfort. Duggan had entered through one
of the two side entrances, which took him into one of the small
holding rooms. A doorway in the metal wall led to a short
connecting passage and then to the control room. The tank was
huge, but even so it was cramped within and the lighting was a
gloomy and subdued green. It would turn red if the tank came
under fire. There were bucket seats along two of the walls, with
five of them currently occupied. Duggan nodded at the soldiers
as he went through.

Corporal Hammond was in the control room – he was broad,
with tousled brown hair and an air of competence. There were
four seats in total and a bewildering array of screens and consoles.
"All systems are operational, sir," Hammond said. "We're waiting
on two more who'll be in here with me, and then we can go when
the order comes."

"That order will be coming soon," Duggan replied. "You're in
charge of this tank?"

"Yes, sir."

Duggan spent a few moments looking around. He knew how
to control the smaller tanks in the Space Corps – those on a
Vincent class were disposable and basic. The Colossus tank was
packed with all manner of extra equipment and was definitely
not classed as a disposable asset. There was much that looked

familiar to Duggan's eye. He guessed he'd be able to get the tank moving and firing, just not as efficiently as someone like Hammond. When it came down to it, much of the hardware in the Space Corps ran off the same back-end programming and many of the interfaces were closely related. It was what allowed well-trained people like Duggan to effectively utilise a variety of military resources. A fleet warship was by far the most demanding and responsible role. Corporal Hammond would be able to handle a tank – generally only the best and most well-trained soldiers went onto a spacecraft - but he'd have no hope when it came to controlling even a Vincent class. It took several years of training for that.

"I'll need the fourth seat," Duggan said. "To coordinate with the *Terminus*."

"We've got nobody sitting in that one, sir," said Hammond, pointing. "It's all yours."

Duggan took the indicated seat. The console was powered up and ready to use and he plugged into the other tanks to find out their statuses. The soldiers knew their stuff and four of the other five were set to go. While Duggan familiarised himself with the menu options on the tank, soldiers Reed and Quinn entered the control room and squeezed into their seats.

"Bridge, this is Duggan, do you copy?"

"I copy," came the voice of Chainer.

"We'll be ready in a few minutes. Commander McGlashan will initiate the launch sequence when I give the go-ahead."

"Right you are, sir. I've got green lights from four out of the six vehicles already and yours just came on to make it five."

"We'll wait for the sixth – everyone goes at once."

"We're holding at forty thousand klicks above the surface. How high do you want?"

"Tell Commander McGlashan to come to five thousand and return to a high orbit as soon as we're away."

"Will do, sir. I've just had the sixth green light."

Duggan muted his mouthpiece. "Corporal Hammond, the bridge sees six green lights. Can you confirm?"

"Yes, sir. All the tanks are prepared for launch."

"Bridge, this is Duggan. Please lock down the cargo bay and initiate launch at five thousand klicks."

"Roger that, we'll be saying farewell in ninety seconds."

As he watched the countdown on his screen, Duggan felt a sense of anticipation about what might be to come. He'd told McGlashan that he wanted her to taste the responsibility of captaincy. His words had been genuine, but the other reason was that he couldn't stay away from danger. The lure of it whispered to him constantly, until it became a struggle to ignore. There were times he wondered if the addiction made him act recklessly and he had no answer to the question.

"We're launching in five seconds," said Hammond to the troops onboard.

There was a clunking of something mechanical, followed by a sickening feeling of intense acceleration. The Colossus tank was hurled downwards along magnetic runners. A hatch in the space-craft's hull burst open to allow the vehicle to eject. A moment later, the hatch closed, leaving the hull smooth and without visible seam. Already far below, the tank tore through the sky, plummeting towards the surface of Trasgor. Inside, the men and women cracked nervous jokes to distract themselves from humanity's innate fear of falling.

# CHAPTER TWELVE

IT QUICKLY BECAME apparent that something was wrong.

"I have negative launch on five of the tanks," said Hammond.

Duggan contacted the *Terminus*. "We have multiple failed launches. Damnit, tell me what's happened!"

It was Lieutenant Reyes who answered. "We're not sure, sir. There are no system errors on the launch hardware. Commander McGlashan is doing her best to rectify the situation."

"Keep me informed," said Duggan curtly. "Less than two minutes in and it's already going wrong."

"We'll do our best," said Reyes.

The three soldiers in the control room had their eyes on Duggan, unasked questions clear on each of their faces. The course and destination of the tank was pre-programmed into its mainframe. There seemed little point in deviating yet.

"We make no changes," said Duggan. "They'll have to get this fixed and send the others to meet us."

Duggan checked the status reports for the tank's critical systems. Perhaps there had been some unrecorded damage from the engagement with the Dreamer warship. It didn't take long to reassure himself there was nothing to cause concern as far as the tank itself went. All the gauges and readings were exactly where they should be.

"We should land in ten minutes," said Corporal Hammond. "Let's have a look at the external sensors and see where we're going."

He activated the largest screen in the cockpit, which filled the area with a startling amount of light. Some tank crews found the main screen distracting and kept it turned off.

"Trasgor, eh?" said Quinn. "I'm sure I've seen this place before."

"Yeah – it's round, grey and cold. A perfect holiday destination," said Reed.

"It's my dream that one day I'll be sent to a planet full of palm trees and beaches," said Quinn.

"It'd be just our luck to find it covered in hostile lifeforms."

"Yeah, that sounds about right."

Duggan let the conversation wash over him. The words were comforting in a way, reminding him of fellowship and cameraderie. After another minute, the urge to contact the *Terminus* became too great and he requested another channel.

"Where're my tanks?" he asked.

"Still in the hold where you left them, sir," said McGlashan.

"Any progress on finding out what went wrong and getting it fixed?"

"Not yet, sir. We've confirmed there's no damage to that area of the ship."

"No damage?" asked Duggan. "That means there's a failure between the AI and the launch tubes."

"That's what I thought and I've checked it out. I can't see any problems."

"Unload the soldiers from the remaining tanks and send them to one of the transport shuttles. They can come to the surface that way. Leave the tank crews in place and you can launch the remaining five vehicles once you've discovered the fault and fixed it."

"Yes, sir. I'll get on it right away."

The minutes passed and a grumbling noise pervaded the interior of the tank. The noise gradually increased in volume, though not loud enough to drown out conversation.

"Gravity engines boosting at sixty percent of maximum output," said Hammond. "They're guiding us in to the landing place. We're going to set down right where we want to be."

Duggan spoke to the *Terminus* again, in the final minutes before the tank landed. There was no apparent cause for the launch failure and McGlashan had narrowed it down to a likely fault with the ship's AI. It was mystifying, since the brain of a warship had so much redundancy a failure of any sort was practically unheard of. The transport shuttle wouldn't be loaded for another few minutes. Duggan told McGlashan and Reyes to keep on with their efforts to fix the problem.

"Here we go," said Hammond over the internal comms. "Landing procedures underway. Keep your sick bags ready." The comment about sick bags wasn't too far from the truth and it wasn't uncommon to feel nausea when a vehicle like this one decelerated. The tanks were programmed to come in fast, and then slow down at the last possible moment to make them less of a target. The main viewscreen showed an image of pitted, uneven ground, before Hammond switched the display off. The tank's engines howled and Duggan swallowed to keep on top of the rising nausea. The sensation remained for too long, but then it passed abruptly.

"We're on the ground, with weapons and propulsion good to go," said Hammond. "Awaiting your instructions, sir."

Duggan pulled up a topographical view of the area on his tactical display. They'd landed fifteen kilometres from the target, which made it eleven to the edge of the energy shield. The surrounding area was bumpy and uneven, thickly covered in a layer of gritty dust and pebbles. The sky was clear and visibility was good. The tank was in a wide channel, with rounded sides and a depth of a hundred metres or so. It prevented them from getting a sight of the artefact, but also gave them cover from any ground attack. There'd been nothing threatening so far and Duggan had taken a chance by having them land as close as this, relying on the *Terminus'* ability to deal with anything that showed up outside the energy shield's perimeter. Time was short and he wanted to get business over with as soon as possible.

"*Terminus*, do we have an ETA on that shuttle?"

"They're loaded up, sir. Another minute and they should unlatch."

"Good. Have them land at our position." There was little choice other than to wait for the other troops to arrive.

"Sir?" said Chainer, with concern. "The shuttle won't undock."

"What the hell is going on?"

"We have no idea. It must be a symptom of what's affected the other five tanks."

"I thought the Galactic class was meant to be the Space Corps' pride and joy."

"That'd be the *Crimson*, sir. The *Terminus* is pretty beat up. I'd say it's put up a decent showing so far."

"Just get me those tanks, Lieutenant, and the shuttle. I don't mind being killed by enemy fire, but I certainly don't want to suffocate in the hull of a tank."

"This baby's got enough power to sustain us for months, sir," said Hammond. "Plenty of time for them to rescue us."

Duggan wasn't convinced a rescue craft was coming any time soon, though he didn't say it. The occupants of this lone tank were effectively stranded on the surface of Trasgor, with no guarantee they'd have any support either from the *Terminus* or from the Space Corps. It wasn't that the Corps had no loyalty to its own – there was simply no appetite to throw men and materials at a lost cause. Duggan had his own code of honour, but he couldn't blame his superiors for refusing to send a fleet every time they lost a soldier and it wasn't realistic to expect them to change. He looked at his wrist to check the time - he'd not worn a watch in years and this was a habit he'd never managed to shake.

"We'll give them another fifteen minutes to fix whatever's wrong and then we'll make our own way to the target."

The fifteen minutes passed quickly. Duggan checked with the *Terminus* several times to see what the holdup was. He hoped for answers and a resolution, and got neither.

"There's definitely no hardware fault," said McGlashan. "I've checked for damage numerous times and there's nothing. I feel as if I'm knocking my head against a wall."

"Could there be an emergency override in place from the AI?" asked Duggan. "Maybe the life support is giving it a false reading that's telling it to keep the ship sealed."

"That doesn't explain why you got away successfully."

"No, it doesn't. I've seen enough things go wrong to know the underlying logic isn't always easy to spot. Keep on it, we're beginning our agreed route towards the target."

"Okay, sir. Good luck."

A notice on Duggan's screen informed him the line to McGlashan was closed. He let Corporal Hammond in on the news which he'd already overheard. "We're not waiting any longer. Take us towards the target."

Hammond wasn't a man to delay. Even while he acknowledged the order, he used the tank's control bars to feed power into its gravity engine. The vehicle lurched once and then moved away, hovering a couple of feet above the surface. Any larger stones which lay in its path were knocked aside by the immense weight of the Colossus tank.

"It'll be fifteen or twenty minutes until we reach the perimeter, sir," he said. "Less if you want us to push our speed."

"Steady as she goes for the moment, Corporal. There's a time to walk and there's a time to run."

Duggan spent the minutes watching the topographical display of the terrain. He called up the feeds from several of the external sensors in order to get a feel for what was outside. The channel twisted left and right. It was reminiscent of a riverbed, though the parched, barren surroundings of this world gave the impression there'd never been water here. It was daytime outside and the sensor feeds were razor-sharp, showing the ruggedness of the land ahead. They were amongst what might be described as hills, which were low and unevenly shaped. Without soil or plant life to smooth off the jutting edges, everything was angular with not a curve to be seen. It was harsh and unwelcoming, though Duggan hardly noticed.

The terrain readings sent down from the *Terminus* were highly detailed. The target object was in a wide, curved valley, with steep sides that sloped to heights of up to thirteen hundred metres. The artefact itself was on the floor of the valley and rested on an area of flat ground. There was no way to tell if the positioning was by accident or design, which made it hard to guess how the defences would be arranged. That was assuming the Dreamers had left something behind to repel a ground assault.

"This channel tapers off a few hundred meters ahead and when we come out we'll be in an exposed position," said Hammond. "There's no cover for the following two klicks until we reach the perimeter."

"We'll be hidden from the pyramid when we reach the shield," mused Duggan. "Once we're through, I'd say we can proceed at least a couple of klicks along the valley before we're in direct sight of the target."

"You don't think the perimeter will be defended, sir?" asked Hammond.

"We have to assume it is," said Duggan. He checked the maps again – once the tank left the channel, it would need to cross the side of a gentle slope. This slope became steeper until it formed the left-hand valley wall. Whatever defences the Dreamers had positioned here would likely have a shot at the oncoming tank. The vehicle's shape was designed to deflect sensor pings but in reality, it wouldn't fool anything remotely sophisticated. After that, all it had to rely on was armour and brawn. Duggan had a thought. "Stop the tank, Corporal Hammond. I need to speak to somebody on the *Terminus*."

"That's done, sir."

Duggan used the onboard comms to reach the warship high above. "Lieutenant Breeze, for the removal of doubt, if we can't fire into the energy shield, are the enemy able to fire out of it?"

"No, sir. The shield will block incoming and outgoing - they'll have to drop their shields to fire out. Their spacecraft was doing the same and I'm sure whatever's on the ground will suffer the same limitation."

"We'll shortly be in line of sight of any perimeter defences. If their shield goes down, be sure to launch missiles from the *Terminus* at whatever you can see."

"No such luck, sir," said Breeze. "They'll not be stupid enough to leave themselves so vulnerable. The shield will go off and come back on within a hundredth of a second. There'll be no time for a missile to reach its target."

"Any sign of my tanks or soldiers?"

"Commander McGlashan is shaking her head and shrugging her shoulders."

Duggan laughed bitterly and closed the line. "I'm going to wring someone's neck for this," he said.

"It'd be nice to have the others with us," said Quinn.

"More glory for us," laughed Reed. "Another story to tell the grandchildren."

Duggan motioned for silence, to allow him to think. The tank was the safest place for the troops and also the largest target. He made a decision and acted on it. "I want everyone apart from the crew outside," he said.

"They'll be unprotected," said Hammond.

"I'm afraid that in this instance, it'll be us taking the risk," said Duggan.

"Sir?"

"We're going to stick our heads out and see what shoots back."

"Sounds like a plan," said Hammond without missing a beat. He used the internal speakers to instruct everyone to put on their spacesuit helmets. "Lieutenant Ortiz asks what I'm playing at, sir."

Duggan was pleased to find her on the single tank they'd managed to deploy. She evidently hadn't known Duggan was onboard as well. "Tell her to stop asking questions and get outside."

"Message relayed," said Hammond. "We're empty apart from the four of us."

"Take us carefully ahead, Corporal. Once we leave this channel we'll be showing our face to the enemy. Be ready to back-track if there's a response."

The Colossus tank's engines powered up again, carrying it in near-silence up the slope and out of the channel. The eleven soldiers who had been left behind watched the heavily-armoured block of metal from a distance of three hundred metres. They were safe between the cocooning rock walls around them, while the tank became exposed to whatever might lie ahead.

In the cockpit, Duggan and the crew watched their various tactical screens nervously. This was the moment which would decide if this part of the overall mission was going to be a success or failure.

"Something's locked on!" said Quinn, calmly and clearly.

"Take us back!" said Duggan.

It was too late to escape. A surface-launched projectile sped outward from the shield, following a low, flat trajectory towards the tank.

"We're not going to make it," said Hammond, his mouth unable to complete the words before the inbound slug connected with the tank.

# CHAPTER THIRTEEN

THERE WAS A HIDEOUSLY LOUD CLANG, accompanied by the screeching of tortured metal. The remaining occupants of the tank felt it rock under the force of the impact. Another strike followed four seconds later, while Corporal Hammond pushed the tank to maximum velocity as he reversed it towards the channel. The hull of the tank shuddered under one final blow before its profile finally vanished from sight in the safety of the channel below.

"Crap, we're going to look like a piece of cheese after that," breathed Hammond. "Give me a damage report."

"There's a minor drop in output from our engines. Weapons okay, sensors okay. They must have deflected away from our armour, sir."

Duggan tried to ignore the ringing in his ears and collated the sensor reports about what had hit them. "I read that as three dense metal strikes from a high calibre artillery piece," he said.

"That's what it was," said Quinn. "A coil gun, somewhere ahead. It's a damn good job we're not in anything smaller than this, else I reckon we might have been completely disabled."

"Or dead," said Hammond, speaking the word Quinn had avoided.

"Yeah, maybe."

"What now, sir?" asked Hammond. "We're tough as hell, but we can't take that level of bombardment over two klicks. If they weren't behind a shield, we could try duking it out with them. There's no fixed emplacement that can stand more than a single round from our main turret."

Duggan knew this wasn't an idle boast – he'd seen what the main cannon on one of these tanks could do. His brain spun through the possibilities. The most important result from this was that the Dreamer defences had shown themselves, yet without getting a kill.

"We need the rest of those tanks," he growled. He patched into the *Terminus'* comms system. "Did you get that?" he asked.

"Yes, sir," said Chainer, with hints of excitement in his voice. "They dropped their shields three times for about a hundredth of a second on each occasion. It was more than long enough for us to get an idea of what's down there. We're just running through the data."

"Give me an outline, Lieutenant."

"There is a total of eight guns covering the pyramid, arranged equally around the perimeter. They've done a poor job, sir. They have almost no overlapping fire and the ship's AI calculates there's only a two hundred and fifty metre area where you'll be under fire from two of the guns at the same time."

"One is more than enough, Lieutenant. They're high calibre, high velocity weapons and they're hidden behind an energy wall that our weapons can't penetrate."

"We'll give you whatever support we can, sir. I've sent you a picture of the nearest emplacement – we got a good view of it."

A rotating three-dimensional image appeared on one of Duggan's screens. It showed a spindly metal frame with a tube running through the middle. A larger alloy cuboid squatted at the rear, presumably to house the power and ammunition. It looked unusually elegant, even if it didn't give away any clues as to the best way to combat it. In fact, Duggan couldn't see a way forward. He could have someone take remote control over the tank, send it towards the shield and hope the onboard weapons system had enough grunt to fire the main turret at precisely the right time for the projectile to arrive in the split second the energy shield went down. He didn't need the *Terminus'* AI to run a simulation to know the plan had little hope of working. The tank's main turret was slow to reload – at least two seconds between each round. There were the two plasma launchers on the shoulders, but they had a reload time of between fifteen and twenty seconds. The Colossus was designed to shatter defences with outright force, rather than with finesse.

"Was there any sign of life?" asked Duggan. "It would be nice to know what our enemy looks like."

"The emplacements are unmanned, sir. The central structure is too dense for our sensors to penetrate."

"Any clues as to what it is?"

"A big power source and an oxygen generator, as we've already guessed. If there's a way inside, I haven't seen one."

"Has Commander McGlashan fixed the nuke launchers?"

There was the sound of conferring. "No ETA at the moment. If we get them working, I don't need to tell you about the blast radius from a two gigaton warhead, sir."

Duggan didn't need telling. The gamma rays would take out the energy shield. The tank was well-insulated, but he had no idea if it would be enough to block the quantities of radiation which would pour forth after the detonation. Radiation wasn't even the primary concern – the explosion itself would extend for hundreds of kilometres in all directions, followed by a shock wave of terrifying proportions. Duggan really didn't want to be on the surface of Trasgor when a massive nuclear warhead exploded.

"I've got an idea," he said. As he spoke the words, he'd already convinced himself it was the quickest option available and one which put the fewest lives at risk.

"I'm all ears, sir," said Chainer.

"Put Commander McGlashan on. She'll need the details."

McGlashan's familiar voice replaced Chainer's and Duggan explained his plan.

"The timing will need to be perfect, sir," she said. "And there'll only be one shot at it."

"I know, Commander. If we had the heavy repeaters we wouldn't need to resort to this sort of crap."

"We can't launch the Lambdas quickly enough to hit the gauss emplacement and the pyramid," she said.

"We'll lose the tank. I can't think of a better way."

"You could call it off and retreat to safety until we get things figured out up here."

"Time is against us, Commander. The reasons we discussed earlier still hold true – we need to destroy this object. I can't accept another war with the Ghasts."

"Nor I, sir. Tell me when you've made the preparations."

"Will do."

Duggan used his headset to create an open channel to the troops on the surface. "Listen up, we're pinned down by an enemy gauss emplacement which is protected by a force shield. Every time it fires, the shield drops for a fraction of a second. We're going to send the tank ahead without a crew and the *Terminus* is going to try and get a Lambda through when the coil gun fires."

"The tank will be destroyed, sir," said Hammond.

"Almost certainly," said Duggan. "There are still problems on the *Terminus*. I'm confident the crew will be able to resolve those problems, at which point they'll send the shuttle to pick us up."

"What if they don't, sir?" said Reed. She had a right to ask the question.

"If they can't get the shuttle to launch, we're stuck here with just our suits, our rifles and each other. This doesn't change anything – we're stuck here anyway. The Space Corps may or may not come for us, so I'm not making you any guarantees."

A few of the soldiers muttered about their lot. In reality, this was what they'd signed up for and none of them came close to mutiny.

"Sir?" said Quinn. There was an unexpected timidity to his voice.

"What is it, soldier?"

"You said you planned to send the tank ahead, didn't you?"

"Unless you want to pilot it yourself?"

Quinn took an audible breath. "We don't carry a remote box for the Colossus tanks unless specifically requested. The crew is expected to stay onboard at all times."

"There's no remote box?" asked Duggan, closing his eyes briefly. He left the open channel and spoke to the *Terminus*. "I need you to patch into the tank and have the AI ride it out towards those emplacements."

The line hummed quietly for a few moments. "I've just tried to access the vehicle's mainframe," said Chainer. "It's not going to work well on the backup comms."

"Speak clearly, man!" said Duggan. "What do you mean it won't work well?"

"I should have been more precise, sir," said Chainer. "I should have said that it won't work." He launched into a hurried explanation about interfaces and the sizes of data packets.

"That's fine, Lieutenant," said Duggan. He turned to the other three on the bridge. "Get your helmets on and go outside with the others. I'll take it from here." They stared blankly at him for a moment as his words sunk in. "Go!" he repeated.

Galvanised into action, the tank's crew released the locks on the exit doorway and went through without a further word. A couple of minutes later, the internal sensors reported there to be only a single occupant. Duggan looked around at the banks of screens. One of them showed the soldiers gathered in a group outside. They milled about with uncertainty. While he was working the steps of his plan through his mind, Lieutenant Ortiz spoke to him privately.

"Need any company?"

"Thanks for the offer, Lieutenant. The troops need you to look after them if something goes wrong."

She didn't push it. "Good luck."

"I'm told these tanks are built to last," he said.

"That they are."

Ortiz wasn't one to overstay her welcome and she left the comms. Duggan felt he was as ready as he'd ever be. He picked up his own suit helmet from where he'd left it on the unpainted metal floor next to his seat and put it on, breathing the scents of rubber and stale sweat like they were old friends. He felt enclosed and safe within the suit, even if it offered no protection against gauss rounds.

"Commander McGlashan. I'm taking manual control of the tank. Please commence your firing routine upon my word."

McGlashan was a professional and knew when it was time to keep her mouth shut and follow orders. "I've programmed in the instructions, sir. The missiles are loaded and ready. We'll need to utilise the rapid reload function on the tubes, so we'll only be able to maintain full launch density for thirty-two seconds. After that, our firing rate will fall by more than half."

"What's your altitude?"

"We're at forty thousand klicks, sir. Sixteen seconds from launch to detonation."

Duggan moved himself to Corporal Hammond's chair and looked at the instrumentation before him. He gave the tank's engines one final check. They were down five percent from one of the earlier gauss impacts. It wouldn't have an appreciable effect on the vehicle's top speed of fifty kilometres per hour and he was just shy of a hundred seconds away from the energy shield. Chainer had sent some additional data from the *Terminus* to show the overlapping fields of fire from the gauss emplacements. Two hundred and fifty metres' worth. Less than twenty seconds. It was going to be rough if he even managed to get that far. His eyes drifted to the external display which showed the place where a single one of the gauss rounds had hit the tank, leaving a two-metre-wide furrow across one of the angular front panels. A direct hit would be far more devastating.

With an effort of will, he buried his doubts and placed his hands on the control bars. "Commander McGlashan, please launch."

Duggan scarcely heard her acknowledgement. He increased the tank's gravity engines to one hundred percent and pushed his right-hand control bar as far along as it would go. The tank had a tremendous amount of power – enough to overcome the inertia of such a heavy object. It burst forward and up the slope which led away from the channel, scattering stones and dust behind it.

# CHAPTER FOURTEEN

THE TACTICAL SCREEN FLASHED RED, before the tank had gone more than fifty metres over the open ground. The vehicle's sensors detected the output from a coil gun and relayed the information to the cockpit. A grooved metal ball, the size of a man's head, thundered into the heavily-armoured front of the tank and ricocheted dozens of kilometres away. Inside, Duggan felt the force of the blow through his seat and through the palms of his hands where they rested on the cold metal of the control bars. The sound of the contact chimed harshly and he was thankful the spacesuit helmet automatically reduced the volume to a safe level. A second round followed the first, again deflecting away from the warship-grade alloy of the tank's armour.

During the earlier engagement, Duggan had discovered the Dreamer gun had a firing interval of four seconds – plenty of time for it to get away a couple of dozen shots. He'd programmed the details into the tank's mainframe, in the hope the computer would be able to calculate all the necessary speeds and distances that would allow it to fire the main turret just when the energy shield dropped. Something rumbled deep within the tank as the mainframe decided it was time to fire. A half-tonne projectile screamed away at such a velocity that it left a bright orange trace in the sky behind it. Two kilometres along its path, the slug struck a shimmering barrier in the air. Streaks of pale blue snaked away from the impact, like sparks of electricity jumping through clear water. The sparks faded and the flattened globe of depleted uranium fell to the ground. On the other side of the energy shield, the Dreamer gun fired again.

Far overhead, the first of the *Terminus'* Lambda missiles hit the top of the shield. The warhead exploded into blinding white, expanding to fill several hundred metres with tumultuous fire. The blast wasn't able to complete its natural desire to form a sphere. Rather, it spread over the dome-shaped barrier generated by the pyramid beneath. A fraction of a second later, another Lambda hit in the same place, followed by another and another. Instead of firing in waves, Duggan had given instructions for the missiles to be launched with a tiny interval between each, in the hope that one might get through when the energy shield was down.

Within the tank, Duggan gritted his teeth as another round hit the tank. The main turret fired again and the shoulder-mounted plasma launchers ejected their own explosives towards the barrier. He'd set up a distance counter to show how far the energy shield was from his position. It already felt as if he'd been under fire for hours but when he checked, the tank was still seventeen hundred metres away. Duggan didn't know quite what he intended if he made it to the perimeter. He had no intention of crashing into it and killing himself. What he did know was the longer the tank kept moving, the greater the chance one of the Lambdas would hit the pyramid. *It had damn well better be enough.*

Duggan quickly learned why there was room for four in the cockpit. An endless quantity of text was thrown across his screens and it was a fight to keep on top of it. On a spacecraft, he'd have managed; on the tank, everything seemed to be in a different place or accessed in a different manner. With little time to think, the overload of data threatened to swamp him.

"Come on!" he shouted.

Another thumping blow shook the tank and the damage reports came in. Amber warnings changed to red and the sensors reported a breach through the tank's front plating where two projectiles had struck near to each other. Other sensors reported garbage – lines of unintelligible code to indicate their failure. Several of the viewscreens merely showed grey static, which seethed in quiet anger.

"Fourteen hundred metres," he said, watching the number count down another digit with painful slowness.

"Sir? You'll be entering the overlapping field in twenty seconds." It was Chainer, his voice welcome but the news not.

"Any luck?" said Duggan, tersely. He was too occupied to say more.

"A couple of near misses," said Chainer.

*No luck, in other words,* whispered the thought in Duggan's mind. "Tell me when there's good news."

The next gauss round destroyed one of the shoulder launchers, catching the plasma round halfway out of the tube. The missile exploded with a low thump, ripping out a lump of the armour. Plasma spilled across the rear quarter of the tank, blistering and softening the alloy. The tank's mainframe fired in response, a nanosecond later than it needed to, leaving the Dreamer weapon unharmed behind the shield.

"Entering the crossfire, sir," said Chainer. "Good luck. I'll let you know if we score a hit."

"Roger."

Dense metal smashed against the tank's front plating. The force of the blow heated the enemy projectile to an extreme temperature, flattening it to a thin disk. It fell away, to be left behind amongst the rocks and gravel. Where it struck, there was a deep crater in the armour, the metal sundered and battered. The projectiles came at two second intervals now, the sound of their blows echoing in Duggan's head with a rhythm of death and ruination.

The tank ploughed on, a damaged mass of plasma-scoured metal. Giddy with battle, Duggan shouted incoherent words of encouragement to the machine. Pride filled his chest at the defiance it showed against the incoming assault - that this projection of the Space Corp's capabilities could deny the inevitability of its own destruction for so long.

*Ten seconds.* He didn't know if he'd spoken the words aloud or imagined them in his head. *Eight.* Still the barrage persisted. The tank was slowing – one of the slugs had put a hole clean through the armour and into the gravity drive. *Four seconds and we're clear. The tank and me.* The last few seconds lasted forever as this battle within a battle struggled on to its conclusion. When the tank finally broke out of the crossfire, it was a mess of burned, punctured metal and still at seventy-five percent of its maximum speed. Bathed in the glow of red, critical alert lights, Duggan had no idea how it was moving so quickly.

"Sir, one of our missiles got though," said Chainer. "It struck the pyramid dead on. The energy output went haywire for a second and then it stabilised."

"Keep firing," said Duggan, his own voice sounding distant to his ears.

"We're not letting up," said Chainer.

The tank had come to within thirty seconds of the shield. Its speed was tapering and the mainframe had to constantly recalculate the time. For each digit the counter fell, it seemed as if another was added to take it back to where it had been. One by one, the sensor feeds winked out as they became too damaged to function. Throughout it all, the Dreamer gun maintained its constant rate of fire, pummelling the tank into a shape that looked like nothing it had been before. Duggan shook his head in wonder – there was no way the tank should still be moving and he should have likely been dead long ago. He was faintly aware of the heat in the cockpit. It had risen past two hundred degrees. *Nothing the suit can't handle.*

With twenty seconds to go, one of the incoming rounds buried itself deeply into the body of the tank. The compressed slug burst through the cockpit wall and fell to the floor near Duggan, glowing fiercely. A siren added itself to the cacophony, warning of a breach into the control room. Duggan crunched his fist against the speaker. The alarm continued to sound, ignorant of his efforts to silence it.

"A second successful strike on the pyramid," said Chainer. His voice squawked and crackled. "The shield is still up."

"I think the comms are failing," said Duggan, raising his voice in anticipation of the next impact. "The tank's dying."

"Hang in there, sir."

Duggan took another look around the cockpit. There were hardly any screens running and the temperature had climbed past two hundred and forty degrees. The suit was an exceptional insulator, but he could feel heat from the burning slug beating against him. Metal shrieked against metal somewhere above the ceiling. *Main turret disabled.*

The tank was travelling at what felt like a crawl, with one side barely an inch above the ground. Duggan checked the timer – one of the three displays which remained active. *Still on fifteen seconds.* It was beginning to seem as if he'd never reach his destination – a long walk where the end faded ever further into the distance. He wondered briefly if he'd live through it. The enemy would surely stop firing once the tank was broken into enough pieces. Perhaps they'd continue their attack long after a human would have stopped. *Thirteen seconds. McGlashan's unlucky number. Today it's mine too.*

One of the sensors was still operating – miraculously it was pointing forward. Duggan peered at its feed and saw his goal. The gauss emplacement looked exactly as it had on his screen earlier, yet bigger than he'd expected it to be. Another punishing strike cracked against the tank. The projectile was far too fast for the human eye. The sensor detected it, however, and showed it as a streak of orange over the display. The trace faded and was replaced by another. A hole appeared in the ceiling, wide and ragged. Duggan noted it calmly without spending time wondering where the projectile had finished up. *Thirteen seconds still on the clock. A sign that my number's up.*

"Sir, we've hit them again! The shield is down!"

Duggan sat bolt upright, the dreamlike quality of the last few seconds banished as if it had never existed. "Get that coil gun for me! I'll be dead in a few seconds."

"You're too close, sir. Commander McGlashan's trying."

Plasma ignited a few hundred metres beyond the gauss gun. It spread with blinding speed, the extremes of the blast engulfing the emplacement. The tank was struck again. When the flames receded, the coil gun was still intact, mocking and stubborn. Here and there, patches of the metal smouldered. There was a second detonation, this time a few metres closer. Once more the plasma fire raged, this time licking across the hull of the tank. Any closer and Duggan could see he'd be burned to a cinder.

"Hold fire!" he said.

The entire structure of the tank shuddered. The engines howled, though to Duggan it sounded like a scream of agony.

"Don't give up!" he roared, thumping his palm onto the console before him.

He had no idea how the tank had so much resilience – a battered husk of metal and engines with its single functioning sensor and a mainframe that seemed to be as obstinate as Duggan himself.

"Get out, sir!" shouted Chainer.

"Negative, Lieutenant, I've got this one," said Duggan.

A third hole appeared in the cockpit and this time he could see clear daylight through it. He looked out, seeing the emplacement only a few metres away, red hot and smoking, with the air shimmering above. The gun fired again. Duggan had no idea what happened to the slug and he didn't care. Through the hole, he watched the tank collide with the structure supporting the gun. The tank was down to eight kilometres per hour, yet it had lost none of its weight. The emplacement was much stronger and heavier than it appeared. Nevertheless, the tank carried a vastly greater bulk and it hardly slowed as it crashed through, bending and twisting struts and beams. The gun barrel was knocked away and the hull of the tank thumped into the housing for the power supply and ammunition. The housing was thick-walled and strongly moored - not enough to prevent it being tipped over and pushed aside.

At that moment, the tank's engine died. The howl of stressed metal faded at once and the tank dropped to the ground, leaving Duggan breathing heavily in his seat. He unclipped his safety belt and prepared to leave in haste. There was only a single screen lit, still showing its countdown. *Thirteen seconds. It must have got stuck. Not my unlucky number – not this time anyway.*

"I'm getting out of here," he said to Chainer.

The inner blast door protecting the cockpit shuddered painfully open and he dashed along the short tunnel to the holding area. It was a mess of sharp-edged holes and there was a wide slash along one wall. Anyone in here would have died a dozen times over. The exit door was gone, ripped away at some point in the last few minutes. Duggan jumped down the steps and into the wan light of day, never so happy to be alive as he was then.

# CHAPTER FIFTEEN

DUGGAN DROPPED to his haunches and looked at the wrecked tank. There were too many scars for him to count, but it looked like it had taken at least fifty rounds. He shook his head in disbelief, having seen smaller tanks get knocked out by a single, well-directed gauss projectile.

"Lieutenant Chainer, please destroy the second coil gun and confirm when the path is clear for me to bring the rest of the troops up."

"Commander McGlashan confirms the target will be destroyed in the next few seconds, sir." There were the sounds of background confusion. "The Oblivion is breaking away from us."

"Have they communicated?"

"Negative. Lieutenant Massey is trying to reach them."

"Don't let them get beyond Lambda range!" shouted Duggan. "Stay close and find out what the hell they're doing. Get the men out of the shuttles and back to their quarters – it'll be safer there."

"Will do, sir. The Ghasts are building up speed – they might be establishing an orbit."

Duggan exhaled. It wouldn't be unusual for a damaged

spacecraft to go into a stable orbit while repairs were ongoing. He wanted to trust Nil-Far, but there was no way he was going to drop his guard. "The order stands. Shadow them and find out what they're doing. They might not have any reason to remain over the pyramid now we've destroyed it."

"It's not completely destroyed, sir. It's far too big for three Lambdas to do that. The energy shield is down and the oxygen levels are stable. I'd say it's disabled and nothing more. Do you want us to complete the job?"

"Not just yet – I'd like to go and take a closer look. We could learn something about why the Ghasts were so keen for it to be left intact. If they're moving away, I assume they've decided it's no longer important to watch what we're doing."

A distant roar caught Duggan's attention. He jerked around in time to see the fading blast from a Lambda strike atop an escarpment, a kilometre or more away.

"There goes the gun," he said.

"We took out five of the eight, sir. The others shouldn't trouble you."

"Thank you. When will we lose comms?"

"Soon. I don't have enough data on their planned course to let you know exactly when the planet is going to get in the way."

"Get me Commander McGlashan, please."

Chainer transferred him over. When McGlashan spoke, she sounded calm and collected, to Duggan's relief. "Sir?"

"You might be in charge for a while. For the sake of certainty – if you need to fire upon the *Dretisear*, you'll do so with my full support. Act according to the circumstances, rather than worrying about what might come from them. We can deal with the consequences later."

"Will do, sir. Thanks."

Her words had developed a faint echo and a hum, which were the usual symptoms of a connection about to fail. He'd expected a little longer to confer with his crew. It wasn't to be - his earpiece went dead, leaving him and his squad on the surface of Trasgor, without immediate backup.

"Lieutenant Ortiz, you can bring the squad forward. Everything's clear, so pick your feet up."

Ortiz didn't answer for a few seconds. When she spoke, it was clear she was running. "We assumed it was over when the noise stopped and we saw those plasma bursts."

"The tank took a beating and won't be going anywhere soon. The *Terminus* has gone out of comms sight so it's just us, and we're going to take a look at the pyramid."

"Have you left anything for us to shoot, sir?"

"For the sake of everyone, you'd better hope not."

"There's always next time. We'll be with you in approximately seven minutes. Should we maintain radio silence?"

Duggan weighed it up. "Don't bother, Lieutenant. I'd rather we had clear comms for now."

"Understood."

Duggan looked into the distance, towards the channel they'd hidden the tank in. The ground was more undulating than he remembered and he couldn't see the approaching infantry. The tank must have been visible all the way, since he couldn't recall a let-up in the punishment it took. Another minute went by and he saw the heads of the lead soldiers appear. A trick of perspective made it appear as if they made no progress at all for another few minutes, until they were almost upon him.

"How'd you get out of *that?*" asked Torres. "And how the hell did it get this far?"

Duggan shrugged, before realising the gesture was hard to interpret when performed within a suit. "They say I'm lucky," he said humbly.

No one said anything more about it, though Duggan detected what might have been one or two shaken heads.

"What now, sir?" asked Ortiz.

"The energy shield is gone. We need to move towards the target object – another four klicks ahead of us along this valley. The emplacements between here and there have been destroyed."

"Any other threats?"

"Nothing known. We're going to assume that could change at any moment. I don't know what other damage the pyramid has suffered and I don't know what it contains – if anything. I'd like to find answers – this could be key to our future relationship with the Ghasts and it may also give valuable clues about why the Dreamers have come and what they want."

"We might need some hardware," said Ortiz. "Carpenter, Reed, get on there and see what you can dig out."

"Is it safe?" asked Reed doubtfully. It wasn't the best response.

"It'll be a lot safer than me shooting you in the leg, soldier. Now move!"

Ortiz had the knack of making threats in such a way that the other soldiers took her seriously, yet without hating her for making them in the first place. Reed hurried towards the open side door of the tank, with Carpenter following. The pair of them emerged a few minutes later, dragging a number of objects.

"A slug went through the weapons cabinet and took out most of the contents," said Reed. "Do we need any of this stuff?"

Duggan and Ortiz had a look at what they'd found. There was a six-feet metal tube with a fist-sized opening at one end. It had two small metal cubes attached to it, positioned near the middle.

"Carpenter, you take the plasma launcher. Check it's working and make sure it's charged. We'll leave it behind if it's empty."

Yes, sir," said Carpenter. He stooped over the tube and

pressed a switch on one of the cubes. "Six rounds, sir. Fully loaded."

Next to it was a stubby cannon with a three centimetre bore. The barrel was about two feet long and joined by a rigid tube to a large cloth-encased metal pack. The pack was designed to be carried on a soldier's back using two straps.

"Torres, you're a strong lad, pick up the repeater."

Torres did indeed look like he could press his own body-weight and he muscled his way through the others. He struggled into the straps and positioned the barrel at his side, where it pointed straight ahead. "And they call this a *light* repeater?" he said.

"Compared to what the Ghasts have, that is definitely a light repeater," said Montgomery.

"Theirs have a lower range and less penetration," said Alvarez. "They need to keep their guns big to keep up with ours."

The summation was partially true. The Ghasts' hand-held weaponry was inferior to what the Space Corps handed out to its soldiers. However, the difference was slight and the average Ghast could carry much more weight than a human. Put them in a mech suit and they could carry a whole lot more again.

"We're not here to talk about the Ghasts," said Duggan. "We've got what we need. Leave the comms beacon here," he said, indicating the final item they'd recovered from the shell of the tank. "The suits' comms should be good enough."

He turned until he was facing in the direction of the pyramid. There were two ways to approach – they could head along the floor of the valley, which curved towards their destination. Alternatively, they could climb the slope and cut over the top of the hill in a straight line. Duggan surveyed the land, trying to decide which way he liked the most. The sides of the valley were only a few hundred metres high at this end. They looked rough, but without presenting a major risk of falling. The valley floor, on the other hand, was easy-going terrain, albeit littered with rocks. If there were known hazards, the high ground was the most sensible place to be. The last report from the *Terminus* suggested there was nothing to worry about within the former perimeter of the energy shield, except the remaining three coil guns.

"We're going up," said Duggan. "Better safe than dead."

It wasn't the preferred route amongst the soldiers. They knew better than to complain and they got their heads down and followed Duggan as he set off in what was a straight line towards the pyramid. The valley wall turned out to be steeper than it appeared, and with a coating of grit that made their footing uncertain. Torres and Carpenter had heavier loads than the others and they fell gradually towards the back of the pack, until Duggan had to slow the pace. Ortiz shouted at them once or twice, but she knew what they were carrying and there was little venom in her words.

At the top, there was a good view of the valley and not much else. On the opposite side, the terrain was uneven, as if it had been moulded purposely to be as irregular as possible. This side was mercifully a lot flatter and with a gentle upwards slope. There was a high cliff a few kilometres away, which they didn't need to go near in order to reach their goal.

Duggan waved the squad forward and they made a good pace. He kept a careful eye on the ground before them – it looked undisturbed. Minefields had once been commonplace, but they were difficult to keep hidden from a warship's sensors. Anything on the ground was vulnerable to a strike from the air, which was why ground offensives were much less significant than they had once been. There were fewer, better trained soldiers, with the flexibility to use a variety of equipment and adapt to whatever surprises the war might throw at them.

The slope continued for more than two kilometres. They didn't venture too close to the valley's edge, since its wide curve would have added time to the run. At the highest point of the slope, the tip of the pyramid became visible, its straight lines and regularity intruding upon the randomness of nature. Soon after, the arc of the valley cut across to intersect their journey and they stopped for a moment on the edge. They were high above the valley floor and shadows from the late-afternoon sun stretched more than halfway over, lengthening rapidly as the day drew to a close. The pyramid was in clear sight and the squad kept low while they surveyed the area. This close, the Dreamer artefact was massive. Duggan remembered it to be equally proportioned, yet it somehow appeared squat and brooding. Its surface was a smooth, unreflective, near-black at fifteen hundred metres to a side. There were patches of obvious damage – with a huge crater midway up the side facing them, surrounded by a lip of melted alloy which had re-hardened into an ugly shape.

"Lots of positrons," said Duggan, cycling through the suit helmet's array of scanning options.

"We should be safe in our suits, sir," said Ortiz.

"Best we don't hang around anyway. I want to take a look and then we can hunker down somewhere to wait for a pickup."

"I make it just less than a thousand metres away," she said. "No sign of movement, no sign of life."

"And no sign of a way in. Not on this side."

Duggan felt deflated, without knowing exactly why. He didn't know if he'd expected that simply laying eyes on the pyramid would give him the answers he wanted. He watched it for a few minutes longer, hoping for something to change, a doorway to open – anything that might give away details about its nature. In the end, there was nothing for it. He got to his feet and set off warily towards the valley floor.

# CHAPTER SIXTEEN

THE WAY down was harder to negotiate than the way up. The squad slipped and slithered, sending a cascade of loose stones and gravel before them. No matter how much care he took, Duggan felt as if he were at a constant risk of tumbling headlong towards the bottom. They made it intact, though Alvarez covered the last fifty metres on his backside. The man got up and patted himself down ruefully. The polymer suits were tough and proof against most abrasion, so the only thing damaged was his pride. The others were too focused on their destination, so the insults sent his way were muted.

Duggan paused to look up at the pyramid's apex. He was used to seeing created objects of unimaginable size and this had no greater volume than a number of the Space Corps' larger ships. Regardless, there was something peculiar about being confronted with evidence that the Confederation's greatest achievements were not unique in the universe. First came the Ghasts, and now this new alien species.

With a start, he realised the *Terminus* had been out of contact for much longer than a single orbit of the planet – even a slow one. He tried to connect and got nothing. He swore under his breath and pushed the uncertainty from his mind.

"Come on, let's see what we can learn about this alien technology," he said.

The base of the pyramid wasn't far and Duggan sprinted across the intervening space, using the heat and movement sensors on his helmet to detect anything he might otherwise miss. The squad followed him, ungainly in their protective suits. When he reached the pyramid, Duggan paused and then pressed the palm of his hand onto the surface. It was neither warm, nor cold, with a hint of vibration deep inside. The glove of his suit numbed his sense of touch, though not enough to block the feeling entirely.

"We're going around," he said on the open channel. "Watch out and shoot anything that moves."

"Those are the kinds of orders I like," said Ortiz.

Duggan led the way, advancing cautiously. As he walked, he noticed the fractures running through the stone at the base of the pyramid. Even with a gentle landing, the artefact was heavy enough to overstress the rock. It took a few minutes to reach the corner. He looked carefully around and saw the next side was in shadow. His helmet sensor kicked in automatically, gathering and enhancing the available light. The result was near-perfect, though a trained eye could tell the difference. In the reduced light, the walls of the valley appeared almost sheer, looming into the sky. There was something eerie about the entire scene – a peculiar contrast between raw nature and alien technology. Duggan walked along this darkened edge, his feet crunching through the gravel. Above, the sky was a blanket of stars, the blackness in contrast with the waning light cast upon the surface of Trasgor by its sun.

"Sir, you've just walked past something," said Ortiz. She was feeling the strangeness too, and her voice was little more than a hoarse whisper.

Duggan stopped and looked around, trying to see what he'd missed. Ortiz helped him out by stepping close to the pyramid and running a finger along a near-invisible seam in the surface.

"A door?" asked Duggan. He continued a few more paces, searching for another seam. He found one and followed it with his eyes. The seam went up at a diagonal for a few metres, and then cut horizontally across to join the other one. It was difficult to judge from so close, but it appeared as if the vertical seams ran exactly parallel to the edges of the pyramid itself.

"Bang in the middle," said Ortiz. "Aliens like symmetry, huh?"

"Anyone got a crowbar?" asked Quinn.

"I thought you always carried one in case you got the chance to do a bit of breaking and entering," said Reed.

"Piss off," replied Quinn mildly.

"Be quiet," warned Ortiz. She didn't need to raise her voice and the others fell silent.

Duggan banged his fist against what he assumed was a door. It was about four metres wide and there was no give in it whatsoever – it could have been a hundred metres thick for all he knew. "We'll need more than a crowbar to get this shifted," he said.

"We've got grenades and explosives," said Ortiz.

"Anything that looks like an access panel?" asked Corporal Hammond.

Five of the squad monitored the area, while the remainder looked for a way to open the door. Garvin was the nearest thing to an explosives expert they had, and she stared at the smooth surface, trying to figure out if they had sufficient kit to get it open. Duggan stepped away, hoping to find some inspiration. There was another Lambda crater on this side of the pyramid – about five hundred metres up. The slope was far too slippery to climb and they didn't have any additional gear with them to help. He found it hard to focus on the solution, since he was distracted by the inevitable conclusion that followed his certainty about this being a door. A door was there to let people in and out. If the pyramid had been nothing more than a power source for whatever created the oxygen, there would have been no need for a way inside.

"Lieutenant Ortiz, we need to be careful," he said. "There must be something – *someone* – inside. Else why have a door?"

"They might not be inside now, sir. The *Terminus* made some big holes in this thing. It may be that the air got sucked out, killing whatever was inside. Assuming they left some of their number behind."

The oxygen levels weren't sufficient to support life, so there was a chance she was right. Duggan itched to face this new enemy, to see what they were made of. If they'd perished inside, the opportunity would be gone.

"I don't care how they die, as long as they're dead," said Cook with uncanny timing. "It means I'll be alive for the next time we fight them. Or the Ghasts. I suppose I don't care who it is."

"There's no way we're getting this open by force," said Garvin. "The tank would have been enough if it still worked."

"No point in crying over it," said Ortiz. "The tank's gone."

"We'll have to wait," said Duggan. "See if the *Terminus* comes back. If not, we'll be here a while."

"Permanently, if you ask me," said Quinn unhelpfully.

"I've been to worse places than this," said Reed. "Admittedly not many."

The squad talked lightly, but the situation was serious. Everyone knew it, though they chose to pretend otherwise. The conditions on Trasgor weren't harsh enough to threaten them while the spacesuits functioned. Regardless, it would be an unpleasant few months counting down the time until the helmet power units failed and they suffocated.

"Should we head back to the tank?" asked Garvin. "One or two of us know how to fix things. Maybe there's something we can do to get it moving."

"It's not going anywhere," said Duggan. "If it's ever recovered they won't even try to repair what's left."

"And there's all that shit spilling out if its engines," said Hammond.

"If we're going to die, we may as well do it trying," said Duggan eventually. "We'll head back and see what we can do. We should finish looking around this pyramid, in case there's a door open on one of the other sides."

They continued onwards until they had completed a full circuit of the pyramid. It was tightly sealed, with no sign of another door. Duggan hadn't pinned any hope on it being otherwise, so he got his bearings and began to walk purposefully back towards the ruined tank. The others came silently after, with no one offering an opinion or alternative.

They reached the tank without incident. Seeing it anew, Duggan was certain there was nothing they could do to fix it. He didn't wish to lower the squad's morale by repeating his earlier words about how broken it was, and regretted saying them. Still, a realist would know any attempt at repairs was a lost cause. Sometimes, a futile task was enough to hold people together and Duggan hoped it would be the case here.

"There it is. I expect it to be running smoothly within four hours," he said, attempting to spur them on with humour.

"Nice one, sir," said Alvarez. "Give me your magic wand and I'll wave it for you."

"I want another search of the shell," said Duggan. "Whatever you can find, bring it outside. Corporal Hammond, I want you in the cockpit. If there's life in any of the systems, bring them online and see if there's something we can use."

A number of the squad got to work with enthusiasm. Others were noticeably less keen and they trudged around the edges of the tank, trying to look busy. Ortiz went amongst them, shouting words of encouragement. No one was fooled, though their activity levels increased.

There wasn't much of the day left and the squad worked for two hours before the light became too bad to work without image intensifiers. It was possible to continue and Duggan considered doing so. In the end, he called a halt for the day. They'd worked hard on fixing the tank and accomplished nothing. All of the internal screens were dead and Hammond hadn't been able to get any form of response from the mainframe at all. The spacesuits were giving amber warnings about positrons, so they couldn't stay here forever. There was little point in trying to outdistance the leakage and they stayed close to the vehicle, with a few attempting sleep in the half-dozen seats that remained intact within.

Duggan sat with his back to the tank's side wall, staring into the distance. Intensified greens and blacks from the landscape mixed into an array of shapes that looked utterly different to how they had during the day. It was tempting to switch off the sensor and enjoy the solitude of darkness. There was little chatter and those voices which spoke lacked their usual humour. There was no anger either and for that Duggan was thankful.

He'd been lost before on other planets and in circumstances as bad as this. He'd been younger then and it had felt like an adventure. Not once had he considered his death as the outcome. Here on Trasgor, the weight of his mortality pressed heavily against him. It wasn't so much his death he feared as it was dying with his duty left undone. Failure was a word he'd spent his entire life running from in one form or another. The older and wiser he became, the harder it was to escape. *I've managed it so far,* he thought, shaking away the gloom. *What's the point in a life without challenge?*

He worked through the possibilities, trying to see if there was a glimmer of a way to control events. The *Terminus* had been gone for too long and it was increasingly likely something was amiss. Lieutenant Chainer had said their initial distress signal through Monitoring Station Gamma would take a couple of days to reach its destination. After that, it could potentially be several more days until a rescue ship got here – perhaps another of the vessels the Space Corps had sent to look for the *SC Lupus* was close enough to arrive sooner. The thought gave him some hope – the Corps might risk a disposable craft if it was in the vicinity. If they lost a Gunner, there'd be little impact on the fleet's capabilities. The biggest unknown was the Ghasts. Nil-Far's interest in the pyramid had been intense and Duggan dearly wished he knew why. Then, there were the Dreamers. While he sat thinking, they could have a dozen warships coming towards Trasgor to find out what had happened here.

His mind wandered off to encompass other ideas, none of which would benefit the stranded troops. Circular thoughts pursued each other, eventually driving him into a fitful doze. Even in sleep there was no freedom from the helplessness and his dreams were vivid representations of death. In the end, he stood and took himself for a walk. When he returned a few hours later, the horizon was brightening and the squad were getting themselves prepared for another day attempting to repair a tank which everyone knew would never move again.

# CHAPTER SEVENTEEN

THE MORNING PASSED SLOWLY. They'd exhausted their few options when it came to repairs. Without proper tools and with only a passing knowledge of how the tank worked, they ran quickly into a dead end. Corporal Hammond had found a hand-held analyser, which he'd plugged into one of the mainframe's interface ports. The device ran through a number of routines to try and kick-start the vehicle's main computer. After a while it, too, gave up, having exhausted its own pre-programmed list of options.

Duggan was just about to call for them to return to the pyramid and plant every last explosive device they possessed onto the door and see if it would blow open, when his suit comms crackled faintly. He jerked in surprise. The crackling didn't go away and he heard a voice amongst the harsh static, repeating a message over and over. He tried to respond, convinced his words would be lost in the noise. After a few minutes, he was able to make it out what was being said.

"This is *Terminus* Shuttle One. Do you copy?"

"This is Captain Duggan. I copy."

"Captain Duggan, this is Sergeant Washington. We're approaching your coordinates. Please hold your position. ETA twenty minutes."

"We're not going anywhere," said Duggan, relief flooding into him. He spoke into the open channel. "We've got a rescue coming. Everyone get off the tank and be ready to give them a wave."

"Damn, I'm glad to hear those words," said Ortiz.

Duggan had plenty of questions, which he kept to himself for the moment. Twenty minutes wasn't long and the shuttle was soon visible in the distance. The vessel was about fifty metres in length and it hovered for a few seconds while its landing computer checked the solidity of the ground below. When it was satisfied, the autopilot set the craft down a short distance away from the tank. The squad ran over, as the boarding ramp folded quietly outwards.

"Sergeant Washington, I'm glad to see you," said Duggan to the first man off the ramp.

"I thought you might be, sir. Want me to fill you in on the details?"

"Fire away, Sergeant. Where's the *Terminus*?"

"The ship's still up there, sir. Commander McGlashan spoke to me directly. The Ghasts are following some crazy pattern around this system. She isn't certain, but she thinks they may be purposefully taking a route that keeps us out of contact with the ground deployment."

"She said that?"

"Yes sir. The Ghasts finally responded to our request for information and they claim they're doing engine tests after the recent damage they suffered."

"What did Commander McGlashan say about it?"

"She believed them, sir. She also believes their deep fission drives have sufficient output to take them into a medium lightspeed. The engines on the *Terminus* won't be ready for another few hours. Commander McGlashan is continuing to shadow the *Dretisear* as per orders."

"How did you get here? There were launch problems."

"Those problems remain unresolved, sir. However, the men and women onboard have worked tirelessly with metal cutters and managed to remove the magnetic clamps from this craft, thereby allowing it to leave the *Terminus*. The Ghast ship came close enough to the dark side of Trasgor for the shuttle to launch. Here we are, sir."

Duggan clapped Sergeant Washington on the shoulder. "Well met, Sergeant. How long till the *Terminus* comes within range again?"

"Hours, sir. We're to fly to a pre-arranged meeting point for an attempted pickup."

"The *Terminus* is moving fast?"

"Too fast for the shuttle to keep up, sir."

"Well, we can't have everything, Sergeant. I don't suppose we can expect a tank to be following in your footsteps any time soon?"

"Not a tank, sir," said Washington, sounding pleased. "We did manage to fit a heavy repeater into our hold. It didn't leave much room for anything else and it's given the engines a workout."

"Sergeant, the news keeps getting better," said Duggan. He climbed up the ramp and looked inside the shuttle. The heavy repeater was fifteen metres long and five wide – a cube of metal with a rounded front and a three-metre-long turret on top. Someone had painted the words *Suck me* on the barrel in rough green letters. The repeater hovered a few inches above the floor and the top almost reached the ceiling. The seats in the personnel bay hadn't been cleared before the gun was loaded and struts of crushed metal were visible, poking out from beneath. There were a few soldiers in the bay as well, waiting to see what was expected of them.

"You powered the gun up to stop it from sliding around?"

"Yes, sir." It was against procedures, since unsecured artillery had been known to rupture the hulls of transport vessels in the past. Duggan recalled it was something about the onboard positioning systems becoming confused by the motion of a shuttle. Here and now, it didn't matter one bit.

"We're coming onboard," said Duggan. "I want to test out the repeater on something close by."

The men and women of his squad scrambled up the ramp. There wasn't a lot of room left once they gave the repeater a wide berth. Nobody wanted to be crushed to death when they were on the verge of rescue. Duggan climbed into the small cockpit, though he let Washington continue as pilot. The shuttle took off with a rumble of stressed engines. Duggan glanced back through the cockpit door and saw the heavy repeater sway gently in position. The troops watched it nervously.

Moments later, the shuttle landed in the valley, about five hundred metres from the pyramid. The occupants jumped out, grateful to be away from the unsecured gun.

"Unlatching the side panel," said Washington, pressing a button on his console.

There was the hiss of a seal breaking, followed by a whining noise. The entire side wall of the shuttle opened outwards, coming to rest gently on the solid ground. These vessels weren't expected to carry large loads, but they'd been designed with flexibility in mind - there were times the normal boarding ramp wasn't big enough. Sergeant Washington left his chair and climbed onto the back of the repeater by means of a set of rusted iron rungs. There was a platform with railings, big enough for a single person to stand on. The gun was controlled remotely, though there were times it was easiest to have someone onboard to fine-tune its movements. When there was a long way to walk, it wasn't uncommon to find the top platform of one of these crowded with men and women.

Duggan jumped off the shuttle, landing with a crunch on the ground. Sergeant Washington rotated the gun with the utmost care. The hull of the shuttle was strong, but it wasn't proof against a collision from an object as heavy as this artillery piece. Slowly, it came down the wide ramp, until it was clear of the vessel. A few of the squad expressed their relief over the comms channel.

"Where should I point it, sir?" asked Washington.

"Over there," said Duggan, pointing at the pyramid.

"This is a big bastard of a gun but I'm not sure it'll go through something as strong as that."

They had landed opposite the single door into the pyramid. Duggan jogged over and indicated the area he wanted the repeater to aim at.

"There's a door. You can't see it unless you're close up."

"Everyone back!" shouted Ortiz. "This is going to be loud."

"What about ricochets?" asked Quinn. "I've seen people killed by the ricochets."

"New model," said Washington. "The firing computer won't eject a projectile if it believes there's a chance of a bounce back."

"I've heard that before. Shouldn't we get the shuttle away just in case?"

Washington laughed richly, the sound carrying undertones of barely-contained madness. "Trust in technology, soldier. Trust in technology."

The soldiers sprinted towards the far side of the shuttle. In reality, a ricochet would smash the vessel apart easily and it might have been for the best to take it a few dozen kilometres away in order to minimise risk. Duggan was high after the turnaround in his fortunes and wasn't in the mood for delay. On top of that, he wanted to be prepared for whatever lay inside the pyramid. He strolled away from the door. The barrel of the floating artillery was a fist-sized circle of impenetrable darkness, pointing directly over his head. He came level with it and thumped the palm of his hand against the side wall.

"Fire," he said.

The repeater poured out its fury. The floating base shook as its gravity drive fought to correct against the recoil. The barrel of the gun rocked violently, its targeting computer making thousands of tiny updates to account for the kickback. The grumbling noise of slugs racing through electromagnetic coils was overwhelmed by a gargantuan clattering of depleted uranium striking a dense alloy surface at several thousand metres per second. Duggan's suit helmet attenuated the sound, reducing it to a level that was just below the pain threshold. He stared impassively at the door as it was subjected to an immense and unrelenting crushing force. The surface began to glow, starting with a dull red and increasing in brightness until it was a vivid orange. The metal swam with movement, reminding Duggan of fingers being pressed into dense clay. Through it all, Sergeant Washington laughed with pure delight.

The door held up well against the assault. The clattering merged into a single, constant sound, which droned and buzzed in Duggan's ears. The Space Corps heavy repeaters fired faster and faster as they warmed up, until eventually the control computer had to shut them down. Without that restraint, they would continue to the point of self-destruction. Duggan pressed his hand gently against the floating base. The metal felt warm, even through the insulation of the glove he wore. It would likely shut down soon.

The fusillade continued unabated and, without warning, a hole appeared in the door. A moment later, it was torn away from its mountings, crumpled and pulverised into a twisted slab of glowing alloy. Sergeant Washington didn't stop and the door was punched away from the doorway and hurled into the pyramid, spreading heat and light around it.

Duggan ran to the back of the gun, meaning to give Washington the signal to stop. He was too late – the noise ended abruptly, leaving Duggan with a ringing in his ears. The Sergeant chuckled to himself as if remembering the greatest joke he'd ever heard.

"Enough," said Duggan.

"Man, I love this shit," said Washington, leaning around the gun to admire the damage he'd caused. Before he could say more, something hit him in the head, taking it clean away along with half of his shoulder and one arm. His body was smashed to the floor, his life taken instantly.

"Get down!" shouted Duggan to the rest of the squad. "We're taking fire!"

# CHAPTER EIGHTEEN

SERGEANT WASHINGTON WAS DEAD, pieces of his body carried away by whatever it was that hit him. Duggan left the corpse where it lay and looked around the side of the repeater. The doorway was three hundred metres away and the ruined door smouldered sullenly in the space beyond. Its glow had faded to a red which showed nothing of the surroundings and also conspired to interfere with the attempts of Duggan's helmet sensors to pierce the darkness.

"Where did the shot come from?" he shouted. There was nothing moving in the Lambda crater above, so the only place was the doorway.

"I'm not detecting movement," said Ortiz. "The repeater's in the way and there's no angle to see in the door."

Something thundered into the base of the artillery gun, knocking it a few centimetres towards Duggan. A second strike followed the first and the repeater was again pushed away. Duggan patched into its computer using his helmet to interface. It was down to thirty percent of its ammunition and several damage warnings flashed up. The gun was hit again.

Without giving it further thought, Duggan instructed the gun to move towards the pyramid door and to fire at maximum rate into the opening. The harsh sound of metal striking metal came again as repeater projectiles tore into the darkness. The gun floated forwards at a fast walking pace, with Duggan keeping behind it. Another damage warning appeared and the gravity engine shut down, causing the machine to drop to the ground. It landed with a heavy thud, sending reverberations through the stone. The gun continued to work and it spewed its missiles into the pyramid. Duggan kept it firing until the ammunition ran out and the muzzle fell silent.

"Did you get it?" asked Ortiz.

Duggan didn't reply at once and waited to see if there'd be any more firing from within. It remained quiet. "I hope so," he said at last.

He looked out from the protection of the now-still artillery. The doorway was a couple of hundred metres away and if there was anything inside, they'd get a shot at him if he ventured out. The shuttle was behind and he saw three one-metre holes through its hull. There was no damage to the cockpit and he kept his fingers crossed that the vessel would be able to get them away from here. He'd erred in leaving it so close and it might be something he ended up regretting later.

"Cover me," he said.

He ran sideways away from the repeater, looking to cut out the angle so anyone deep inside the doorway wouldn't have much chance to fire at him. He heard the fizz of gauss rifles – not those of the enemy, but those of his soldiers as they fired into the doorway. When he was a few metres clear of the gun, he changed course and sprinted directly towards the pyramid, reaching it a little way to the side of the opening. He inched along until he could look within. The spacesuit helmet had a sensor near the top, so he didn't need to put too much of his head around the corner. The broken door had faded to black and though it emitted enough heat to cause a shimmering in the air, it no longer interfered with the suit's ability to penetrate the darkness. There was a passage which led further into the pyramid. It opened out into a space after fifty metres or so. The inner walls were as dark and featureless as those outside and it was hard to distinguish edges. There was a mass within – an indistinct shape somewhere beyond the corridor. Nothing moved and there were heat signatures coming from both the door and the unknown object. Duggan turned his visor towards the Corps repeater – there were several large holes in its front surface.

"Clear?" asked Ortiz.

"I can't be certain. There's something inside that might be a weapon. Hard to tell if it's working."

"The repeater should have taken it out?" She phrased it as a question, clearly unsure herself.

"Maybe. I wonder why it wasn't destroyed when we knocked the door down."

"Automated defences? It could have moved into place when it detected a breach."

"We can't sit around waiting to see what happens. Move up. One at a time."

The first shape broke out from behind the shuttle. It was Ortiz, never one to hide behind others. The repeater was between her and the doorway, but there was a space of a few metres where she'd be visible. She made it to the pyramid without being torn to pieces by high calibre gunfire.

"Next," she said. "Move fast and don't stop."

"I want two to stay behind," said Duggan. "People who can fly that shuttle. Check it works and get it out of here before any more holes appear in it."

"Reed, Quinn, that means you," said Ortiz.

Soon, nineteen of them were lined up to the right of the four-metre doorway. There hadn't been any further shots from within and Duggan was sure the weapon inside the pyramid had been destroyed. He wasn't quite sure enough that he'd run headlong towards the wreckage, nor send one of his squad to do the job for him.

"Damn, there's wasn't much left of Sergeant Washington," said Alvarez.

"There isn't time to think about him yet," said Duggan. He waved Carpenter over and the soldier came closer, still carrying his shoulder-fired plasma launcher.

"Are you a good shot with that thing?" asked Duggan.

"Pretty good, sir. What's the target?"

"There's something in there, it's giving off heat. I think it's a movable gauss turret. I'd like you to hit it again."

Carpenter carefully leaned out. "That thing back there?"

"If you're looking at the shape about eighty or ninety metres away, then that's what I want you to hit."

"You got it, sir," he said. Carpenter lifted up the launcher tube. It was heavy and he grunted with effort. He took four paces backwards, still remaining out of sight. The tube emitted three quiet beeps and its coils whined. Carpenter leapt into the doorway and something whooshed from the launcher. There was a whump inside the pyramid and the walls of the corridor were briefly lit in bright light. Carpenter jumped back even before the plasma light had started to fade. "Direct hit," he said.

Duggan had a look. The plasma light had gone, leaving a strong heat signature at the place it had detonated. There was no way to tell for certain if the weapon in the pyramid was disabled. The shoulder launchers were effective against most things this side of a tank. It was time to act, rather than hide behind endless precautions.

"I'm going in," said Duggan.

He didn't hesitate and darted around the corner, pushing

himself into a fast run along the passageway. His breathing sounded loud in his ears and he gritted his teeth. As he ran, he noticed furrows in the walls, which hadn't been obvious from outside. The repeater slugs had scarred everything. The broken door covered most of the corridor's width and he jumped over it. *I'm still not dead.*

The object became clearer – it was a mangled lump of metal, with bits half-ripped away. Duggan saw what it was – a smaller version of the coil guns the Dreamers had left positioned around the perimeter of the energy shield. There was no way to tell if this was a fixed emplacement or if it had moved itself into place as part of an automatic self-defence system. *Or been moved here by our enemies.*

It didn't take long to reach the end of the corridor. The gun didn't fire and Duggan was pleased to find he was still alive. As he'd guessed, there was a room at the end and he crouched near to a wall and looked inside, using his helmet to detect anything potentially hostile. The chamber was a good fifteen metres square and had corridors leading away from the other three walls. Duggan's breathing settled from his sprint and the flood of adrenaline his body had produced. He noticed the humming he'd felt the first time he touched the pyramid, leaving him surer than ever that this was just a power source, left behind to make Trasgor inhabitable for its makers. Knowing it didn't explain why the Ghasts would have such an interest.

Duggan took a gamble and crossed the room, keeping low. His rifle was in his hand and he aimed it ahead. He skirted around the ruin of the Dreamer gauss gun, dimly aware of the heat it continued to emit. He reached the opposite passage and pressed himself to the wall on one side. The corridor went on, deeper into the artefact. The humming was infinitesimally louder and there was more sign of repeater damage to the walls. The pyramid was only fifteen hundred metres across – the projectiles could easily have covered the distance if the passage went all the way to the other side. There might be another door there, he guessed.

"Lieutenant Ortiz, bring the squad in," he said. "We're going to have a look."

There was no response. He frowned and checked the comms were functioning. There was no problem with the hardware. "Too much metal," he muttered to himself. "Blocking the comms."

He hurried towards the entrance. A few metres from the doorway, his earpiece came to life again.

"Do you copy?" said Ortiz.

"I do now, Lieutenant," he said. "This place is too dense for our signals to penetrate. It'll add to the danger, but we're going to search it."

"How many squads?"

"Three – a six, a six and a seven."

The troops were quickly divided. Duggan was in a group of six, with Alvarez, Cook, Hunter, Smith and Corporal Wong who'd come down with the shuttle.

"We go in for exactly one hour and then we come out," said Duggan. "Is that clear?"

"I'm not sure I want to be in there any longer," said Torres. "Not if I have to carry this repeater everywhere with me."

"You'll be pleased you have it when the bullets come flying," said Ortiz. "Now let's move out!"

They went in one squad at a time, leaving a ten second gap between each. Duggan's squad was first and he chose the straight-ahead route, which took them directly towards the centre of the pyramid.

"The middle's got to be the most dangerous," whispered Smith without any particular sign of worry.

"The most exciting," said Hunter. "That's where they'll keep all their alien women."

"You're stupid," said Smith.

"Quiet!" Duggan ordered. It wasn't the time for banter and he wanted them focused on the task in hand.

The sound of footsteps told him the other squads were on their way through the two side exits. Duggan got his feet moving and advanced along the corridor at a measured pace, hearing the others fall in behind. The side walls sloped inwards, so he couldn't keep as close to them as he preferred. It left him feeling exposed, even though the safety offered by the wall was ephemeral at best. After sixty metres, they reached another room. This one was empty and with no sign of defensive emplacements. Duggan had been worried the place might be riddled with them and his soldiers only had rifles and grenades. They were in no way prepared to face heavy armour or high-calibre guns.

The comms to the other squads were dead, leaving the six of them alone in the depths of the unknown. Duggan checked his timer and was shocked to find seven minutes had elapsed. It felt as if only seconds had gone by. With a deep breath, he and his squad pressed on deeper into the pyramid.

# CHAPTER NINETEEN

THEY CROSSED over two more rooms, each with the same number of exits as the one before. These places were empty and there was no apparent need for them to exist. It could have been a result of the method used to create the pyramid, Duggan supposed. It didn't seem likely. The trouble was, he was a man who liked to think there was a reason for everything. When the reason wasn't apparent, his mind would search endlessly for an answer.

After the fourth room, they entered another passage. There was still the occasional sign of repeater fire on the walls. Here and there they came across flattened discs of metal, where the projectiles had ricocheted away from the sides and come to a rest on the floor. Duggan turned one over with his foot – it was heavy yet made little sound when he flipped it.

The corridor opened out into a vast space that filled the centre of the pyramid. The ceiling was lost somewhere in a darkness their suit helmets struggled to make sense of. The walls to the sides were visible, about four hundred metres away. These walls sloped up until they, too were gone from sight. In the centre

of the space was a pillar. It wasn't a pillar in the conventional
sense – this was a vast, cylindrical monolith of stone which glittered faintly without any light source to reflect. Duggan estimated the diameter of the object to be five hundred metres and it
blocked his view of the chamber's far walls. He couldn't guess at
the height – certainly it went beyond the extents of what he
could see.

"What the hell is that?" asked Smith.

Duggan shook his head. "I don't know. A power source,
perhaps. There are no detectable emissions."

"My suit's picking up light over there, sir," said Wong. "Not a
lot, though."

Duggan pointed his visor towards the left of the room. The
pillar blocked his line of sight, but there was the faintest increase
in light on the floor and walls. It was easy to miss if you were
concentrating on something else. He tried to figure out their position in relation to the exterior damage the pyramid had suffered.

"We landed two Lambdas on this place before the third one
shut it down. The last missile must have damaged this pillar."

"It's big," said Hunter doubtfully.

"Could be delicate," said Alvarez. "Whatever it is, I don't
think it's metal."

"Let's check it out," said Duggan, setting off across the floor.
"Keep your lights off for now and stay alert."

The metal underfoot was dense and thick. It seemed to
absorb the sound of their footsteps as they walked over it. Neither
was there any perceptible echo from the subdued noise of their
passage. The effect was one of walking in a tight, enclosed space,
rather than in a huge chamber. The sensation wasn't altogether a
pleasant one. Duggan looked about, jerking his head in all directions in case there were any more automated defences left here
by the enemy. He considered turning on his light and rejected it.
The helmet torch would interfere with the sensor's image intensi-

fiers, without being powerful enough to illuminate the walls or ceiling.

He reached the pillar – huge chunks had been ripped from it and they were scattered on the floor everywhere around, along with spent repeater slugs. It looked as if it had taken thousands of hits, making a hole many metres across and deep. Duggan craned his neck and he could make out shapes high above, with no way to discern exactly what they were. The material in front of him was utterly black when viewed from straight on, yet it twinkled with a hint of the metallic when seen from an angle. Stepping forward, he pressed his hand against the column. His suit helmet provided him with an urgent warning and he pulled his hand away.

"It's cold," he said. "Very cold. Yet there's no chill emanating from its surface."

"It reminds me of obsidian," said Cook. "That stuff you get around volcanoes."

"Yeah," said Smith. "With a sprinkling of metal in it."

Duggan had no idea what it was made of, though it did look exactly like obsidian with a metallic sheen. "We should try and take a piece of it for testing," he said.

"Want me to pick some of it up, sir?" asked Hunter.

"Not yet, soldier. If it got hit by a Lambda, there might be other pieces on the floor further around."

"The repeater really smashed it up," said Alvarez.

Duggan moved on, walking close to the pillar while taking care not to touch it again. The suits were particularly well-insulated against cold, but there was no point in taking unnecessary chances. He checked his timer. *Twenty minutes.* Time was running out and he didn't want to leave here without learning more. It was an option to come back later, though one he hoped he wouldn't need to exercise.

The light increased, a miserly quantity coming in through a

gap overhead. "There's a hole in the ceiling, right near to the pillar," he said.

"With pieces on the ground," said Wong.

More black shapes covered the floor, most of them small. Duggan stooped over one – it was fist-sized and shaped like a dagger with an edge that could have sliced easily through his suit. He remembered hearing that obsidian was brittle, yet its edges could be sharper than any metal.

"Careful what you pick up," he warned. He walked a few paces on, to see if there was anything suitable for him to collect. There was plenty of choice and he tentatively touched one with a fingertip. "It's broken away, yet it's just as cold as the main cylinder," he said.

Hunter and Smith walked further along, looking curiously around them.

"Some big pieces here, sir," said Smith. "This one must weigh a hundred tonnes."

"I've found something," said Hunter.

There was a note to the man's voice which made Duggan take notice. "What is it?" he asked.

"I think it's a ladder, sir."

Hunter was twenty metres further around the pillar, walking and looking up at the same time. Duggan jogged towards him. "Hold up," he said.

The soldier stopped walking and raised an arm to point. There was a series of rungs protruding from the side of the pillar. They appeared to be made from the same near-black metal as the pyramid's walls, widely spaced and climbing into the dark. When Duggan looked closely, he saw there were sockets to either side of the rungs, like there'd once been a safety cage fitted around the ladder. There was no sign of it any longer. The ladder was almost indistinguishable from the pillar and it was a wonder Hunter had spotted it. He touched the third rung and his suit informed him it wasn't any colder than the surrounding air. A part of Duggan wished Hunter's eyes hadn't been so sharp, since he knew what he was going to have to do.

"I'm going up," he said.

"Shouldn't we look for some stairs?" asked Wong.

"If I find some stairs when I'm at the top, I'll be sure to come down that way," said Duggan. He had no relish for the climb, yet was reluctant to go looking for a stairwell or a lift he might be unable to operate. "I don't want to us run into another gauss emplacement either."

"Can you make it to the top and back down in time, sir?" asked Hunter.

"Probably not – unless there's a quicker way down that doesn't involve me falling. We need a sample of this pillar. If I'm not back when the sixty minutes are up, I want you to do whatever it takes to return one of these chunks to Lieutenant Ortiz and let her know where it came from. Wait here for as long as you can."

With a deep breath, Duggan stretched out a hand to the highest rung he could reach and put his foot on the lowest. He pulled himself up to the next rung, discovering the wide placement made it difficult to climb without putting extra strain on his arms and shoulders. In addition, it was hard to avoid brushing against the pillar itself. A whispering internal voice told him he was being stupid and he agreed with it. The part of him that was a stubborn bastard took control of his limbs and made him press on.

Duggan was fit and strong. However, the spacesuit was heavy and his gauss rifle knocked against his back in an irritating manner. The weapon would have been better left on the ground, yet he was reluctant to leave himself completely defenceless. He climbed higher, with pain building in his muscles. He grimaced and stared directly ahead, trying not to think of anything but the climb.

Minutes passed and each rung became a challenge to overcome. Duggan cursed his obstinacy and concentrated on lifting his arms and dragging himself upwards a single step at a time. He didn't think about falling, refusing even to accept the possibility. Instead, he occupied his mind by counting each rung he climbed. At four hundred metres, a readout within his helmet advised that his heart rate had climbed to an unsustainable level and advised him to take a shot of battlefield adrenaline. Duggan hated the thought and he ignored the suggestion.

He paused to look upwards and wished he hadn't. The change in perspective, allied with the blood rushing through his head, made him dizzy. He closed his eyes, but not before he'd seen an outline of a rough hole from the Lambda strike against the pyramid. Where the ladder went, he couldn't see. The dizziness passed and Duggan began once more, repeating a mantra in his head. *Grip, pull, climb, six hundred, grip, pull, climb six hundred and one.*

By seven hundred metres, the suit was unable to regulate his body temperature adequately. Sweat covered his forehead, dripping into his eyes and stinging them constantly. There were a series of red alerts on his HUD about the physical state of his body. It wouldn't be long until the suit took matters into its own hands and started injecting him with whatever concoction of drugs it felt he needed. Luckily, the pillar had begun to taper, presumably coming to a point like the pyramid itself. Therefore, Duggan was no longer climbing vertically and the going was fractionally easier. He growled at the imaginary person which inhabited the spacesuit mini-computer and told it where it could shove its battlefield adrenaline.

It took him a while to realise he was no longer in an open space. He glanced around and discovered that he'd ascended through the ceiling and was in a semi-circular shaft which continued through the metal. Heartened, he tipped his head back and his eyes told him the shaft ended in another fifty metres or so. His body's reserves were depleted and the last part of the climb took a huge expenditure of effort to complete.

At last, he made it. The shaft ended at a metal ceiling. There was no way to tell if the pillar went higher and in truth Duggan was beyond caring. There was a square opening in the wall on the opposite side of the shaft. It was large, wide and more than a metre away from the ladder. Duggan cursed and used his feet to push away from the rungs. His legs were leaden and he didn't get the distance he'd wanted. Nevertheless, it was far enough and he landed with a thump in the opening. He was in a passage, approximately two metres wide and three high. There was no light to speak of and he turned on his helmet torch. His heart fell – the passage continued for only a few metres before it ended at a dull, black-metal door.

He advanced, flexing his shoulders to try and get the blood flowing into his tired muscles. As he'd feared, the door didn't open automatically for him. However, there was something attached to its surface which didn't appear very often on the doors which Duggan habitually used. It was a heavy metal handle - nothing more than a horizontal bar. It looked stiff, but when he pressed down upon it, the handle moved silently and easily. He switched off his torch, in case there was something unexpected on the other side. The door gave the impression it had a great weight when he pulled on it, yet it opened without requiring much effort.

There was a room beyond. It was unlit, except by the tiny quantity of light which came through an irregular six-metre opening in the ceiling. The metal around the hole had been melted and then reformed as it cooled. Duggan had seen plasma damage often enough that he knew this was part of the crater resulting from a missile strike. Through the gap he could make out the pinpricks of stars which filled Trasgor's night-time sky.

The ceiling itself was five metres above and the room was five metres across, with the opposite wall being vertical, rather than sloped like the sides of the pyramid. The floor went to the left and right away from him. Duggan stopped for a moment while he struggled to make sense of the overall shape. Then it came to him – the room went around the inner perimeter of the pyramid. Ten metres away on each side there were corners and the room continued at a right-angle to each. He was sure if he went in either direction, he'd end up at this door. There was no sign of furniture, however there was a row of screens running along the far wall. They were all dark, as if the power had been switched off.

There was something else – a misshapen object a few metres away. When Duggan focused, he saw there were others with it. His motion and heat sensors were clear and there was no sound to be heard, so he walked over to the nearest shape. It was a body, so badly damaged by the ingress of plasma fire that it was unrecognizable. *Dreamers,* thought Duggan. He pulled at the remains, hoping there might be something for him to look at – to see the features of humanity's new enemy. The body was little more than charcoal and ash. It crumbled under his grip, giving away nothing of how it once looked. He checked the other remains without learning anything further about these aliens.

He got to his feet, feeling the early signs of aching in his limbs. Stepping carefully over the bodies, he made his way to the place where the room turned left. He peered around the corner, uncertain if there were any active defences. It was clear and the room continued until it reached another corner. There were more screens embedded in the wall – a row of dozens, each as blank as the next. He went across to one and pressed it, wondering if he could activate it. The screen remained off, but there was something vaguely familiar about everything here. The idea tugged at his brain and told him this was significant.

Duggan turned left again. There were more screens and a door in the centre of the wall. He hurried over to it. This door had no handle and it was closed. There was a clear square plate on the wall adjacent. He pressed the plate, knowing before he did so that it wouldn't activate at his command. He was sure this had been the main control room for the pyramid, or at least a secondary one. The answers he'd hoped to find continued to elude him and his frustration grew. He kicked the door with the front of his foot and swore at it.

The realisation that he might have to climb the ladder came to the fore in his mind. He didn't want to contemplate it – the way up had left him with little spare for the way down. He called up the timer. *Sixty-five minutes – I've got to hurry.* Leaving the door, Duggan moved to the next corner, which would take him around the full perimeter of the pyramid. There were more screens and another closed door. Next to the door was a slumped figure. Now he'd ascertained there were no defences in this room, Duggan switched on his helmet torch and light illuminated the body. It was partially charred, though there were signs it had escaped the worst of the plasma. He walked towards the corpse, hearing his heart beating in his ears. His mind had reached a conclusion that he didn't want to accept, at least not until his eyes gave him no choice.

The Dreamer had been dressed in a flexible, dark silver material, which had burned away and allowed the exposed flesh to be eaten by plasma. Its head pointed away, the dead face looking at the metal floor. Duggan didn't want to see it and he put out a hand slowly, hating his weakness. He closed his eyes and pulled at the body. It rolled over with a quiet sigh. Duggan opened his eyes again and found himself looking at the lined, grey face of a Ghast.

# CHAPTER TWENTY

DUGGAN STARED DUMBLY at what he'd found. The alien's eyes were open and they looked back at him, blank and lifeless. He wasn't a man to be frozen by shock or indecision and he stood up, turning his attention away from this revelation and onto the task of escaping the pyramid.

The nearby door was sealed and also lacked a handle. There was another activation plate to one side, which he pressed without any more luck than the last time. The fingers of the dead creature were curled up tightly into its palm. With an effort, he straightened them, feeling the thick digits crackle as tendons stiffened by rigor mortis were stretched. The body was heavy and difficult to move, seeming to weigh more than its size suggested. It took a few seconds for Duggan to haul it into a position where he could push the grey palm onto the door's activation plate. His hopes were dashed when the door stayed close. Before he could think of anything else, he heard a crackling in his earpiece and a female voice spoke, the words unclear.

"The hole!" he said, looking through the damaged ceiling and to the stars outside. He dashed over, until he was standing directly beneath it. "*ES Terminus*, this is Duggan, do you copy?"

There was a response, clear and crisp this time. "Sir, this is Commander McGlashan. Where are you?"

"I'm inside the pyramid – there's a hole in the roof for the signal to get through."

"You've got to get out. The Ghasts are going to destroy it!"

"What do you mean?" he asked. "They were the ones who asked us to leave it untouched."

"They must have received orders to the contrary. They're planning to wipe out any trace it was here."

"What about the squad? Have you told them we have people down here?"

"They gave us sixty minutes to evacuate and we only have fifty-five remaining."

"Do what you can to stall them," said Duggan. "I'll be out of comms sight in about five seconds and won't be able to speak until I exit the pyramid."

"Understood. I'll do what I can, sir. The shuttle will need to leave in fifty minutes to be sure of getting clear."

Galvanised by his determination to bring news of his discovery away from this place, Duggan ran towards the open door he'd first entered through. He sped along the short passage-way, the light from his torch sweeping aside the darkness and glinting off the surface of the black pillar. The rungs were clear to see in the artificial light and he sprang for them, grabbing the closest tightly with both hands.

He started to climb, now knowing why the rungs were spaced so far apart. After a hundred metres, the effects of his earlier exertions caught up with his willpower. A hundred metres later and exhaustion threatened to overcome him.

"Damnit, I won't die because I'm too proud!" he said angrily.

What he'd found was too important for the information to be lost because he'd fallen from a ladder.

He ordered the suit to give him some battlefield adrenaline. He felt the prick of the needle, sharp and intense. The drug coursed through his veins, giving strength to his limbs and making him feel like he could run a thousand miles. His heart hammered in his chest, his pupils widened and his jaw clenched tightly.

Down he went, his arms and legs metronomic as they carried him towards the floor below. *Four hundred metres to go,* he thought with surprise. *Feels like I've just started.* The fifty-minute timer ticked steadily downwards on his HUD. *Plenty of time, I could get used to this.* He shook the feeling away – the adrenaline was dangerous if it was overused. It took something out of the user and never gave it back. It was a trade – the drug helped you live in exchange for an undying lust to use it again and again. Duggan had seen the effects of long-term abuse and there was no way he'd give in to that.

His leading foot struck something unyielding. For a split second, Duggan thought he was in the process of slipping away to his death. Then he saw that he'd reached the bottom of the ladder. The adrenaline's initial rush was already subsiding - the drug would keep him going for a few hours yet, but the first big kick had faded. He took a few seconds to get his bearings and then made a run for it. There were broken pieces of the pillar around him on the floor. He was tempted to grab one, before telling himself that he trusted his squad to do as they were told.

"It's too important to leave to someone else," he said, scooping up a piece from the ground and resuming his sprint around the base of the pillar. The suit detected the extremes of temperature and offered a warning. Duggan held onto the rock and exited the huge central room, passing the chunk from hand to hand. His palms got colder and colder and the material of his suit became stiff and brittle. He dashed through the rooms he'd passed and the pain in his hands got worse, until he had to grit his teeth against it. The battlefield adrenaline had strong numbing properties and Duggan knew the coldness was doing him real damage.

An object appeared in his path. He leapt over it before remembering it was the pyramid's outer door. A few paces more and he emerged into Trasgor's night, his eyes searching left and right for the transport shuttle. There was no sign of it and he was forced to drop the pillar shard for a moment.

"This is Duggan, where the hell are you?" he shouted into the comms.

"Sir, we're still here," said Ortiz. "I've got a lock on you and we'll be there in a moment."

A searchlight appeared on the ground a couple of hundred metres away, moving towards his position. He squinted up and saw the shuttle hovering in the sky, level with the top of the pyramid. It dropped towards him and thumped heavily into the ground, the pilot sacrificing finesse for speed. Duggan picked up the rock and ran towards the transport, feeling the deep chill rush into his cold-blistered palms. The entry ramp opened and Duggan jumped onboard, throwing the pillar sample onto the floor. The pain was intense and the suit injected him with a strong painkiller without his intervention. The visors of the men and women in the passenger bay looked at him, giving away nothing of the expressions within. Duggan fell into one of the seats which had survived the damage from the heavy repeater and closed his eyes, the pain already fading.

"Let's get out of here," said Ortiz, leaning out of the cockpit to be sure Duggan was safely inside.

The door closed and the shuttle lifted off, accelerating faster than procedures allowed for. Duggan checked the timer. *Seven minutes.*

"Want to stick around for the fireworks, sir?" asked Ortiz

"We'd best not, Lieutenant. I'd rather we weren't accidentally hit by a stray missile."

"I'm sure they wouldn't do that," she replied.

"I'd have agreed with you only a few days ago," said Duggan, wondering what he believed about the Ghasts after recent events. "We're escaping by the skin of our teeth. Let's not slow things down."

"Right you are, sir."

The transport flew into the sky, still accelerating hard. It had a life support system that could mitigate the effects, though not one that was able to withstand the abuse of a determined pilot. There were rough metal patches over the holes through the hull. Duggan had no idea where the soldiers had got the materials to make them. This was the sort of thing they were good at.

The shuttle docked twenty minutes later, with Ortiz allowing the autopilot to take control over this final manoeuvre. Duggan was first off, eager to return to the bridge and resume command of the ship. When he exited the docked craft, he saw where the soldiers had cut through the metal clamps which had previously held it in place. Without them, the shuttle might not survive the jump to lightspeed.

Before the squad could return to their quarters, Duggan took his helmet off and thanked them for their work on the surface. There were nods and acknowledgements, with more than one person speaking of their eagerness to become reacquainted with the food replicator. The suits sustained their occupants but they couldn't replace the feeling of having a full stomach.

"I need a medic," said Duggan. He knew his hands were going to be a mess and he wasn't looking forward to seeing what state they were in. The gloves of his spacesuit were splitting and he knew he'd put himself at great risk to bring the sample of the pillar.

"You should have left that piece of rock, sir," said Ortiz. "Your squad brought a couple of pieces already."

"Damn," said Duggan ruefully. "I should have trusted them more."

"You're like me, sir. You don't want anyone to do something you could do yourself." She smiled at him, her features softening. "I'm glad you got out."

"Me too," he said. "Though the information I discovered won't be welcome when I hand it on."

Ortiz was a professional and she didn't pry further. "I'll send Corporal Bryant to the bridge. She'll have you sorted in no time."

"And have those samples locked up somewhere safe. Have one brought up to the bridge in a cold-proof box or something – Lieutenant Breeze might know what it is."

"Will do, sir."

Duggan returned to the bridge. The crew were happy to see him and greeted him warmly, except for Lieutenant Nichols who didn't smile and only said enough to avoid giving insult. There was little time for pleasantries and Duggan got straight on with business.

"Have the Ghasts done what they said?" he asked.

"Right at the time they promised," said McGlashan. "They didn't hold back either. We tracked just shy of one hundred missiles inbound to the pyramid. Here's what it looks like now." An image came up on the bulkhead screen. Duggan had to take McGlashan's word that the Dreamer artefact had once been there. After the *Dretisear*'s missile bombardment there was nothing recognizable, just a cluster of craters and an area of heat-blackened rock.

"Where is their spaceship and what information have they given you about why they wanted to destroy the pyramid?"

"They're ten thousand klicks away and moving in a tight circle over the target area, same as we are."

"No more information?"

Lieutenant Breeze was the next to speak. "We've got a fission signature from the *Dretisear*."

"Get Nil-Far on the comms!" said Duggan loudly.

After a few moments, the Ghast captain's voice reached Duggan's earpiece. "Captain John Duggan," he said, the interpretation giving away no hint about the Ghast's demeanour.

"Shut off your engines, Nil-Far. I want answers!"

"I have been ordered to leave this place. You have found what happened to your missing ship, therefore our mission is completed."

"What was that object on the surface? Why the secrets?"

"I do not have the authority to say, John Duggan. Nothing has changed."

"Ten seconds and they're gone," said Breeze.

Duggan's earpiece had become quiet and he thought Nil-Far was gone. The Ghast was still there and he spoke one final question.

"Did you see anything within the pyramid?"

"I saw nothing," said Duggan.

"They're gone," said Breeze. "At a healthy speed from what I can tell. They're either good at repairs or we overestimated their damage."

"How long till our engines are ready?" asked Duggan.

"They came online half an hour ago, sir. Not enough to attain maximum velocity, but it'll get us where we need to be."

"Fine," said Duggan. "Warm them up and set us on a course for the *Juniper*. The shit is about to hit the fan."

He caught McGlashan staring at him with one of her expressions. He didn't know if he had anything to say to her just yet, so he didn't meet her gaze. The engines on the *Terminus* took a few seconds longer than usual to prepare and then they sent the heavy cruiser away into lightspeed.

# CHAPTER TWENTY-ONE

WITH A FEELING OF DÉJÀ VU, John Duggan paused for a moment outside Admiral Teron's door. He clenched his fists, feeling the new layers of artificial skin flex uncomfortably. The *Juniper*'s AI scanned and recognized him, before opening the way for him to proceed. There were no perceptible changes to the office, except for the presence of an additional person who sat opposite Teron. This woman turned to look at Duggan as he walked inside, her eyes narrowing briefly, as if she had already found him wanting. For his part, Duggan kept his gaze neutral and even, having recognized her to be another officer of Admiral rank.

"Have a seat, Captain," said Teron. "This is Admiral Franks."

Admiral Franks was lean and her face was hard. Her hair was pulled away from her face and tied in a bun at the back of her head. Duggan wasn't a good judge of ages, but thought her to be somewhere in her fifties. They exchanged polite greetings, during which Admiral Franks' accent showed her to be originally from New Earth.

Teron got straight on with business. "I've read your preliminary report and I'm not pleased. This puts us in a very difficult situation."

"I can appreciate that," said Duggan.

"However, it may do little beyond bring forward other plans we have."

Duggan was caught unawares. "What do you mean?"

"We'll get to that shortly. Admiral Franks was here on other business and it seemed wise to invite her along to our discussion. I don't have the authority to deal with this on my own."

"Have you spoken with the Ghasts about what happened on Trasgor, sir?"

"We have, albeit only briefly. As far as they are concerned, they were within their rights to destroy the pyramid and claim their actions have no bearing on the peace we are negotiating. They also claim there were no threats made to members of the Space Corps or its warships."

"All of this is close enough to the truth that it's hard to refute, sir," said Duggan. "Except you weren't there. The Ghast captain was rattled when we found the pyramid and I believed there was a significant possibility the *Dretisear* would receive orders to fire upon us. The *ES Terminus* is a powerful warship but it is not a match for an Oblivion, no matter what the Space Corps might hope."

"Was there much of a difference between the two?" asked Teron, with an unmistakeable interest.

"Enough, sir. They had more of everything and they were tougher and faster than us. I think the AI core on the *Dretisear* is ahead too. The biggest difference continues to be their missile targeting."

"Well over a million kilometres," said Franks with a slight drawl. "They *have* been keeping secrets, haven't they?"

"Not secrets, sir. They've just continued to do what they've been beating us at for the last ten years – building and improving."

"That won't last forever, Captain," said Teron. "We're gaining on them technologically and there's nothing they can do to stop it." He paused to consider his next words. "We've had a few people working to estimate the Ghasts' theoretical industrial output, and do you know what? Even the most pessimistic results suggest that the Confederation has a fifty percent greater output than the combined Ghast worlds. Give us the time and we will overtake whatever technology they can create."

"That's by-the-by, sir. There was a damned Ghast in a terraforming power source left on Trasgor," said Duggan. "We need to find out why. Have the Ghasts secretly allied themselves to the Dreamers? They could have encountered each other around the Helius Blackstar and somehow come to an agreement."

Teron and Franks went quiet for a few seconds. It was Teron who broke the silence. "We need more proof, Captain."

"I saw the body, sir. It was a Ghast."

"I'm not doubting what you saw, nor am I going to humour you whilst I secretly believe your eyes deceived you or some other such nonsense. However, I *do* need more proof before I'm certain. If you'd been able to recover the body, we'd have been able to do tests."

"We couldn't do a recovery because the Ghasts blew it up," said Duggan. "They must have known what we'd find there, which would explain why Nil-Far was unwilling to tell me anything."

"You told the Ghast captain what you saw?" asked Franks.

"It was in my report, sir. I told Nil-Far I hadn't seen anything. I wanted to tell Admiral Teron about it first."

"The Dreamers destroyed as much of the Ghast fleet at the

Blackstar as they did of ours," said Teron. "Why would they be allies? On top of that, the Ghasts willingly assisted you with destroying the Dreamer warship which was guarding Trasgor."

"I don't know, sir. We know so little about the Ghasts and how they are governed. Could they have different factions, some of whom allied themselves with the Dreamers?"

"It doesn't seem likely, does it?" asked Franks. "The Ghasts have always acted in concert against us. Why should they suddenly be split now?"

Duggan shrugged, aware none of it made a lot of sense. "I'm worried we might arrange peace, only to find ourselves betrayed later. The Ghasts alone are a powerful foe. The Dreamers have only a limited presence in our space and they are looking to prepare entire worlds, presumably for them to populate. They will send more ships after the others and we could be caught in the middle."

"What are you suggesting, Captain?" asked Teron.

"Caution. Any peace deal with the Ghasts should be accompanied by a reduction in their armaments and a commitment by them to share their Shatterer technology. At least that will cut what advantage they have over us."

"We're trying," said Teron. "They aren't buying it."

"Will they eventually agree?" asked Duggan.

"Who knows? They may or they may not. I'm not really permitted to talk to you about it, Captain. Negotiations such as this are invariably delicate."

"If the Ghasts won't accept a reduction in their armed capabilities, they will eventually become a threat again," said Duggan. "Who is to say they aren't working on their own version of the Planet Breaker? They used a series of incendiary devices on Charistos and Angax. If they find where our home planets are, they could use them against us. And who knows what could happen if they are allied with the Dreamers?"

Teron gave a barked, humourless laugh. "I thought you wanted peace!" he said. "Here you are talking like we should make contingency plans to betray the Ghosts!"

"I do want peace, sir. Most of all, I want the Confederation to survive. I've fought too long to be on the losing side. Too many of my soldiers have died in the cause." His anger grew. "I simply do not want peace at any cost, sir."

"This is all for the future, Captain Duggan," said Teron, his eyes glittering. "The very near future. Rest assured, the details in your report have been taken seriously. I've said before that you always come with baggage – every victory has a downside."

"That's how it is, sir," said Duggan.

"I know," Teron replied. "It's something I've come to accept. For the moment, you'll need to leave certain matters in the hands of others."

"What next for me and my crew?"

Teron didn't answer directly, a trait Duggan had become familiar with. "You brought back samples of the Dreamer power source from Trasgor. Your Lieutenant Breeze made some preliminary findings about its nature, which have got a few of our scientists excited. *Very* excited."

"I believe it provided power for the energy shield and also for the structure itself – to create a new oxygen-rich atmosphere for the planet," said Duggan.

"I don't think there's much doubt about that," said Franks. "However, the idea of a power source based on stone rather than metal is what has got us interested."

"I thought stone was too brittle to use in a military capacity?" said Duggan. "Hence we use metal for everything."

"That's what we've always believed," agreed Franks. "Our researchers have started to think that the output from a metal-based power source will never be sufficient for a number of objectives we would like to pursue. Not because we lack the knowledge, but because the material itself is unsuitable."

"Cutting to the chase, we want more of what you found," said Teron.

"I've just arrived back!" said Duggan. "There's been no time to study the samples, let alone decide what we need!"

"That's only partially true. We have past research projects into generating power from materials other than metal. Many of them reached a dead end, though in some cases this was because of our own limitations, not a limitation of the materials we hoped to utilise."

"There are times you know something is possible, yet lack the capability to make it happen," said Franks.

Teron performed another one of his topic shifts. "How many of our spacecraft do you think it would take to destroy the Dreamer vessel you encountered in the orbit of Trasgor?" he asked.

"It depends how many of our craft you expect to be destroyed," Duggan said. "Without Shatterer missiles, we'd need to get in close enough to bring down its shields with nuclear blasts."

"How many?"

"Three like the *Terminus* would stand a chance. I'd want many more for certainty."

"We've lost another ship," said Teron. "In the Garon sector, a couple of days' high lightspeed from Trasgor."

"This time it was a warship, the Anderlecht *Bulldozer*."

"Travelling alone in an area known to hold a threat to our fleet?" asked Duggan sharply.

"Rest assured there'll be a reckoning," Teron replied. "All you really need to know is that they sent a low-speed distress signal from the surface of a planet, describing the presence of a large pyramid-shaped object on the ground."

"We don't know if the Dreamers can trace our broadcasts," said Duggan.

"The crew of the *Bulldozer* didn't consider that," said Teron. "What's happened has happened."

"What else have they told you?"

"They were destroyed by an unknown warship which hit them with beam and missile fire. We've not heard from them after their first message."

"We're sending you to recover the pyramid," said Franks. "You'll likely encounter another enemy warship, which you'll need to destroy, before picking up the target object and bringing it to New Earth for study."

"I'll require a heavy lifter," said Duggan.

"We're currently looking into what vessels we can make available for this task," said Teron. "It's a high priority, so resourcing isn't an issue. It's the time and distances which we're struggling to overcome. We need you to go as soon as possible."

"What if the pyramid broadcasts distress signals from the hold of the MHL?" asked Duggan.

"You'll have to make sure it doesn't," said Teron. "This is your chance to take another look inside and capture whoever happens to be operating the device."

"If I can't be certain I've locked down their transmissions, I'll have to destroy it," said Duggan.

"We'd rather you didn't," said Teron.

"And what about the crew who sent the broadcast?"

"They're a secondary concern, Captain Duggan," said Franks.

"If I can find them, I'll bring them back."

"Of course," Franks said. "I'll repeat they are secondary to your primary goal." She didn't need to spell out what she meant.

Duggan thought the meeting was over and that he was about

to be dismissed until the time came when Teron had gathered enough warships.

"There's more, which I'll let you know about while you're here," said Teron, his expression showing the news wasn't going to be palatable. "The Confederation Council are looking to cut costs. To reap the benefits of peace before peace has arrived."

"We're having a stand-down from total war?" asked Duggan.

"Not yet. They're seeking to justify it and the decision is in the balance."

"Unbelievable," said Duggan. "We're facing two dangerous alien races, both of whom have the capability to wipe us out."

"They're not looking to cut us to the bone, Captain," said Franks with a thin smile. "Just bring the costs back to what they describe as a more acceptable level. Existing ships will be built and more will follow. Inevitably there'll be a degree of scaling back."

"You know all about Military Asset Management," said Teron. "They're one of the monitoring tools the Council asked to be implemented." He raised a hand to forestall Duggan's next words. "Yes, I've read about Lieutenant Nichols in your report and yes his behaviour was unacceptable. I will have words with the right people, but we have to put up with it for the moment."

"Sir, he questioned my actions at every opportunity. He could have jeopardised the mission."

"In truth, I am furious, Captain Duggan," said Teron. "My hands are tied for now. Nichols is a senior figure in MAM - his rank of lieutenant is not representative of the power he wields. You need to be careful with him."

"He's coming with you," said Franks.

It wasn't the sort of news Duggan had wished to hear. He'd hoped to be rid of Lieutenant Nichols and anyone else from MAM who took an interest in what he was doing. The stern faces of Teron and Franks told Duggan his complaints wouldn't go anywhere. "Is that all?" he asked with a calm he didn't feel.

"That's all, Captain."

Duggan stood and left the office, feeling two pairs of eyes drilling into his back as he went.

# CHAPTER TWENTY-TWO

WITHIN THIRTY-SIX HOURS, Duggan had his warships. It wasn't exactly what he wanted, but he grudgingly admitted there was probably enough firepower to get the job done, even if it wasn't the overwhelming force he wanted. He stood on the bridge of the Galactic class *ES Rampage*, with the crew and soldiers from the *ES Terminus* already brought onboard. The *Terminus* wouldn't be going anywhere for a while, except to a shipyard for extensive repairs.

"We've got Anderlechts *Vestige*, *Lustre* and *Extraction* with us," said Chainer. "The *Brazen* is due within the hour."

"How many Gunners?" asked Duggan.

"We've got *Furnace*, *Paranoid* and *Fencer*, sir. New models."

It was good to have the Vincent class fighters with them, though they probably wouldn't contribute too much. Duggan had in the past thought these smallest of warships could be made to fight like tigers. He'd had a lot of time to reflect and it was increasingly apparent the Gunners were being gradually left behind and their significance diminishing. They couldn't hold many Lambda clusters or nuclear missiles. They were definitely not big enough for a beam weapon. As time passed, the former workhorse of the fleet was heading for irrelevancy. Duggan wasn't usually sentimental but there was something sad about the idea.

"Where's our lifter?" asked Duggan.

"It's coming later," said McGlashan. "The details arrived a few minutes ago. There wasn't anything suitable near the *Juniper*, so they're having one sent directly to Kidor – that's the name of the place where the *Bulldozer's* crew found the pyramid. The lifter isn't fast and it might not be there at the same time as we are."

"That's for the best," said Duggan. "We don't want it getting involved in the fighting."

"It's the *MHL Goliath*," said McGlashan, her face perfectly straight.

Duggan shook his head and turned to Chainer. "We're instructed to leave at once. Please coordinate our departure with the other vessels."

"I've already done so, sir," replied Chainer. "We'll leave within five minutes of the *Brazen's* arrival."

There wasn't much to do while he waited and Duggan fidgeted with impatience. The cruiser was five minutes later than scheduled when it winked into normal space, a good distance from the *Juniper*.

"Send them my greetings and tell them to get ready," said Duggan.

"I've provided them with the coordinates," said Chainer. "They've confirmed readiness to depart."

After another five minutes, the eight Space Corps warships surged into lightspeed within a millisecond of each other. The *Rampage* was capable of Light-M, yet the heavy cruiser was obliged to travel no faster than the slowest accompanying vessels.

"We're at Light-H," said Breeze. "It feels like a bit of a crawl, these days."

"How long till we arrive?"

"Another five days, sir. Kidor is a lot closer to the central zones of Confederation space."

"I know," said Duggan. "It has me worried."

"Do you think the Dreamers are looking?" asked McGlashan.

"They know there are at least two intelligent species here," said Duggan. "Our technology is clearly not as advanced as theirs, but we've managed to destroy two of their ships. If they're not specifically looking, they're certainly alert to our presence."

"What's the plan when we meet the enemy?" asked McGlashan.

"We hammer them with nukes and conventional missiles," said Duggan. "Even though we'll take some damage, we should be able to defeat them."

"Not too much damage I hope, Captain?" said Lieutenant Nichols.

"My orders come from an Admiral of the Space Corps," said Duggan. "I've been trusted with their execution. If you have anything you wish to discuss, please feel free to get on the comms and speak to whoever it is you wish to speak to. I will not have you questioning my orders when the missiles start flying."

Nichols gave one of his infuriating smiles. "I'm sure neither you nor your senior officers wish to appear profligate when it comes to the assets purchased with the Confederation's funding."

"I will complete my mission," said Duggan. "I can't believe you're still here. You've seen what we face, Lieutenant Nichols. I'm surprised you're not begging your superiors to maintain our war footing."

"If we believed the military about everything, we'd have to give you so much money there'd be nothing left for any other facilities our citizens like to have provided for them. Warships, tanks and shuttles, Captain. Our people cannot eat them and they cannot sleep in them. Money cannot be wasted when the need is unproven."

"Did you prevent the tank deployment from the *Terminus*?" asked Duggan. The bridge went silent.

"I have a job to do, Captain. Please let me get on with it," Nichols replied, sitting down.

Duggan returned to his own seat. He didn't know where the accusation had come from – he hadn't been conscious of thinking the words, yet they had arrived unbidden from his mouth. The more he thought about it, the more the idea developed a twisted appeal. He remained in his seat for a few minutes and then got up, before leaving the bridge. A short while later McGlashan found him in the hold, inspecting the array of tanks and other weaponry within.

"Why would he do that?" she asked.

Duggan didn't regret his words. "When nothing adds up, I have to ask what other reasons there could be."

"The *Terminus* was damaged, sir. Not much of anything worked."

"Only one tank launched and that was mine. There was no reason for it to happen, Commander. We spent most of the return trip investigating and then all of a sudden we got green lights on the release commands."

"The AI could have fixed the problem. It's happened before."

"I've seen enough strange things happen to accept there's not always an easy answer. Still, it seems peculiar for only my tank to launch and for everything else to remain in a failed state until a short time before we returned to the *Juniper*. It's conceivable that Lieutenant Nichols has codes to lock down the assets his department claims to manage."

"What you're suggesting is that he tried to murder you?" she asked, uncertainty clear across her features.

"No, Commander. I despise the man, yet I can't see why he'd

want to kill me. I think there's a power struggle going on some-where in the echelons above me. Nichols has greater power than his Space Corps rank suggests. It could be as simple as one organ-isation trying to discredit another."

"In the middle of a war?" she asked. "They could have picked a better time."

"These things never stop, Commander. Believe me, I've seen it happen. You heard Nichols – he talked about money, rather than the extermination of our species. He expressed scorn about the military and how much we could be believed. If he's as blinkered as he sounds, he may think it's his duty to undermine us at every opportunity. The worse we look, the better it is for him. In his eyes, the Ghasts are neutralised and the extent of the Dreamer threat is undetermined. What better time to try and claw back some of the money invested into our warfleet?"

"Whatever it takes?"

"I don't know," said Duggan at last. "It's the only reason I can think of for the launch failures on the *Terminus*. I can't be certain of his motives, so I'll have to give him the benefit of the doubt for now."

"I suppose if you'd died on Trasgor and the mission had failed, the Space Corps would look incompetent," she said.

"Maybe. Or maybe he's just an overzealous bastard who's acting outside his orders."

"I'll try and keep an eye on him," said McGlashan. "I can record what commands he makes from his console. If he gets up to any funny business, I'll throw him into space myself."

Duggan took a deep breath. "I found bodies in the pyramid on Trasgor."

McGlashan looked at him closely, aware he had more to tell. "Dreamers?"

"Several of them were burned beyond recognition. There was

one which wasn't - the very last one I found. It looked like a Ghast."

Her eyes widened. "What does that mean?" she asked.

"It throws everything we know out of the window. Other than that, I have no idea what will come from it. I told Admiral Teron. He believed me, yet he wants more proof. We might find that proof where we're going."

"How can the Ghasts and Dreamers be working together? The Dreamers have been equally hostile to both of us."

"I really don't know. There's got to be an answer. Nil-Far acted so strangely once he realised what was on Trasgor. He knew something and he didn't want to tell us."

"You like Nil-Far."

"I'm not sure *like* is the best word for it. I saw something in him that made me feel hope our two races could finish this war. I thought if there were others like him, we may have a chance for a working peace. After what happened on Trasgor, I am utterly confused."

"That makes two of us," she said, trying to smile. "What happens if we find more Ghasts in this next pyramid?"

"It's going to become much harder to make a lasting peace. There's no way we'll be able to trust them. We'll build up the fleet until we feel safe. Eventually hostilities will resume one way or another. Someone in the Confederation Council will ask why we have the Planet Breaker if we aren't going to use it. I'm sure you can guess what will happen."

"What about the Dreamers?"

"They're the big unknown and the greatest threat we face. If they need new worlds to live in so badly that they'll throw themselves through a wormhole to find them, I dread to think how numerous they are."

"At least if we're told to build up the fleet, it'll put Lieutenant Nichols out of a job."

"Every cloud has a silver lining," said Duggan.

They returned to the bridge and settled down to their usual duties. Duggan occupied himself by running through the logs of the previous encounter with the Dreamer warship. The few examples he'd seen so far showed their vessels to have flat, rounded noses, with broad struts running parallel to a low-slung main hull. They looked delicate in a way, as if they lacked the mass to hold the weapons Duggan knew they carried. In comparison, the sleekest of the Space Corps ships looked heavy. Not quite clumsy, but lacking in flair. The Corps had always built for purpose, rather than to make their ships look pretty. Duggan wondered if the Dreamers' technology was so advanced they had the luxury of building their ships to impress visually as well as being able to destroy. Ultimately, it wasn't important for him to know.

Over the next couple of days, Duggan spent time with the soldiers onboard. There hadn't been much opportunity to speak to them on the *Terminus* and he liked to put names to faces. Everyone looked the same in their spacesuits and he preferred to know who he was talking to. The troops had accepted Lieutenant Ortiz, having been initially resistant. Duggan hadn't doubted for a moment she was capable of handling them, else he wouldn't have asked her to do so. When they returned after this mission, he planned to recommend her promotion to lieutenant be made permanent.

With the inevitability of time, the five days passed. On the bridge, Duggan took his seat, gave his instructions to the crew and waited for the AI to decide when it was time to disengage the engines and put them into normal space.

# CHAPTER TWENTY-THREE

"I'M DETECTING gamma radiation twenty thousand klicks to starboard," said Massey.

"There's something else," said Perry. "Wreckage at about a hundred thousand klicks."

"Wreckage of what?" asked Duggan. "Tell me what's out there!"

"Need time," said Chainer, his head down in concentration, an empty can of hi-stim on his console nearby.

"We might not have any time," said Duggan.

"Our comms are down," said Perry.

"Activate the backup systems."

"Switching over now," said Chainer.

"Weapons systems ready to fire," said Reyes. "As soon as we've got eyes on the target."

"Do we have any of our ships in the vicinity?" asked Duggan.

"The *Vestige* and the *Brazen* have just arrived," Breeze told him. "Their fission signatures have come up on my screen."

"Send them a red alert. Presence of hostiles," said Duggan,

hoping the rest of the fleet had been sharp enough to activate their own backup comms.

"The *Furnace* and *Extraction* got here before us," said Perry. "Two hundred and fifty thousand klicks off."

"Damn they didn't come in close enough," said Chainer. "Sir, I've got a confirmed sighting of a Dreamer warship. It's more than two klicks long - the same type we saw before."

"I'm reading it," said McGlashan. "Just out of Lambda range."

"*Lustre* and *Paranoid* are here, sir," said Perry. "*Lustre* at fifty thousand closer to the enemy and the *Paranoid* twenty thousand further away."

Duggan swore loudly and banged his fist against the bare alloy of his console. "This is meant to be a military operation. We've come in spread across half of the damned galaxy!" He glanced at one of his screens. The ES *Rampage* was fifteen minutes out from Kidor, with the rest of the group scattered all about. He didn't have a chance to open his mouth again before red dots appeared across his tactical screen.

"The *Lustre*'s launching her nukes, sir," said Reyes. "Six Lambda-mounted warheads fired, along with sixty conventionals. They've disabled the targeting. There's zero chance of a unguided warhead strike from that range."

"Fifty missiles coming in response from the enemy," said McGlashan.

"The wreckage is the ES *Fencer*, sir," said Massey. "Evidence suggests they got burned up by a beam strike."

"I'm bringing us into range," said Duggan, hauling on the control bars. "I want those bastards to be swimming in so much radiation their home world can see them glow. Our other ships should know what to do. Lieutenant Perry, get in touch and remind them, just in case they've forgotten."

---

"Aye sir!" said Perry. He'd been timid at the start, though his confidence had noticeably grown since the first time he'd met Duggan.

"The *Vestige* has launched as well," said Reyes. "Six more nukes and another cloud of Lambdas."

Duggan called up a sensor feed onto the main bulkhead screen. It showed the *Lustre*, which was the closest to the enemy vessel. The image sparkled with pinpricks of silver light. The Anderlecht had launched countermeasures and the shock drones interfered with the *Rampage*'s sensor readings. The cruiser's Bulwark projectiles were tearing up the sky around the vessel as well, with four out of six firing at the incoming missiles.

"Not enough to stop fifty missiles," said Duggan to himself. He pushed the control bars harder in a pointless effort to extract more speed from the *Rampage*.

"Beam hit on the *Lustre*," said Breeze. "Damage unknown."

More than just the beam weapon hit the cruiser. Spheres of white appeared, partially hidden by the vessel's hull.

"Several successful missile hits," said McGlashan. "I can't tell you how many exactly, since their Bulwarks might have knocked out a few at the last moment. The *Lustre* is probably out of the fight."

"None of their Lambdas hit," said Reyes. "They've remote-detonated their nukes. I don't think they've come close enough to disable the enemy shields."

"I'm feeling distinctly under-powered," said Chainer as he watched events unfold on his sensor feeds. "Bring back the *Dretisear*."

"Unfortunately, you're right, Lieutenant," said Duggan, his eyes not leaving his console. "I hadn't anticipated we'd be taken by surprise and I'd hoped to combine our firepower. Instead, we're spread out and easy pickings."

"Luck's only great when it's with you," said Chainer. "Otherwise it's like a kick in the balls with a hobnailed boot."

"Focus, Lieutenant," warned Duggan.

"We're in range," said McGlashan.

"Fire Lambdas only," said Duggan. "Keep the fast reload till we're closer. Let's see if we can overload their countermeasures with numbers."

"One hundred and twenty missiles away," said McGlashan.

"They're launching more missiles. Two waves of fifty," said Reyes.

"One for us and one for the *Vestige*," said Duggan. The *Lustre* was disabled, though not yet destroyed. Luckily for the crew, it appeared as if the Dreamer vessel had decided to concentrate on the other inbound threats.

"The *Vestige* scored a hit," said Chainer. "Bang on their shields."

"One hit on a warship that size isn't going to cut it even if they didn't have shields," said Breeze.

"Six more nuclear detonations in the vicinity of the enemy," said Reyes.

"There are fluctuating readings from their shields," reported Chainer. "Something's given them a shock."

"Shields down?" asked Duggan. "We're still too far away." It was becoming painfully obvious how under-equipped they were for this encounter. The *Dretisear* had brought two weapons that could damage the Dreamers. The Space Corps warships could only fire nukes and keep their fingers crossed.

"The enemy ship is coming towards us," said Duggan. "Maybe we look like the biggest threat."

"Their course will take them near to the *Lustre*," said Chainer.

"We just took a beam hit on the nose," said Breeze. "I hope those nukes are well-insulated."

"They are," said McGlashan. "We've lost some of our front tubes, though."

"How long till the other ships get close enough to fire?" asked Duggan.

"Minutes," said Chainer. "Quite a few minutes for the *Extraction* and the *Furnace*. They won't get here before it's over."

The enemy missiles approached the *Rampage* at a terrifying speed. Duggan tried his best to time it right and swung the spaceship at an angle which allowed more of their Bulwarks to fire. The grumbling of the cannons echoed through the bridge.

"Countermeasures away," said McGlashan. "Plenty of shock drones for their missiles to find a way through."

Several pairs of eyes watched the inbound warheads and there was more than one release of pent-up breath when the *Rampage*'s countermeasures dealt with all fifty. The Dreamer missiles were fast and with a good range, yet they didn't seem vastly more advanced than the Lambdas. In fact, Duggan thought, the enemy missiles were in many ways inferior to what the Ghasts possessed. The Dreamer beam weapons were exceptionally powerful but they weren't a game-changer. It was the energy shields which made the difference.

"The *Vestige* has taken a couple of hits," said McGlashan. "No way to confirm the damage yet."

"Our missiles have passed by the enemy warship," said Reyes. "No hits."

"I've detonated the nukes," said McGlashan. "That's got to be close."

"There's a shuttle launch from the *Lustre*, sir," said Chainer. "They're abandoning ship."

"Are they so badly damaged?" asked Duggan.

"Must be," said Breeze. "There's a lot of heat spilling off them."

The tactical screen was now a mess of pin-point lights.

Lambdas poured from the *Rampage*'s remaining forward tubes, followed by four nukes. The *ES Vestige* continued to unload from its own arsenal, while the *ES Paranoid* had come close enough to fire its two missile clusters. The enemy ship responded with a barrage of its own, each wave consisting of exactly fifty missiles, spaced out at irregular intervals.

Another particle beam struck the *Rampage*, near to the previous one. Red alerts appeared on the bridge status displays and a siren began its alarm. Two missiles penetrated the barrier of countermeasures, crashing into the side of the warship and tearing ugly holes through the armour.

"One of our missiles scored a hit," said Chainer. "Their shield is still up and looking as healthy as ever."

*We're going to lose this,* thought Duggan. He didn't speak the words out loud. Instead, he ordered McGlashan to use the rapid reload and fire the Lambdas as quickly as possible. She acknowledged the order and missiles continued to spill from the warship's launch tubes.

"We've received another missile hit aft," announced Breeze. "Our engine output is falling. If we take another one there we're screwed."

"The *Lustre*'s moving, sir," said Chainer. "They must have left someone onboard."

The news caught Duggan by surprise. Sure enough, the large dot representing the Anderlecht was moving at a decent speed. "Going fast too, from the looks of it," he said.

"Are they trying to ram the enemy?" asked Massey in shock. "There's no way they'll be quick enough!"

"They'll get close," said Chainer. "The enemy's changed course to avoid an interception."

Duggan still had his eyes on the tactical screen. The dot representing the *Lustre* vanished without warning. "What?" he asked.

"The *Lustre* has exploded, sir!" said McGlashan. "What the hell?"

Duggan cycled through the options on his tactical display and saw a vast cloud of radiation, expanding at enormous speed away from its centre. The cloud engulfed the Dreamer vessel and continued beyond.

"The enemy shield is gone, sir!" shouted Chainer.

"Engines too, from the looks of it," said Breeze. "Their output is close to zero."

"Fire everything!" said Duggan.

"Continuing as before, sir," said McGlashan. "We might not need to bother."

Duggan realised what she meant. There were still hundreds of Lambdas in flight. Four of them hit the Dreamer ship within a hundred metres of each other. Duggan called up the external feed and zoomed in on the enemy vessel. The Lambda blasts had opened up a huge, deep breach into its hull. Duggan didn't know enough about the design of the Dreamer ships, but the damage looked severe.

With its engine output reduced, the Dreamer warship wasn't able to take effective evasive action, making it easy for the *Rampage*'s AI to predict the enemy's course. Duggan watching intently as another twenty Lambdas cascaded against the length of the spaceship. Plasma washed over and through its armour, hiding much of the hull behind a fierce glare. More missiles plunged into the stricken vessel, tearing it into three parts. Still the barrage continued, until the enemy ship was scattered in glowing pieces over a huge swathe of Kidor's sky.

There was no cheering, only relief, tinged with sadness. Duggan fell into his seat and wiped his forehead with the back of his hand. "See if you can get in touch with the other ships and find out who we've lost. Then speak to the people on the shuttle and ask what happened. Whoever was on the *Lustre* has saved a lot of lives."

"Aye, sir," said Perry.

"There's got to be a better way to defeat them," said Duggan. He set a course for Kidor, though not before he'd caught the unreadable expression on Lieutenant Nichols' face.

# CHAPTER TWENTY-FOUR

THE EIGHT SHIPS which had set off from the *Juniper* were reduced to six, with the loss of twenty-two soldiers and crew. The captain of the *Lustre* – a woman called Anya Gottlieb had issued the evacuation order for her ship, but had stayed behind to activate the self-destruct facility in case the Dreamer ship came close. Duggan silently congratulated her for her prescience and sacrifice. There queue of tributes to pay was building.

The shuttle had nowhere to dock and shadowed the other ships. The *ES Rampage* had two docking bays, both of which were occupied. Duggan was more than happy to jettison one of his two shuttles and this he did, programming its onboard computer to keep the craft stationary in case anyone ever came to recover it. Lieutenant Nichols offered no protest. A short while later, the shuttle from the *Lustre* docked and ninety additional personnel boarded the *Rampage*. There was room for them, though it was a little cramped.

"We took some hits," said Breeze. "This time we came out of it mostly intact. Even if we lack the weaponry to destroy the enemy, we can still ride a few punches."

"I agree," said Duggan. "The Space Corps have come up with a solid design here. Once our weapons technology catches up, the Galactic class will be a force to reckon with."

"What are our orders now, sir?" asked McGlashan.

"Ensign Perry, contact the other vessels - order them to stay close and in standard formation. We need to be on guard against the possible presence or arrival of another enemy warship. This time we will be clustered tightly enough to focus our fire, instead of being spread halfway across the solar system."

"I'm advising them, sir," said Perry.

"We'll approach slowly until the *ES Extraction* and *ES Furnace* join with us. Then we will do a controlled sweep of the planet's surface to find this pyramid we've been sent to locate."

"The *Extraction* or *Furnace* might have already located it," said Massey. "I'll find out."

"When is the heavy lifter due, sir?" asked Breeze. "I reckon we got lucky on Trasgor when the enemy didn't send reinforcements."

"I'm sure you're correct, Lieutenant," said Duggan. "We've got between four and six hours until the *MHL Goliath* comes. That's plenty of time for something to happen, so we'll remain on high alert."

The search would have been finished quickly if the six vessels had been able to disperse into different orbits. Duggan was insistent they stay together, which slowed things down. In common with Trasgor, this planet was mid-distance from its sun and not otherwise remarkable. There was no sign it held great quantities of rare metals or anything resource-wise which would make it a specific target for settlement. However, its distance from the sun would ensure it would be neither too hot, nor too cold, once it had a suitable atmosphere to support life.

"The oxygen levels are higher than I'd expect and they're on the way up," said Chainer. "Same as we found on Trasgor."

ANTHONY JAMES

"We've had a confirmed sighting of another pyramid, so it's here," said Duggan. "Can you track the source of the oxygen?"

"That's what I'm doing now, sir. The concentrations are higher close to Kidor's equator. I've sent you the details."

"Got them," said Duggan. "I'm changing course. I'd like you to keep scanning for any further emergency broadcasts from the people on the surface."

"Of course, sir," said Massey smoothly.

"Got it!" said Chainer excitedly. "They've left this one in pretty much the same place as the one on Trasgor."

"I'm sure there's a reason," said Duggan. "What're the readings from it?"

"There's an energy shield with an eight-kilometre diameter, which comes as no surprise."

"No sign of anything else?"

"Nothing our sensors can pick up. There might be defensive emplacements like Trasgor. In fact, I'd bet money there's something inside the perimeter."

"Are we going to disable them with the nukes?" asked McGlashan.

"We'll hold for a moment," said Duggan. "Let's make a very quick sweep for the *Bulldozer*'s missing crew."

"I think I've already found them, sir," said Massey. "There's a beacon on the ground about two klicks from the energy shield perimeter."

"I see it," said Chainer. "It's firing out a signal along the floor of a valley and almost flat across the planet's surface. No wonder we didn't spot it sooner."

"Why would it be doing that?" asked Duggan.

"I don't know, sir. Maybe something's disturbed it. The signal is strong, but it's going nowhere except a hundred trillion miles out into nothingness."

"What's the terrain like around it?"

"There are high hills. Rock, stone, the usual stuff. The beacon is near a cliff face. And look! Something has exploded right at the top. There's a big chunk of the rock missing."

"A missile?"

"I'm certain that's plasma damage," said Chainer.

"Any sign of the people who operated the beacon?"

"Nope. They might have been killed, sir."

"I'm not so sure," said Massey, chewing her lip.

"What do you mean?" asked Duggan, standing at her shoulder.

"If the beacon was originally broadcasting directly upwards, it would have been found by anyone determined to do so. I wonder if the Dreamer warship fired a missile at the source of the signal, only they hit the top of the cliff by mistake. If they caused enough rocks to tumble down, they could have buried the beacon or knocked it over."

"Then the signal apparently vanished, making the enemy think they scored a hit?" asked Duggan. He wanted to believe, but wasn't yet convinced.

"It's a possibility, sir."

"It's a poor job if they managed to miss a ground-based target," said Reyes.

"Stranger things have happened," replied Duggan. He stood abruptly. "I'm going to send a few of the troops in a shuttle to take a look. We can't launch a two gigaton nuclear warhead at the energy shield if the *Bulldozer*'s crew are holed up somewhere close by. Lieutenant Nichols, you're going with them."

Nichols couldn't conceal his surprise. "I'm needed here," he spluttered.

"To do what? Keep an eye on me? You're going to go and have a look at what we have to do in the Space Corps from time to time. How can you make a firm decision on how we treat our *assets* if you don't experience it first hand?"

Nichols gave Duggan a look that was not at all friendly. "I have done this before, Captain," he said. Even so, he had no choice in the matter and climbed from his chair.

"Ensign Perry, please tell Lieutenant Ortiz that she is to choose eight of her men and women to go on a short trip to the surface, leaving from Shuttle Bay One as soon as they're ready. Make her aware that Lieutenant Nichols will be joining them and that this should be a quick in and out, without the need for gunfire."

Nichols left the bridge, glowering as he did so. He wasn't stupid enough to outright mutiny, but he made his displeasure obvious. Duggan didn't care – if Nichols wanted to involve himself in how the Space Corps used its equipment, he should be prepared to get his hands dirty.

"The atmosphere has improved in here already," said Chainer, taking a swig from a can of hi-stim.

"Lieutenant Chainer," warned Duggan.

"I was just saying, sir," Chainer replied.

A short time passed, before Ensign Perry announced he'd received notice from Lieutenant Ortiz that she was ready to depart.

"Good. Tell them to make haste. Find out what happened to the crew of the *Bulldozer* and get back here," said Duggan. Ortiz wasn't known for taking her time and the shuttle departed swiftly. It backed out of its bay, rotated smoothly on its axis and then raced off towards Kidor.

"There's no sign of hostile activity from the Dreamers," said Chainer. "No change whatsoever."

"Good - keep watching. Commander McGlashan, destroy anything that emerges from the energy shield."

"They'd have to be foolish to stick their heads outside," said Breeze.

"I know," replied Duggan. "However, for all their technology,

I'm starting to believe our enemy are not completely infallible. They've made mistakes before."

Duggan ordered Perry to request regular updates from the shuttle. A moment later, the voice of Lieutenant Ortiz came through the bridge speakers. "I'm going to bring us in low and flat and stick close to the valley floor. Everything's clear so far, though I'm sure you know better than we do, sir."

"There's no sign of anything hostile," said Duggan. In truth, a surface-launched missile could destroy the shuttle before there was time to blink, let alone try and intercept it. There was a risk in sending the shuttle to look for the missing crew and Duggan was fearful. In other circumstances, he'd have gone himself, yet he carried too much responsibility now to go out on a limb to save people who might already be dead.

"Want me to order a bombardment on the shield in case they let their guard down?" asked McGlashan.

Duggan cursed himself for not thinking of it earlier. "Thank you for the reminder, Commander. It's too late, now though. The shuttle is too low for the enemy to target it with surface missiles. If they were going to do anything it would have happened already."

"We're at the landing area, sir," said Ortiz. "I'm going to set the shuttle down."

"What do you see?"

"It's rough. This area of the valley is filled with rocks. I can read the signal from the beacon clearly and it's somewhere amongst the mess."

"Any signs of life?"

"Nothing I can see. There's a cave in the cliff wall."

Duggan looked questioningly at the comms team. "I'm sure there is, sir," said Chainer. "We could easily miss something like that from directly overhead. Particularly if there's an overhang."

"We're down safely," said Ortiz. "We'll have to go outside and take a look around."

"Keep us informed," said Duggan.

He paced back and forth for a few minutes, impatient to hear an update. The bridge had begun to smell of ozone and metal, where previously there had been little discernible odour. It had been the same on the *Terminus*. The scents would have been comforting in other circumstances.

"The cave looks deep," said Ortiz. "We're going inside. I'll leave Flores at the entrance in case we lose the comms. I have no idea how far they'll work through the rock."

"Roger."

"Sir?" said Breeze, alarm in his voice. "I've just read a fission signature, about a third of an orbit away from us. It's massive and it's not one of ours."

"Ghast or Dreamer?"

"Bigger than an Oblivion. And the Ghasts don't know we're here," Breeze replied.

Duggan swore. If the newly-arrived warship was bigger than an Oblivion, that made it at least five kilometres in length. The Ghasts' capital ship was far larger than that, which left only one possibility.

"There's no way we've got the firepower to beat a Dreamer ship as large as that one," he said. "We've got to assume they'll come towards the pyramid."

"I'd say so," said Breeze.

"How long have we got?"

"Minutes if we're lucky," said Chainer.

"Sir, I'm receiving several requests for orders from the other ships," said Perry. "They've detected the arrival and they want to know what to do."

The possibilities roiled in Duggan's head. He chased each one, finding nothing but dead ends. The odds were too great and the dangers too much to face. "Order an immediate retreat. Full speed to the *Juniper*."

"What about the shuttle, sir?" asked McGlashan.

Duggan gave her a grim smile. "The *ES Rampage* is not going anywhere, Commander."

# CHAPTER TWENTY-FIVE

"LIEUTENANT ORTIZ, we've got hostiles – more than we can deal with."

"Sir, Lieutenant Ortiz can't hear you." The voice belonged to Flores. "She's inside the cave with the others."

"Get them out of there and be ready to board the shuttle. We're going to do a couple of orbits and see if we can pick you up."

"Yes, sir," said Flores.

"We should leave with the rest of the fleet, sir," said McGlashan.

"I don't want to abandon our soldiers, Commander."

"There may be little choice. The enemy clearly knows we're here. They're going to hunt us down and they're going to destroy this ship and everyone onboard."

"What about the *Goliath*?" asked Duggan. "We can't communicate with them when they're at lightspeed. We need to do something!"

"A couple of hours till the *Goliath* arrives," said Chainer.

"And another hour after that until they can return to light-speed," said Breeze.

Duggan stayed quiet, though his mind was in turmoil. The mission had failed and he accepted that. The enemy ships significantly outclassed those of the Space Corps, so in a way they'd fared better than could be expected. However, he couldn't stomach the thought of abandoning Ortiz and the others. He'd also made a promise to Captain Erika Jonas and it was a promise he wasn't going to break. He realised how angry he was and did his best to push the emotion aside before it swamped his rational thought.

"The *Vestige*, *Extraction* and *Brazen* have gone to light-speed," said Breeze. "The *Paranoid* and *Furnace* are almost ready."

Duggan got into his seat and took the control bars. He swung the ship until it was facing the opposite direction to the Dreamer warship and increased power to the gravity drives. He brought them low to the surface and the hull temperature climbed at once. McGlashan came over and stood next to him. She spoke quietly.

"Sir, we have to leave. There's no way to tell if the enemy ship will pursue us or if they'll stay directly over the pyramid. Whatever happens, the shuttle is too easy a target. We're both going to get shot down if we try to let them dock."

"I know, Commander," he replied with equal quiet. "I have no choice but to try."

"There is always an alternative, sir, but these decisions are the hardest of all. You wonder why I've not pushed for a promotion. This right here is the reason for it."

"Sir, there's another fission signature," said Breeze. "High overhead at a distance of two hundred thousand klicks."

"What is it?" asked Duggan sharply.

"It's the *Goliath*, sir," said Chainer. "It's arrived early."

"Try hailing them! Tell them to swing around and get away!"

"I'm getting nothing when I try to contact them," said Chainer. "Their comms are down and they won't be equipped with a backup facility."

"I'm detecting missiles," said Reyes. "The curvature of the planet stops me from seeing the source, but it can only be from the enemy warship."

McGlashan ran the few paces to her console. "Fifty in the air," she said. "They're targeting the *MHL Goliath*."

With his heart sinking, Duggan watched the wave of missiles speed across his tactical display. He zoomed out until the *MHL Goliath* appeared as a distant, green circle. Time slowed and everything around him faded into a dimly-realised blur. He opened his mouth to speak, unsure what he wanted to say. In the end, no words came out. The red dots of the enemy missiles reached the larger green circle. Without ceremony, the screen went blank.

"The *Goliath* is gone, sir," said Chainer. "They managed to shoot down about six of the incoming missiles with their Bulwarks."

"Gone," repeated Duggan slowly, his grip on the control rods weakening.

"Sir, you need to act, else we'll follow the same way," said McGlashan.

Duggan felt as if he were wading through treacle, with his thoughts slowed down to a crawl. Instead of making them easier to control, they became more elusive and swam easily away from him.

"Sir!"

"Yes, Commander, I hear you," he said.

One part of his mind remained detached. It evaluated the possibility of recovering the stranded shuttle, rejecting the idea immediately. *I must get something out of this,* he thought. With a flash, he realised there was no reason he had to do so. *Or maybe I need to accept this and face the consequences.* Duggan had never been a man to hide. Whatever difficulties had been thrown into his path, he'd always faced them square-on. The trouble was, he now knew, none of what had gone before had remotely prepared him for this. Commander McGlashan had spoken to him about these most difficult of choices. In reality, the only choices were the ones you permitted yourself to make. There was only one option and Duggan forced himself to take it. Not for himself, but for everyone he had responsibility to command.

"Activate the fission engines," he said. "We're going to the *Juniper.*"

"Aye, Captain," said Breeze. "They're coming online, we'll be able to leave in just shy of fifty seconds."

It happened without Duggan realising it. The *ES Rampage* burst away from its low orbit of the planet Kidor. It left behind the wreckage of broken spaceships and an uncertainty about the missing soldiers. On the planet's surface, the alien artefact continued to generate oxygen in vast quantities under the protection of the Dreamer battleship.

"A little less than four days until we arrive," said Breeze. "We're not held back by the slower warships on this run."

"Sir?" It was Chainer. "We received a transmission via the emergency beacon on Kidor a split second before we escaped."

"What did it say?"

"The message came from Flores. It said they found Ghasts."

"Thank you, Lieutenant."

No one spoke on the bridge for a few hours. As their shifts ended, the crew took turns to head off for sleep. Chainer seemed to be constantly heading to and from the replicator, bringing with him a variety of grease-laden foods, coffee and cans of hi-stim. Eventually, the ozone smell of the bridge was replaced by the smell of cooked meat, interspersed with coffee and the sharp-edged tang of booster drinks. Duggan hardly noticed, so lost was he in his own thoughts.

"You should get some sleep, sir," said McGlashan. Duggan couldn't remember when she'd last gone for sleep either, but she looked fresh and alert.

"I don't feel tired," he replied, surprised at the truth of his words. He should have felt drained, when in fact he felt nothing.

"Something to eat, then."

Duggan looked at McGlashan's concerned face. She wasn't going to let up until he made at least a small concession. "Very well," he said. "I haven't eaten in a while."

"Good, neither have I," she said. "I think I'll join you."

Duggan shook his head in mock-despair and got to his feet. He left the bridge, with McGlashan walking alongside. They continued in silence until they reached the mess room. There were a few soldiers inside – any place on a spaceship where you could get food was rarely empty. Duggan got himself a tray and ordered the replicator to produce a steak and fries, which he took over to his table. McGlashan sat opposite, with two cheeseburgers and a coke. Duggan raised an eyebrow.

"I don't eat healthy food all the time," she said, patting her flat stomach. "Believe me, I'd far rather be eating cheeseburgers than fruit for my lunch."

"Yeah, me too," said Duggan. He looked at his own stomach to reassure himself there was nothing spare and then took a bite of his steak. It was dry in his mouth at first, but then saliva flowed to let him know that his body was hungry.

McGlashan looked around furtively to make sure there was no one paying attention. "You liked Captain Jonas a lot?"

Duggan took a deep breath, aware that he'd been brought into an ambush. "I hardly knew her," he said. McGlashan stared hard, insisting he continue. "She reminded me of what I've missed," he continued. "I thought I saw this one last chance to find what the war has denied me."

"A wife? A family?" she asked gently.

"Maybe. Not just that. Everything. So I can forget the past and move on to the future."

"You're tired of war?"

"Part of me wants to keep fighting forever. Another part is tired and wants a change. I sense it growing within me. All the fighting takes it from you. Each time we escape by the skin of our teeth, I feel diminished. I want to get away before there's nothing of me left." The words were hard to speak and Duggan focused on nothing but the voice coming from his mouth, refusing to run away from what he had to say.

"You could ask to be taken away from active duty," she said. "Heaven knows, you've done your fair share on the frontline. With Admiral Slender gone, there's no one left to hold you back. I bet Admiral Teron would have you on his team without hesitation."

"I'm not sure I can do that," he said. "There's a part of me wants to see the war through to its end. We aren't there yet."

"You'll never win if you keep thinking like that. What about the Dreamers? Are you going to fight until we've defeated them or the Confederation is wiped out? You can't carry everything on your shoulders."

Duggan sighed. "It feels as if that's what I have to do. I'm not so stupid that I think I can manage, nor so untrusting that I believe I'm the only one that matters. Still, I'm driven. I can't let go, Lucy."

"You're a stubborn man, John Duggan. You always have been and you always will be. It's going to kill you in the end." She took a deep breath. "And I don't want to see that happen."

He looked across and saw something in her face which he didn't recognize. *Maybe something you don't want to recognize,* said an unbidden voice. "I don't want any of us to die," he said lamely.

McGlashan sat back, not willing to let him wriggle off the hook. "You've experienced real, proper, hands-tied failure for the first time and it's going to eat you alive if you let it."

"The larger the stakes, the more it hurts," he admitted. "And the stakes on Kidor were very high. I don't so much care that we had to run away. I can't accept that I've lost Ortiz, I've lost ships under my command and I've lost what I hoped was a chance at my future. A slim, remote chance, but a chance nonetheless."

"You did your best, John - you always do. When we get back to the *Juniper* you need to be over this. You need to be strong, because you can be sure there'll be hard questions to answer. An innocent man who feels guilt will hang for crimes he didn't commit. You're leaving yourself open to a punishment you don't deserve." She put her hand briefly on his and then pulled it away. She stood to leave, with half of her meal untouched. "There's more than one future," she said quietly.

# CHAPTER TWENTY-SIX

THE *ES RAMPAGE* arrived at the *Juniper* before the other ships. Duggan found he was as fascinated as ever when he saw the slow-turning orbital on the bulkhead screen.

"The *Juniper*'s AIs have greeted our arrival," said Ensign Perry. A moment later, he spoke again. "It's Admiral Teron, sir. He wants to know how you got on."

"Tell him our mission has failed. He can have my report when I see him."

Perry looked nervous at the instruction, though he carried it out at once. "Admiral Teron has acknowledged the response and nothing more," he said.

Duggan nodded to show he'd heard. "I'm bringing us closer to the *Juniper* and then I'll take the shuttle. The rest of you will need to stay here until you hear otherwise."

The *ES Rampage* was a lot faster than the shuttle it carried, so there was no point in disembarking quite yet. Duggan closed the distance with the orbital at a speed which comfortably exceeded the recommended maximum. The *Juniper* issued several warnings, which he ignored. There were other warships in the vicinity, but there was no chance of a collision so it seemed reasonable to be as quick as possible.

The shuttle was cold and its interior light seemed too bright. Duggan climbed into the cockpit and undocked from the *Rampage*, feeling the emptiness of space only a few feet away from him. He set a course towards the orbital and dutifully engaged the auto-dock routines when the *Juniper* asked him. The approach felt needlessly slow and Duggan was relieved when a green light showed he was able to enter the airlock.

The corridors of the *Juniper* were busier than usual and people bustled around. A few smiled at Duggan politely as he went by, though most kept their eyes aimed at the floor, or fixed on a point somewhere in the distance. Teron wasn't in his office and had asked to speak to Duggan in one of the orbital's countless meeting rooms a few extra minutes' walk away.

He arrived at the door to Meeting Room A-212 and waited. The door didn't move. With a sigh, he pressed his palm to the security panel off to one side and the door whisked open.

"What happened, Captain Duggan?" asked Teron.

Duggan looked around very briefly, his eyes telling him at once there was nothing of interest here. It was just another meeting room with a square table in the middle, surrounded by chairs. There were a couple of screens on the wall and a series of motivational framed images dotted about the place. Teron sat upright in one of the chairs. The sheets of paper arrayed in front of him suggested he'd recently finished a meeting in the room. Duggan took a chair.

"We lost two warships, one heavy lifter and didn't recover the pyramid, sir," said Duggan, with a set to his jaw. "And we've had to leave some people behind on Kidor."

Teron didn't say anything for a while, his grizzled face giving nothing away. "What went wrong?" he said at last.

"We were outgunned, sir. We engaged another Dreamer

warship. Nukes work on their energy shields, but without targeting it comes down to luck. We destroyed that one only because of a brave woman's sacrifice. Then another arrived and I ordered our ships to retreat. Before the *Rampage* could escape, the *Goliath* came out of lightspeed and the enemy destroyed it."

"Could you have done anything differently?"

Duggan had thought about the answer to that very same question for much of the voyage to the *Juniper*. The mission had gone wrong from the outset – they'd lacked firepower, technology and had emerged from lightspeed scattered too far apart.

"There's always another way, sir. The way I chose didn't work out. I don't think we'd have succeeded whatever choices I'd made."

Duggan had a patchy knowledge of Teron's background. Some he'd guessed, some he'd learned from other sources. On top of that, he had his own opinions about the Admiral. On this day, Teron impressed Duggan greatly.

"Our best isn't always good enough, Captain Duggan. Some of us learn that early on, some of us learn it later. In all my years in the Space Corps, I've not yet met a man who lasted as long as you have. If you accept what's happened, you'll come out stronger for it. If you don't accept it, there's nothing that can save you."

"Yes, sir."

"Your mission went wrong. I'm sure I'll learn the details later. The Space Corps needs you, Captain Duggan. Are you ready to carry on?"

Duggan met Admiral Teron's eye and saw the steel that underpinned the person. "Yes, sir. I'm ready to carry on."

"I didn't expect anything else. Now, we have things to discuss. The information you brought back last time has been the cause of much head-scratching, particularly your report about the dead Ghast in the alien pyramid."

"We received a transmission just as we were leaving Kidor, sir. We found an emergency beacon from the *Bulldozer*'s crew and sent a shuttle to look for them. The message from our soldiers told us they'd found Ghasts."

"Nothing more specific?"

"No. The message was incomplete and we weren't able to wait any longer, so I can't tell you more than I have."

"As it happens, I believe you. There are lots who don't believe or simply don't *want* to believe. However, the legions of stats and predictions analysts we employ have decided that there are avenues we should investigate."

"What avenues, exactly?"

"Naturally, we are concerned at the possibilities of a Ghast-Dreamer alliance. Also, we are concerned that we lack enough information to make an educated guess at other possibilities."

"I'm not sure I follow."

"If you think about it, we know nothing about the Ghasts. Equally, we know absolutely nothing about the Dreamers. Therefore, in our ignorance, we are unable to see other reasons for what you encountered. I've heard this referred to as *unknown unknowns*."

"What reasons could there be other than an alliance?" asked Duggan.

Teron smiled grimly. "I wish I knew. I always search for logic, Captain Duggan. Even amongst chaos, I am convinced I will find order. Everything we know contradicts itself, leading to a never-ending circle of what-ifs. There are occasions when I fail in my search, but I never give up looking."

Duggan nodded, hearing a description of himself in Teron's words. "Have you found anything yet, sir?"

Teron snorted with laughter. "Would that I had! The questions haunt my every waking minute and pursue me into sleep. Amongst it, one thing keeps returning. I ask myself why the

Ghasts were so interested in the pyramid and wouldn't tell you the reason."

"I haven't found an answer to that either," said Duggan. "However much I've thought about it."

"It doesn't seem right. One minute they wanted you to leave the artefact, the next they destroyed it themselves. It appeared as if they were willing to return to war over it."

"I'm certain it was a possibility."

"I gave these snippets to some of our best statistical analysts. And you know what? They believe there's something significant behind it – not merely a result of an uncertain situation."

"How significant do they mean?"

"Enough that we have to find an answer, Captain Duggan. We're working on something. As it happens, we were already intending to use this particular resource for something else, yet a new opportunity has arisen."

"Can you explain, sir?"

"Not at the moment, I can't. I'm awaiting clearance. The ability to use this resource is also contingent on the progress of the peace negotiations we're in the middle of."

Duggan was curious and wary in equal measures. He was aware of the need for secrets, yet he'd fallen foul of them before. With a humourless smile, he reminded himself it was the secrets that weren't even hinted about which were the ones to be most careful of. Here, Teron was talking openly about the existence of a secret, without giving away the details. *Let's see where this one goes,* thought Duggan.

"Are you telling me there's another mission?"

"Not quite yet. There's a chance it'll happen." Teron sighed. "You're a good man, Duggan and I don't want to lie to you. Suffice to say, if my plans become an option, you're the man I'd like to bring them to fruition. I'll also tell you it's something you won't like one little bit."

"I appreciate the honesty, sir."

"No, don't say that. I'm not being honest, am I? An honest man would tell you exactly what is required."

Duggan laughed. "Fine, in that case I'll amend my last sentence to 'I understand the need for secrets', if that sounds better."

Teron smiled. "That suits me."

"If there are no plans ready and there is nothing to tell me, what am I assigned to in the meantime?"

"Something I'm sure you'll like far less than what I have in mind."

"Desk duty?"

"I'm afraid so. The Space Corps requires a full and comprehensive report of what happened on Kidor. Every encounter with the Dreamers gives us valuable insights and – believe it or not – has an immediate effect on the direction our weapons research takes. We're making progress. It might not seem quick when you're out there launching missiles without guidance systems, but I can assure you we're making some incredible breakthroughs. It also helps that you brought us an example of the Ghast Shatterer launch tubes and some of their missiles. It's much easier to copy than to build from scratch."

Duggan was heartened by the words. He could read from Teron's animated body language that the Admiral truly believed what he was saying. "If our targeting systems were better, that would make the difference."

"We've got more than one hundred thousand people working on that aspect of our weapons design alone. *One hundred thousand*, Captain Duggan. We'll get there. Anyway, I didn't bring you here to talk about that. A man like you can find out the details if he's determined enough. I want you to leave for the Atican shipyard on Pioneer. Take the ES *Rampage*, since I believe it needs a few minor repairs which they have the capacity to accomplish."

"Yes, sir. I'll leave at once and wait until I hear further." He hesitated. "What will happen to the soldiers on Kidor?"

"I can't promise you anything. You know if we send more ships, more troops, they'll be killed?"

"Yes, sir, that seems the probable outcome."

"If they're in their spacesuits, they have a few months yet. Leave me to think on the matter," said Teron. "Dismissed."

Duggan was almost to the door when he asked a question he'd meant bring up earlier in the conversation. "What about the samples of the power source we brought back from Trasgor, sir? I thought they were more important than anything."

"They are. We've missed this opportunity to capture an intact Dreamer power core. If another one arises, we'll try again."

This time, the meeting room door slid open automatically. Duggan exited the room and retraced his footsteps until he reached the shuttle. It was exactly where he'd left it. He boarded the craft and piloted it away from the *Juniper*. A short time later, he was back on the *ES Rampage*, relieved, yet with no idea what the future had in store for him.

# CHAPTER TWENTY-SEVEN

"PIONEER IT IS," said Breeze.

"What're we going there for, sir?" asked Chainer.

"Admiral Teron's got something for me. He says I'm not going to like whatever it is."

"It must be bad if he's keeping it to himself," said Chainer.

"I don't think he has the details either, Lieutenant. We're going to twiddle our thumbs at the Atican shipyard complex until he decides what he's going to do."

"You mean this top-secret mission might never happen?"

Duggan shrugged. "That was the impression I got."

"Maybe we should head back to Kidor and see if we can rescue Lieutenant Ortiz and the others," said Breeze, his face deadly serious.

"We can't," said Duggan. "The time isn't right and we'd get ourselves killed for nothing. I promise you our soldiers aren't forgotten, Lieutenant. I'll see what I can do."

"They're going to be bored sitting in that cave," said Chainer.

"I'd prefer them to be bored, rather than dead," said Duggan.

"We're at Light-M," announced Breeze, almost sounding

surprised himself. The transitions on the heavy cruisers were smoother than any other vessel. "Less than three days till we reach our destination."

On this one occasion, the time flew over. It was unfortunate for Duggan, since he wanted the time to think. He had shaken off the lethargy he'd felt in the aftermath of the mission to Kidor. The chains of it were still there, but they no longer held him back. Their presence was a reminder of his duty and he chose to take strength from them, rather than be weighed down. He focused his mind on the future instead of the past and his determination built, filling him with endless energy. Captain Jonas was gone and Lieutenant Ortiz was stranded on a hostile planet. He couldn't fix the first, but he could try his best to come to terms with it. There was little he could do about the second for the moment - his words to Lieutenant Breeze about the time not being right were true and Duggan did his best to accept that. As long as he eventually got a shot at getting his soldiers away from Kidor, it would be enough.

Within five minutes of its predicted time, the *ES Rampage* arrived into a high orbit over the planet Pioneer, forty thousand kilometres above the surface. Chainer scanned the vast shipyard far below.

"They've got a couple of free trenches for us," he said. "I assume we're landing in one of them?"

"Yes, Lieutenant. Get permission from the shipyard mainframe and we'll set down nice and easy."

Chainer got the clearance he needed and Duggan prepared to bring the *Rampage* closer, in order to engage the automatic landing system. Procedures dictated a slow, steady approach and since Duggan wasn't in the mood to deal with an angry computer, he kept to the recommended guidelines. Something caught his eye and he brought up an image on the bulkhead viewscreen.

"They're making good progress on the new flagship," he said.

"Last I remember, there was hardly anything more than an outline."

All eyes were fixed on the growing hull of the new warship. It was nearly ten kilometres long and planned as a replacement for the *Archimedes*, though the latter would remain in active service.

"They're going to call it the *Aristotle*," said Massey. "That's what I've heard, anyway."

"Someone likes their historical figures, huh?" asked Chainer. "I wouldn't have been surprised if they'd named it the *Admiral Slender*."

Hearing the name gave Duggan a start. At one time it would have brought unpleasant memories to accompany it. Duggan was pleased to find it did no such thing, as if the dead man had finally relinquished his grip.

"What about that Hadron next to it?" he asked, pointing a finger at a vessel in the adjacent trench. This one was a lot closer to completion. "Have you heard what that will be called?"

"I have no idea," said Massey. "Most of the excitement is around the flagship."

"We should take heart from seeing this," said Duggan. "It's a profound example of what humanity can achieve when it's pushed. The Ghasts' fleet has grown enormously over the last few years, but it's nothing close to what we're doing now." He opened his mouth to say something else and decided against it.

"What else?" asked McGlashan.

Duggan sighed. "I didn't want to dampen anyone's spirits, because in truth the Confederation has improved so much in the last couple of years. It's just that our weaponry has yet to catch up. We're working on so much that's new, yet I can't see any of it being ready in time to fit into these new hulls. We'll have dozens of ships at Galactic class and above, each of them stunted by weaponry that is behind what our opponents can put against us." He smiled with sudden conviction. "However, each day which passes brings us closer to parity. After parity comes superiority. I'm convinced we'll pull through this if we're given the time - even against the Dreamers."

The image on the viewscreen panned away from the Hadron and onto the next ship docked here. This one looked different – it had more lumps and curves than the others, like a mixture of shapes thrown together. The front was crumpled and there were indentations along its flanks. Even so, there was no mistaking it for anything other than a fighting spaceship. It was different to the Space Corps' designs, yet just as threatening.

"The Cadaveron we brought back," said Breeze. "No sign of antimatter leaks, so they must have sealed it up tightly."

"Given it a coat of paint as well," said Chainer.

"Yeah, it looks a lot tidier than when we picked it out of that hole on Everlong," said McGlashan.

"There must be thousands of people working on it," said Chainer, zooming in for a closer look. "They've got all the heavy-duty kit around the hull."

"Maybe it's heading for the museum," said Breeze. "It would make an impressive exhibit."

"As long as they keep people off the bridge," joked Chainer. "I seem to recall the engines were still working."

"I imagine quite a lot of it was still working," said Duggan. "We got lucky in taking out the life support section."

"Well, we've been asked to land right next to it," said Chainer. "There'll be a good view when we disembark."

They were close enough to activate the auto-land and Duggan handed control of the ship over to the AI. It brought them in carefully, so as not to create turbulence on the ground.

"They've not stopped work on the Cadaveron for us," said Breeze. It was usual practise to move workers on adjacent trenches away when a warship as large as the *Rampage* came in to land.

"Probably want to get it done and free up that space for something else," said Chainer.

"The fifth dry dock is free already," said McGlashan.

"Never mind," said Duggan. "I'm sure they know what they're doing."

A few minutes later, the ES *Rampage* landed dead-centre in trench four. Each of the dry docks contained an enormously powerful gravity field, which supported much of the docked spaceship's weight. The power draw on the field generators was immense, and each had what was effectively a warship gravity drive buried underground to provide the necessary power. The crew on the *Rampage* experienced a barely-perceptible thump as the spaceship's weight settled on the reinforced alloy surface.

Duggan was first to his feet. "Let's go and find out what they want us to do while we await the next mission from Admiral Teron," he said. "Ensign Perry, send a message to the troops below. They're dismissed to the barracks until they're called upon."

The crew followed Duggan off the bridge and to the front boarding ramp. It was mid-afternoon and heat from the desert air washed inside the interior bay. There was a woman in uniform waiting at the bottom. She greeted Duggan and handed him a clipboard with a pen. There was a form to sign in order to hand over the warship and Duggan scribbled his name, wondering why this anachronistic procedure still existed.

They took a lift out of the docking trench and paused briefly to say their farewells. Each had received orders as to where they needed to report once they reached the shipyard. The Space Corps considered all of its officers to form a pool into which it could dip for the personnel it needed. There were a few senior captains like Duggan who could generally get their way and retain the same crew from mission to mission. For now, the people from the ES *Rampage* would be split.

The damaged Cadaveron loomed out of the adjacent trench, its hull a non-stop hive of activity. The Ghast vessel was a little smaller than the *Rampage* and it looked in surprisingly good condition compared to the last time they'd seen it close up. The Space Corps had a lot of funding, yet Duggan didn't think it likely they were doing the repairs without a specific purpose in mind. He felt a strange attachment to the vessel given what had gone before, and decided he'd try and find out why so much effort was being expended on fixing it up.

There were ranks of shuttle cars parked in a line near to the dry docks. Duggan wished the others good luck and climbed into the nearest car. He knew where he was going and pushed the vehicle to its maximum permitted speed in the direction of a large building in the distance. His destination was a square, utilitarian slab of greyness, its surface pocked with darkened windows and with a Space Corps flag outside the main entrance. He pulled up in front of it. Usually at a time like this, his morale would ebb away like water through his fingers. Today, he felt energised without knowing exactly what had changed.

Half an hour later, he'd been assigned a new office and provided with new quarters close by. He breathed in the warm air, happy it wasn't over-chilled like most of the military's buildings. At his desk he powered up his computer. It sprang immediately into life, helpfully displaying his inbox. The page was already half-full of notices, warnings and memos about this, that and the other. He read each in turn, finding nothing important. He deleted everything, only to find a new message appeared a few seconds later. He shook his head and deleted this latest one, aware he was trying to hold back the tide with a wall of sand.

He turned his screen off and sat for a time in quiet contemplation. There were so many questions to which he had no answer. Where once his powerlessness would have angered and frustrated him, now he felt only calm. He remembered the words from Admiral Teron. *If you accept what's happened, you'll come out stronger for it.* Duggan pondered those words and knew that he *had* accepted his failure, or at least was close to acceptance. The unfinished business of leaving Ortiz behind would gnaw at him until he concluded it one way or another. Whatever happened, he was going to do something.

Outside, the soothing orange glow of day was fading. Night came quickly in the desert, though work on the warships would continue around the clock under artificial daylight. Duggan heard his stomach growl, reminding him he hadn't eaten in several hours. He sat for a few minutes longer, before putting a call through to McGlashan and arranging to meet up for some food.

## CHAPTER TWENTY-EIGHT

A FEW DAYS WENT BY, during which Duggan used his contacts to find out whatever information there was to learn. What he discovered was that the details he wanted to know were so well-guarded, no one had anything to tell. The negotiations with the Ghasts were top-top-secret, with the Confederation Council refusing to give out anything whatsoever as regards their progress or lack thereof. This was no surprise, since the subject of peace continued to be a touchy one with the general populace, no matter what positive swing was given to it.

There were reports of sporadic rioting on a few of the Confederation planets. This news was harder to suppress, if in fact it was suppressed at all. The people were sick of war and they were sick of their money being spent to finance that war. Many had decided peace was a given and therefore it was time to scale back the eye-watering level of expenditure on new spaceships and technologies. Duggan couldn't blame them. They had a vision of the war which was passed through many filters before it was made available for their consumption. He doubted any of them had even heard of the Dreamers. Still, it drove home the reason why new departments such as Military Asset Management had sprung up to provide oversight on how money was spent. Duggan accepted the principle, if not the implementation.

Otherwise, there wasn't much to learn that he wasn't already aware of. The one remaining mystery was that of the Cadaveron and why the Space Corps was diverting so much effort in restoring it. Duggan had taken himself out to the dry dock on a few occasions and spoken to the technicians working there. Some secrets were hard to keep and generally there'd be rumours flying around, waiting to be plucked from willing mouths. This time there was nothing and he was reduced to guessing - a game he wasn't especially fond of. When the mystery of the Cadaveron was finally answered, he wasn't sure if he wanted to laugh or cry.

"Sir, there's an inbound call from Admiral Teron," said an androgynous voice in Duggan's earpiece. It was the shipyard's automated comms system, which was designed to act exactly like a human secretary. Duggan was in the middle of a video meeting with a number of senior members of the ballistics research team, who wanted his input on various matters relating to the armaments on the Galactic class warships. He was alone in the meeting room, while the engineers were sat in a research lab on another world, several thousand light years away.

"Can it wait?" he asked the automated voice, knowing what the answer would be.

"He wants to speak to you now," it replied, with just the right degree of sheepish insistence.

"Very well."

The six men and women on the other end of the video link stared quizzically at him. "I take it our meeting is going to be cut short?" asked one of the men churlishly.

"It is," said Duggan. "We can reconvene later." He switched channels without further delay. The wall screen went blank for a second, before the image of Admiral Teron appeared. There was someone else in the room with him, sitting just off camera.

"Captain Duggan, I hope I'm not interrupting anything." He didn't look as if he especially cared one way or another.

"Nothing that can't wait, sir."

"I told you I might have something for you."

"Yes, sir." The words sparked through Duggan's body, though he tried not to show it.

"We've been held up by a few things. Nothing is straightforward these days. There are times I wonder if it would be easier if we simply declared war on the Ghasts again in order to bring things to a conclusion."

"I'm sure there's a better way."

Teron laughed. "Don't patronise me, Captain Duggan. A man is allowed to let off steam every once in a while."

Duggan smiled in response. "What do you need, sir?"

"The Ghasts want their Cadaveron back."

"I see," said Duggan.

"The peace negotiations aren't moving as easily as we'd have liked. It's hard to offer the hand of friendship whilst the other hand is pointing a gun. The talks are meandering."

"From our end, or theirs?"

"Mostly ours."

"Because we can't trust them."

"That's it exactly. We're in a situation where we don't really trust them. There is nothing about their approach that appears anything less than genuine, yet we can't be certain where we stand. It's down to what you found on Trasgor."

"We've been negotiating since before Trasgor," said Duggan.

"Of course we have and everything was going well until that point. A few weeks ago, we were determined to achieve peace on our terms. Now we're stalling in the hope we can find clarity on the matters which worry us. If the Ghasts can't be trusted – and remember how ruthlessly they conducted the war – we don't want to let down our guard. Equally, we don't want to begin hostilities again. The Planet Breaker is the only game-changer we possess. If it was destroyed somehow or malfunctioned, we'd be back to square one."

"The Ghasts' best warships are better than ours."

"Yes, they are. I suppose if it came to it, we could bombard their worlds with nuclear warheads and lose much of our fleet in the process. That's assuming they don't have ground-based defences that can nullify such an attack."

"Are we planning to negotiate forever?" asked Duggan. "Or are we close to a breakthrough on some new weapon or other that will significantly increase our odds if we lose the Planet Breaker?"

Teron rubbed his thick fingertips across his close-shaven scalp. "We have a status quo that suits us. I'm aware we're kicking the can down the road, and in truth our time is running out. We've seen the early signs that the Ghasts are beginning to doubt our sincerity. We don't want that to happen."

"I take it we've offered to return their heavy cruiser as a gesture of our continued goodwill?"

"That's an excellent summary," said Teron. The other person in the room with him shifted position, their face still away from the camera. It didn't look like Admiral Franks and Duggan wondered if there was a reason this person chose to remain anonymous.

"And I'm the man chosen for the job?"

"This is something I'm offering you, Captain Duggan. As I'm sure you're already thinking to yourself, this isn't going to be a simple handover of their warship. We're going to send the *Ransor-D* to them, however we won't surrender it without getting some use out of it. That warship is going straight to their home world Vempor."

"Without their approval?"

"Yes, without their approval. We want you to keep it in orbit for as long as possible in order to scan the surface for signs of Dreamer activity. You'll send the details on to us via Monitoring Station Beta."

"You're expecting to see signs of warships?"

Teron shrugged. "Anything, Captain Duggan. At this point in time, I'd gratefully take whatever you can find that ties the Ghasts to the Dreamers."

"What if there's nothing?"

"It'll go some way to alleviating our concerns."

"Just to be clear - you want me to fly the Cadaveron to Vempor, do a few circuits to look for signs of a Ghast-Dreamer alliance and then come home?"

"You might not be coming home. We're planning to arrange the handover in a neutral place. When the *Ransor-D* doesn't arrive, we'll tell them you've gone rogue and chosen of your own volition to go all the way to Vempor. Like a man chasing infamy and glory, if you will."

"This is a suicide mission!" said Duggan.

"I said you wouldn't enjoy what I had planned," said Teron. "Once you're there, you have my blessing to do whatever you wish to escape, short of starting hostilities again."

Duggan didn't know what to say. He sat in thought for a few seconds, while Teron watched impassively through the video screen. "Assuming I agree to this, how am I expected to fly the damned thing? Or use the onboard systems? They look similar to ours in design, but I can't read their language."

"We've installed some of our own systems. Language modules and a few of our sensor arrays. After all, the Ghasts can't expect us to have left a captured warship entirely untouched. Naturally we were going to learn what we could from it!"

Duggan thought long and hard. "If I agree to this, will I be left high and dry?"

"I don't make promises lightly, Captain Duggan. If you do this, we'll do what we can to get you back."

"I want more than that, sir."

Teron raised an eyebrow - a gesture it looked like he'd practised often. "What do you want?"

"I want the opportunity to get the soldiers back from Kidor, sir. A ship and a crew, if I can find one willing to give it a try."

"I can't give you the *Aristotle,* if that's what you're looking for. Very well, I'll give you the commitment you're asking for, as long as your expectations are reasonable."

"They will be, sir."

"Does that mean you'll take the *Ransor-D* to Vempor?"

"It does."

Teron cleared his throat. "It needs more than one to fly the Cadaveron."

"I know, sir. With permission I'll speak to my usual crew and see if they want to come along."

"If not, you'll be assigned the required personnel. I doubt there'll be many volunteers, but I'm sure we can find the people you need. You've got four hours to get back to me with an answer. Time is short and now you've agreed to this, we're going to give the Ghasts a time and place to return their ship."

Duggan nodded his acceptance and waited until Admiral Teron ended the connection. With the room silent, he shifted in the hard-backed chair while his mind turned over the details of what he'd heard. There was a part of him wanted to call Teron immediately and say he'd changed his mind. The trouble was, he couldn't do it. He felt entirely caught up in a web that was partially his own making, and partially woven by the machinations of other people he couldn't control. The only way out was to reverse his decision, yet his stubborn loyalty wouldn't let him.

There was more than that – this was a war he'd fought for the whole of his adult life. He was tied to it and couldn't let go, whilst still being desperate for the chance to put it in his past and move on. This mission could make a difference. It could bring peace from uncertainty or it could reveal treachery before any harm could result.

Duggan wasn't prone to flights of fancy, but an image came to him. In it, he was holding the strings of a puppet and making it dance stiffly at his command. When he looked closer, he saw the puppet was a perfect likeness of himself. He shook away the thought and opened up a communication channel to Commander McGlashan.

# CHAPTER TWENTY-NINE

"MINIMUM CREW OF FOUR, EH?" asked Chainer, looking up the scarred side of the *Ransor-D*.

"Apparently so," said Breeze.

"I think he just wanted the company," said McGlashan. "After all, we won't need to fire the weapons."

"Yeah, it's not as if we're going into a combat situation," said Chainer. "Not from what he said, anyway."

"Fly in, do a bit of surface scanning, get arrested for spying and get thrown into a Ghast jail," said Breeze. "I don't see why that needs more than one person to accomplish."

"I wonder if the Ghasts have the death penalty," said Chainer.

"They might inject us with a lethal dose of hi-stim," said Breeze. "Except there's not enough of it available to kill you, Frank."

"Come on," said Duggan, recognizing the nervousness beneath the light-hearted conversation. "We've got to get used to the bridge if we're to fly this thing."

"I'm excited," said McGlashan. "And worried."

"Me too," said Duggan.

"It can definitely fly, can't it?" asked Breeze. "I mean, the hull looks okay, if a little beat up. It took a lot of damage when it crashed."

"Apparently it flies perfectly well when they run the simulation," said McGlashan. "Goes like a charm."

"That's good enough for me," said Chainer sarcastically.

It appeared as though there were still hundreds of people and machines working on the ship. They acted with purpose, as if there was much left to do. It didn't inspire confidence, though Duggan knew the Space Corps well enough to trust the ship would get off the ground. There were likely to be a few things unfinished, which he hoped wouldn't impact on the warship's effectiveness.

There was a boarding ramp right in the middle of the underside. It was steep, with metal steps ascending into the cold-blue light of the interior. Duggan went first, finding it an effort to climb smoothly. McGlashan came next, with Chainer huffing and puffing behind her.

There was an airlock at the top, with a team of three technicians studying a readout from one of their hand-held analysis devices.

"Is everything in order?" asked Chainer. "You know we're meant to fly this thing away in an hour or two, don't you?"

"Last minute checks, sir," said a woman. She smiled disarmingly, cutting off Chainer's smart reply.

"Fine, fine," he muttered, suddenly lost for words.

"When will the vessel be clear of shipyard personnel?" asked Duggan.

"We've been asked to keep working right until we receive your confirmation that you're ready to leave," the same woman answered.

Duggan wasn't entirely pleased with the idea of having repair crews scrambling to exit at the last minute. On the other hand, he wanted everything to be ready. "Very well," he said. "Do what you can to patch us up."

"The patching up finished a while ago," the woman replied. "We can't get the hull looking any prettier than it is without a complete rebuild. It should hold together, which is all we've been asked to achieve. The life support took a lot more work and we've only recently finished testing it."

"Why all these people, then?" asked Duggan.

"We've been studying and mapping the design," she said, laughing at the look of realisation on Duggan's face. "Not only that, we've fitted a number of our own systems to run in parallel to the Ghost ones. Not our latest hardware, for some reason. Most of it's at least ten years old. What are they planning to do with the ship? It's not going out to fight is it?"

"It's going to a museum," said McGlashan.

The woman's smile faltered as she tried to decide if she was being mocked. She recovered quickly. "We've replaced some of the control systems. The missiles and countermeasures work fine. There's a disruptor that works sporadically and one of the beam weapons operates at a reduced output. You probably don't want to let people onto the bridge when it goes on display at the museum, in case there are any accidents."

"What about the Shatterers?" asked Duggan.

"I believe it has two theoretically functioning launch tubes. Most of the missiles themselves have been taken away for reverse-engineering."

Duggan wasn't reassured by the technician's use of the word *theoretically*. It wasn't her fault, he knew, since the Space Corps couldn't make these weapons from scratch, let alone repair broken ones.

"So, everything that runs the ship will be familiar to us?" asked Breeze.

"As best as we could make it in the time available," she replied. "Haven't they briefed you on this?"

"They've done the best they could in the time available," said Duggan, echoing her words. "Thank you for your time ma'am." He made to walk past her and then pulled up short. "Which way is the bridge?"

The technician smiled and pointed through the wide exit doorway. "Then you turn left. It's much smaller inside than it is out, something I'm sure you're familiar with."

They followed her directions and entered a wide, high corridor, lit in the blue which the Ghasts seemed to favour. Duggan had been on this ship before, yet it looked completely different to last time. Circumstances were different and he'd come in through the access ramp instead of a missile crater in the armour plating. They passed a couple of large rooms, devoid of feature or furnishing. There were screens in the walls at intervals, some of them dark, while others showed gauges and level meters.

"This is still in the Ghast language!" said Chainer. "I thought they'd stripped this lot out."

"I doubt they've had time for a complete refit," said McGlashan. "Look – here's one of our own screens. I can read what's on this one."

"We shouldn't need to leave the bridge," said Duggan. "If we do, something's gone so badly wrong we won't be able to fix it whatever language these screens show."

The corridor branched right and a set of wide steps went up before them. Memories flooded back and Duggan knew the bridge was just ahead. He walked faster and climbed the steps to the top.

"They fixed the door we blew off," said Chainer.

Duggan didn't answer. The replacement bridge door was activated by a panel to one side, which responded to his palm print. The heavy door slid open and revealed the bridge. "They've changed this around," he said.

"The blue light is like I remember, but not much else is the same," said Breeze.

McGlashan hadn't been here before and she looked with curiosity. "This is a big space," she said.

"There were more than thirty seats last time," said Chainer. "They've pulled most of them out, as well as a lot of the Ghast consoles."

The bridge was fifteen metres square. Previously there had been chairs, along with clusters of screens against the walls and in the middle of the floor. Since then, it had been transformed into something which closely resembled the control deck of an Anderlecht cruiser, albeit bigger. There were eight seats, divided between comms, weapons and engines, with a single, additional chair for the captain to sit in. The room was too large for its contents and the consoles looked small and lost in the middle of the floor.

"There's a locker here," said McGlashan, looking at the adjacent security panel. She tentatively pressed her fingers against it and the locker opened to reveal a row of spacesuits and some light armaments. "We won't have to go far if there's a hull breach," she said.

"They've had to make a few holes in the floor to patch everything in," said Breeze, looking under a number of the fixed consoles. "Quite a few holes."

"As long as it works," said Duggan. "We need to get to going. The trip to Vempor is a long one, so there'll be plenty of time to learn how it works on the way, but we need to get this ship off the ground first."

Chainer practically leapt into one of the comms seats, his hands sweeping across screens and touchpads. "This is standard kit, sir," he said, "Just like the lady said."

"Yeah," said Breeze in agreement. "The designs are a bit old. I've not seen this particular interface since I was fresh on a warship."

"The technician said they were fitting older systems," said Duggan. "We don't want the Ghasts to have a copy of our latest designs."

"They must have begun fitting this before the decision was made to return the ship," said McGlashan, furrowing her brow as she worked out the timescales.

"I imagine they planned to send it out against its makers," said Duggan. "It's got a disruptor onboard, which our own ships don't."

"I can't believe we're giving the ship back with all its weapons," said Chainer. "Particularly the ones the Space Corps is lacking."

"You heard the technician say they've removed most of the Shatterers," said Duggan. "I think it's a safe bet that if the disruptor is still here, the Space Corps is close to being able to make its own. They've had plenty of time to study the *Crimson*."

Duggan took his seat and glanced at the screens around him. As Chainer said, everything was familiar, though some of the secondary displays updated sluggishly instead of instantly. The Ghasts' AI technology was good, so he assumed the tiny delays were a result of the interface between the Space Corps equipment and the Cadaveron's core. It wasn't bad enough to be a concern.

"Begin your checks," said Duggan. "If you see something you don't like, tell me at once."

There was little sound on the bridge for fifteen minutes while the crew did their checks and tests. If this had been a Space Corps warship, Duggan would have been confident to take it straight out of the dry dock. While simulations had their value, he wasn't willing to trust four lives to one, particularly since he'd witnessed how much damage the heavy cruiser had suffered when it crashed on Everlong.

"Update me with your findings, please," said Duggan when he felt enough time had passed.

"Looks good to me," said Breeze. "We can output ninety percent of our maximum power according to the readouts. There might be a little more, depending on what the core can do with the burned-out sections of the engines."

"Funnily enough, the sensors and comms are in tip-top shape," said Chainer. "We're covered in them and they've installed some further processing hardware on the underside arrays."

"Those are the important ones," said Duggan. "We won't have long to do what's necessary."

"If the Ghasts are allied to the Dreamers, won't they block our comms?" asked McGlashan. "I assume we've got a backup system, but does it have the capability to transmit to Monitoring Station Beta?"

"There's plenty of bandwidth to send at a low-to-medium resolution. Full details will take longer. I think we'll be okay."

"Is everything ready on the weapons?" asked Duggan. "If we need to use them the mission has gone disastrously wrong, but I'd prefer to know they're available."

"They're all in order, sir. The *Ransor-D* is low on ammunition – it must have been away from its base for an extended period."

"As long as there's something in the arsenal," said Duggan. He cleared his throat. "I'm going to bring the gravity engines online."

"Should we ask the technicians to get clear?" asked McGlashan.

Duggan knew it was the right thing to do and he didn't want to risk other lives through his own impatience. "Lieutenant

Chainer, order everyone onboard to leave. There shouldn't be a problem at this stage – they've had long enough to get it ready."

"I think I'll strap in," said Breeze. "Just in case."

It took twenty minutes before the warship was clear of personnel. As soon as the last technician had gone, Duggan issued the command to feed power into the engines. The whole ship vibrated faintly, before it settled into a low hum.

"Nothing to worry about," said Chainer.

"Sounds like one of ours," added McGlashan.

"They use the same metals in the same way," said Duggan. He'd been on an Oblivion before and had known what to expect. "I'm ordering the shipyard mainframe to remove the cranes and gantries."

"You think we're ready, sir?"

"As ready as we'll ever be."

It took another twenty restless minutes before the hundreds of machines surrounding the Cadaveron were moved away from the hull. During this time, Duggan and Breeze cycled the engines through a series of tests, to see if they could trigger an alert. The monitoring tools remained green.

"Everything's clear, sir," said Chainer. "The shipyard has informed me we've got a fifty-minute opening to leave."

The heavy cruiser had been fitted with a standard Space Corps pilot's console. Duggan gripped the bars and pulled them carefully back. The humming increased in volume and there was an imperceptibly slight feeling of weightlessness. Outside, thousands of men and women stopped to stare as the *Ransor-D* rose silently from its berth. Higher it went, until the watchers had to shade their eyes against the strong desert sun. The huge warship became smaller as it accelerated, until all that remained was a tiny dot in the clear blue sky. Then, the dot vanished from sight and the workers at the shipyard returned to their duties.

# CHAPTER THIRTY

AT TEN THOUSAND KILOMETRES, Duggan released the breath he'd been holding. The monitoring readouts were a sea of green, reassuring calmness. "Do you have the coordinates, Lieutenant?" he asked.

"I do, sir. Vempor is a long way from here. I can't tell you how long it'll take until we reach lightspeed and see what sort of speed we can achieve," said Breeze.

"I assume we've stripped out the ship's monitoring logs, so it can't report the location of Pioneer when we hand it over?" asked McGlashan.

Duggan hadn't thought about it. "They can't have missed something so obvious, surely?" He wasn't certain enough that he was willing to leave it to chance. He made a snap decision and used his command authority to push open a priority channel to Admiral Teron.

"What is it?" asked Teron. He didn't sound particularly flustered or upset.

"Have we cleared every scrap of data from the *Ransor-D*'s

memory arrays, sir? I realise it's an obvious question, yet I don't want to leave without knowing for definite."

"There's nothing there which can betray us," Teron said. "I'm assuming none of you have memorised the five-hundred-digit coordinates of our populated planets?"

Duggan looked around and was greeted with shrugs and headshakes. "Doesn't appear so, sir."

"You're clear what you have to do. Good luck, if I haven't already said it."

"Thank you, sir," said Duggan, switching off the comms channel. He turned to the others in disbelief. "We've had clearance to leave on a mission of such importance and only now does he remember to ask if we've memorised the coordinates of Confederation worlds."

"I know the first fifteen or twenty digits," said Breeze. "There didn't seem much point in remembering the others, since computers do the hard work."

"Even so," said Duggan, wondering if Teron had thought this whole mission through properly. It wasn't too late to turn back, but there'd be repercussions if he did. The questions about the Ghasts' allegiances needed to be answered and time was a luxury they didn't have. "Prepare us for lightspeed," he said.

"Beginning the preparations," said Breeze. "Fifty-five seconds. A little slower than the *Terminus* and *Rampage*."

Chainer looked about with a worried expression. "I hope they've fitted decent life support."

The technicians at the shipyard had worked hard on the *Ransor-D* and installed equipment which was adequate for the task of keeping the crew alive. When the warship switched from gravity engines to deep fission drives, there was a noticeable bump. Otherwise, the sense of dislocation was muted.

"We're at Light-L," said Breeze. "That's what I'd expected to see."

"How long to Vempor?" asked Duggan, aware it was going to be a long trip.

"Twenty-eight days," said Breeze, "With a likely margin for error being an hour or two either side, judging from the processing power of the AI."

"Twenty-eight days to contemplate our fate," said Chainer. "I feel like I'm on death row and we've only just set off."

"You should have told me if you had doubts, Lieutenant," said Duggan. "I asked you to come because you're one of the best. I would have found someone else if I'd thought you weren't certain you wanted to be involved."

Chainer had always been a man of highs and lows. He laughed, tinges of bitterness in the sound. "You aren't the only one tied to your duty, sir. We're here because we're the same as you. We follow you and we put ourselves on the frontline because we're driven to do it. I could have requested a transfer dozens of times over the last few years and I'd have got one." His voice strengthened. "It's never been an option, sir. Never has and never will, just like it is for you."

Duggan nodded and looked at the other two. It was McGlashan who spoke first. "I've given up everything to be here. There wasn't a chance I'd refuse to come along. In truth, you knew it when you asked, sir. I don't blame you and I chose to come willingly."

"You're not as willing as you think," said Duggan quietly. "There's not one of us who could let ourselves do otherwise. I've often wondered if I'm exercising free will, or if I've taken that away from myself, leaving me incapable of escape. I don't know if I'll spend my life taking risks in the name of duty until my luck runs out - or I meet an opponent who's just plain better than me."

"Have you found answers?" asked McGlashan.

"Not yet. One day I'll be old and wise enough to let go. If I live that long."

"We're still needed," said Breeze. "If we get back from this one alive, maybe I'll hand in a request for early retirement. That should get me out of the Corps in four or five years. I don't think I can face the rest of my life fighting."

"Perhaps you can, if you decide it's what you want" said Duggan. "One thing is sure – while the Confederation is facing the possibility of war with two different enemies, I'm going to offer everything I have to give."

"What do you think will happen when we get to Vempor, sir?" asked Chainer. "I agreed to come but I don't really want to die if I can avoid it."

"Me neither, Lieutenant. You're not permitted to die. Admiral Teron's made a promise that he'll support a mission to Kidor to rescue the men and women I left behind. I'll need a crew I can trust."

Chainer laughed, this time it was filled with unsullied humour. "You don't demand much, do you?"

"I take it the Space Corps aren't planning a rescue?" said McGlashan.

"I don't think so." Duggan sighed. "From a purely logical standpoint, I don't blame them. Even if we sent half the fleet, there's no guarantee they'd be able to destroy the Dreamer warship at Kidor. We're only talking about a few soldiers and a shuttle. We lose people every day and in greater numbers."

"Doesn't it make you angry?" asked Chainer. "They're still *our* people."

"At what point do the risks become too great?" asked Duggan. He looked at McGlashan "Someone recently told me that these are the hardest decisions to make. Besides, I blame myself for it happening. It should be me – us if you'll come – who attempt the rescue."

"It wasn't your fault," said Breeze. "A blind man could see as much."

"I can't help but take responsibility for what happens as a result of my actions," said Duggan. "I'll never be able to change that."

The conversation ended and the crew turned their attention to their consoles. The controls and interfaces were familiar and presented no obstacles. However, this was still a Ghast ship and many of its operating methods were unusual or activated in a different manner. It was mostly subtleties and when Duggan stopped to think about it, he realised what an awe-inspiring job the Corps had achieved in such a short time. He was a believer in underlying order and the notion that different species would find broadly similar methods to perform a given task appealed to him. None of that detracted from the accomplishment of making it comparatively easy for humans to pilot a Ghast heavy cruiser. However, there was one disappointment, which Chainer felt most keenly.

"Look at this crap the replicator spat out!" he cried. There were items on his tray which he insisted on showing to everyone in turn.

"What's that?" asked Breeze.

"Precisely my point! What *is* it? I asked for a cheeseburger and this looks nothing like a cheeseburger!"

"That clear fluid could be liquid grease," said McGlashan.

"It should be inside the burger, though. Not in a puddle on the plate."

McGlashan wasn't able to take the matter seriously. "It'll do you good to cut down, Lieutenant. Just think what you'd look like after twenty-eight days of eating decent-quality replicated cheeseburgers. At least now you might consider getting some decent proteins and fats instead."

"No chance of that," muttered Chainer, taking a bite of the lumpy, off-colour product. "It's going to be a long journey."

"It appears the Space Corps is concerned about sharing our

latest food replicating technology with the Ghasts," said Breeze. "Hence they've installed one of the older models."

"One of the very oldest, it would seem. Closer to an antique if this *stuff* is anything to go by."

Duggan didn't wait to hear the conclusion of the discussion. With the Cadaveron travelling comfortably towards its destination, he set out to explore the interior. A greater proportion of the vessel was given over for soldiers and crew than was usual on Space Corps warships. Duggan remembered how some Cadaverons had been known to carry more than a thousand mech-suited Ghast warriors. More recently, the Ghasts kept fewer of their soldiers onboard. The nature of the war had changed until there was little need for warships to deploy enormous numbers of soldiers and armour onto a planet's surface. Battles were usually won and lost in space. Afterwards, dedicated transport vessels would be used to deploy ground forces if they were needed in significant numbers.

The *Ransor-D* was an older design, with plenty of rooms and open areas. He remembered finding smashed lockers and broken chairs in one such room. Now, that room was spotlessly clean, with the contents removed and presumably disposed of at the Atican shipyard.

Duggan found his way to one of the barrack rooms and recognised it as the place he'd first boarded the vessel after it had smashed into the surface of Everlong. The light here was more muted than elsewhere and a shiver ran down his spine when he contemplated the living beings who had been killed in this room. There were other barrack rooms close by and Duggan found himself counting the bunks. At the end, he estimated the Ghast ship could have housed approximately eleven hundred soldiers, plus whoever else might have slept elsewhere within the labyrinthine interior of the hull.

Aside from the troop-carrying potential, the Cadaveron was

remarkably similar to a Space Corps warship. Internally it looked the same, sounded the same and had its own unique odour which filled every room. The smell wasn't unpleasant, though Duggan wasn't able to pin down exactly what it was. He discovered several rooms, separate from the others and clearly intended for officers. There was bedding here, laid out on the oversized beds. There was no decoration and everything was plain and for a specific purpose.

After a few hours, he returned to the bridge, to find it exactly as he'd left it, with everyone at their stations and focused on a variety of minor tasks.

Chainer looked up. "Where do we sleep?" he asked.

"They've fitted out a few rooms," said Duggan. "Probably where the Ghast officers bunked."

Chainer nodded and returned to what he was doing. Duggan took his own seat and tried to busy himself with the onboard systems. It only took a few minutes to realise he was wasting his time. He'd not used these older interfaces in many years, but for some reason they were still as fresh in his mind as they'd ever been. He sighed and looked at his wrist for the watch he no longer wore. It was going to be a long trip.

# CHAPTER THIRTY-ONE

AS DUGGAN FEARED, the days dragged slowly by and each one which passed brought them closer to an uncertain fate. Duggan hated the helplessness of being unable to face the coming challenge. He knew he should savour the time, since it could be the last remaining to him. He'd told himself similar things in the past and it had never been enough to alleviate the boredom of travel - Duggan would always be a man who preferred to arrive, rather than depart.

Time seemed to pass gradually, yet its progress was inevitable. Twenty-eight days become twenty, then ten and then seven. With excruciating slowness, the seven days were reduced to one, until all that remained was a short time before the *Ransor-D*'s planned arrival at the Ghast home world of Vempor. The crew were rested and at their posts, awaiting the Cadaveron's emergence from lightspeed.

"We know absolutely nothing about Vempor, right?" asked Chainer for the dozenth time since they'd left Pioneer.

"The Ghasts won't allow us near any of their worlds as a

condition of the ongoing peace negotiations," said Duggan. "I can understand why."

"So, they're going to be pretty angry when we show up out of nowhere," said Chainer, again for the dozenth time.

"We'll have to handle it, Lieutenant," said Duggan. "There's no point in trying to make predictions about this. Once we arrive, there'll be a short time during which we will attempt to gather the information requested of us."

"I'm not sure what I want to find. Nothing would be better than something," said McGlashan.

"If we find sign of Dreamers, I imagine it won't be long until the ESS *Crimson* turns up in Vempor's orbit, with the Planet Breaker refitted," said Duggan. "I can't imagine either the Space Corps or the Confederation Council will be willing to sit back if they think those two races are collaborating against us. Far easier to neutralise one threat quickly – a lesson they've learned the hard way."

"If we find nothing then there'll be a few insincere apologies about a rogue captain and his crew seeking to overturn the peace process?"

"We're meant to be glory-seekers, not peace-breakers" said Duggan. "We're here to show off to all and sundry how brave we are for facing the Ghasts alone."

"We'll either be shot down by the Ghasts or thrown to the wolves by our own side," said Chainer. He raised his hand to acknowledge he'd been made aware of the threats long ago.

"We know the score," said Duggan. "From now on, we play it by ear and hope we can somehow obtain a good outcome."

"I really hope we get a clear look at the surface and find nothing unexpected," said Breeze.

"That's what I'd prefer," said McGlashan, repeating her stated view. "It'll still leave questions unanswered."

"Let's not worry about the aftermath before we've arrived," said Duggan. "I want everyone on top form for the task ahead."

"It'll not be long," said Breeze. "I've got a peak arrival likelihood of fifty minutes from now." There was a rumbling, which caused one or two of the retrofitted consoles to buzz loudly. "Well damnit, we've just exited lightspeed."

The news caught Duggan off guard. He sprang into action. "Give me a sensor scan of the vicinity. I want to know what's about. Prepare countermeasures against possible attack."

"We've come in pretty close," said Chainer. "Large sun, seven planets. The middle one is above average in size with surface patterns indicating the presence of life forms."

Duggan didn't wait to hear anything more. He pushed the *Ransor-D* to maximum velocity. "We're hardly making a thousand klicks per second," he said angrily.

"We've benefitted from that before," McGlashan reminded him. "Lots of wasted space in these old models where they could have fitted engines."

"Nine minutes until we reach a high orbit," said Chainer. "I'll have a good chance of gathering what we need from twenty thousand klicks up."

"Any sign of alarm?" asked Duggan.

"Nothing yet. There are two small objects between us and the planet – they're moving slowly. Civilian transports I'd guess."

"What can you see on the planet?"

"It's heavily built up on the exposed side, sir. There might be more than twenty billion Ghasts living here."

"We're sending this data back, aren't we?" asked Duggan, unwilling to leave it to chance.

"Yes, sir, though there's nothing much to tell yet. The surface is too crowded to make much sense from this distance."

"Commander McGlashan, please assist Lieutenant Chainer

until I say otherwise." She nodded in response. McGlashan had once been a comms officer and she'd spent a couple of years assigned to that role.

Duggan tapped into one of the sensor arrays and fed the image onto the bulkhead screen. It showed a planet covered in mighty oceans, with comparatively little land mass. He zoomed in and saw the signs of vast, sprawling cities, which covered huge areas of the surface. There was one large continent visible and this too was covered in cities - they showed as irregular grey-white shapes, with mottled greens spreading away.

"Vempor," said Duggan quietly. The original home of mankind's once-deadliest enemy.

"Something's pinged us," said McGlashan.

"What was it?"

"It wasn't hostile. I think it's one of their ground bases querying our arrival."

"I wonder how long until they realise who we are," said Duggan.

"The ship has sent a response," said McGlashan. She held her hands out to show it wasn't something she'd intended. "The Cadaveron must have a system to respond automatically to signals from its base or other Ghost warships."

"A friendly handshake," said Duggan. "They must be aware there's something amiss – that we shouldn't be here."

"I've located two areas on the surface which may be military bases, sir," said Chainer. "They're damned big."

"Are they scrambling to meet us?"

"There's one gravity drive burning hot. Otherwise, nothing."

"If the *Ransor-D* has provided the correct response to base, they might not have realised yet."

"The response will surely have contained encoded information specific to the ship," said Breeze.

"You'd have thought," said Chainer. "There's no sign of alarm yet. No, here we go - perhaps I spoke too soon. There's someone hailing us."

"Ignore them," said Duggan.

"He's quite insistent," said Chainer a few moments later. "The shipyard technicians have installed the language modules on our ship and the instructions we're receiving are very clear. The Ghasts want us to stop pissing about and tell them who we are."

"I don't think that's wise," said Duggan.

"There are other signs of activity on the surface," said Chainer. "Seven more engines have lit up. Some big, some small."

It was the expected response. Duggan clenched his jaw, partially relieved to have had even this short respite before the Ghasts became alarmed.

"Got twelve engines in total now. One is certainly an Oblivion. The rest are smaller – mostly Kravens."

"It doesn't matter since we're not going to fire at them," said Duggan.

"Four minutes till we can establish a suitable orbit," said McGlashan.

"Can you pick up much surface data from here?"

"Bits and pieces, sir," said Chainer. "We're logging the top-level details as we go and sending them to the monitoring station."

"Two Ghast vessels have left the surface of the planet," said McGlashan. "Kravens, I think."

The image of Vempor gradually increased in size on the bulkhead screen. Previously unseen details were resolved into shapes of huge structures, while areas of green became a patchwork of fields. Farming was still a vital industry within the Confederation and it was no surprise to find the same on this Ghast planet. There were some things technology couldn't entirely replace.

The Cadaveron had been fitted with a huge number of extra

sensor arrays and the data they gathered streamed into the core's memory banks. Duggan kept a close eye on the utilisation. "Any sign of us choking yet?" he asked.

"Not a chance, sir. We're hardly tickling our available capacity. We could gather at ten times our current rate without concern. When we get closer we'll see if the comms can send it off quickly enough."

A number of circles appeared on Duggan's tactical display. He didn't know what colour the Ghasts used for friendlies, but the Space Corps equipment showed the inbound ships as green circles. The largest dot moved faster than the others – an Oblivion battleship had been sent to investigate. Other ships appeared on his screen, some coming from the dark side of Vempor. Duggan counted them at fifteen in total.

"How many orbits will you need, Lieutenant?"

"As many as you can give me, sir. The more time I have to look, the surer we can be."

Duggan checked how far away they were from the planet. They were approaching a distance of twenty thousand kilometres and he adjusted their approach to ensure they'd come into orbit heading in a direction which would allow the first circuit to cover as many of the populated areas as possible. The Oblivion had almost reached them and it, too, changed course in order to follow the *Ransor-D* at a few hundred kilometres away.

"Think they'll fire at us?" asked Breeze.

"Definitely," said Duggan. "Keep your fingers crossed we can find what we need before they think it's necessary."

"Let's have a quick look at what we've got," said Chainer. The bulkhead view split in two. The left-hand image displayed a feed of the surface beneath. To the right, the Ghast Oblivion shadowed them, keeping exactly parallel to their course. The clean lines of the battleship were marred by pits and scars caused by strikes from missiles and particle beams. Duggan had to do a double-take when he saw what it was.

"The *Dretisear*," he said.

# CHAPTER THIRTY-TWO

"WE'RE BEING HAILED AGAIN, SIR," said Chainer. "This time from the battleship."

"Who is it speaking?"

"It's Nil-Far. He wants to know what the hell we're playing at."

"Maintain silence," said Duggan.

"He wants to know why we've come to Vempor instead of the prearranged meeting place."

"Sounds like our secret is out," said McGlashan.

"Have we found anything from the surface scans?" asked Duggan.

"Nothing that springs out as unusual. We're gathering sights, sounds and thousands of emission types. It'll take me a while to make sense of the raw data."

"We don't have a lot of time, Lieutenant. Once we've found what we've come for, I'm going to surrender the ship."

"I'll tell you anything of significance, sir."

Duggan kept the Cadaveron on its course, wondering how long until the Ghasts decided enough was enough. They'd already held fire for longer than he dared hope. In a way it was a hopeful sign – if the Ghasts intended treachery, they would have destroyed the heavy cruiser already.

"It's Nil-Far again. He's asking to speak to you. They are prepared to launch missiles at us."

"Talking might buy us some time," said Duggan. "Patch him through on the speakers."

The connection was made. "Captain John Duggan, you are a long way from the place we'd expected to meet." There might have been the subtlest hint of anger in the Ghast's words.

"We've brought your warship," said Duggan.

"So I see. You were not invited to our world. It was agreed in the first week of peace negotiations that your Space Corps would not come to any of our planets."

Duggan took a deep breath. There was no doubt Nil-Far had already heard the pre-planned response about maverick captains taking matters into their own hands. He didn't want to jeopardise the Space Corps' position by saying otherwise, but he wanted to see if the Ghast would offer up more information about what had occurred on Trasgor.

"I have seen things which throw doubt over the Ghast commitment to peace," he said.

"What have you seen?"

"Ghasts on a Dreamer world."

"The pyramid," said Nil-Far. "Are you convinced we will always be your enemy?"

"I would prefer to be sure before I accept there is no hope of peace."

"You have come here seeking evidence of treachery? There is none to be found."

"Without certainty there will never be trust."

"You will find no answers here John Duggan, only more questions."

"I thought the Ghosts took pride in speaking the truth."

"We do and I have told you no lies."

"You may not have told lies, but you evade the truth by refusing to answer the questions, or giving only partial answers. Amongst humanity, that is tantamount to lying."

"Will you land the *Ransor-D* and hand it over peacefully?"

"I will not fire upon your spacecraft," said Duggan.

"Now who is giving incomplete answers?" asked Nil-Far. He made a sound which may have been laughter.

"He's gone," said Chainer.

"Keep scanning," said Duggan.

"We're not going to stop?" asked Breeze.

"Not until we're done. We didn't expect to be greeted with open arms."

"We didn't know *what* to expect," said McGlashan.

"There's something strange happening on the AI core," said Breeze, raising his voice to be heard over the others.

"What's wrong?" asked Duggan, frowning.

"I don't know. The utilisation gauges are jumping all over the place."

Duggan checked their speed and saw a problem immediately. "We're slowing down."

"The core is getting flooded with data," said Breeze. "It'll affect most things onboard."

"Whatever's happening, it's holding things up, sir," said Chainer. "The core acts as the conduit for sending the data we're gathering. It's getting patchy."

"You mean we're losing data?" asked Duggan sharply.

"No, sir. It's simply taking longer to send what we're picking up. There's already a five second backlog."

"Can anyone tell me what's happening?"

"I think they're trying to take control of the ship, sir," said Breeze.

Duggan wanted to reject the idea out of hand. Then, he remembered some of the earliest Space Corps warships had been equipped with the facility to take over control of other fleet warships. He vaguely recalled it was intended as a protection against officers who went off the rails and decided to use their warships to commit mass murder - they could be shut down before they caused too much damage.

"You might be right, Lieutenant. Can we stop it happening?"

"Maybe. I'm sorry but I don't have a clue how," said Breeze.

Duggan looked at Chainer and McGlashan in turn. Both shook their heads.

"Twenty seconds backlog on our data stream."

"Can you compress the data?" asked Duggan. "We need to get it back to base."

"I can knock it down to ten percent of its original size if you want. It'll lose some detail and we could end up missing what we're looking for."

"Do it anyway," said Duggan. He stared briefly at one of his screens and found he'd just been locked out of the weapons systems. It didn't matter – they weren't going to get out of this with missiles and disruptors.

Chainer pressed furiously at his console, a look of consternation on his face. "Too late. They've blocked our transmission."

Duggan cursed and suppressed the urge to kick his console in pointless anger. "What's left?"

"The engines have dropped below twenty percent," said Breeze.

"They're not going to let us crash, are they?" asked Chainer.

"I think it's more likely we'll be brought in to land slowly under the control of the *Dretisear*," said Breeze. "They're not going to want a huge crater or mile-high tidal wave that would result from letting us come down without guidance."

Duggan was shortly locked out of each major system on the

heavy cruiser. He tried a few things to get his access back – nothing worked. The control bars would still move, though they no longer affected the direction of the warship.

"I think we're coming to the end of the road," he said.

"Yeah, I can't get anything working over here," said McGlashan. "I can view a few bits and pieces, but they won't respond to my commands."

"Can we get through to the *Dretisear*?" asked Duggan.

"Certainly can, sir. That's something I've not been denied access to," said Chainer.

"Get Nil-Far."

The Ghast spoke almost at once, as though he'd been waiting patiently for Duggan to make contact. "We have control of the *Ransor-D*, John Duggan. We will take it to one of our landing fields and set it down."

"What will happen to my crew?" asked Duggan. "They were obeying my orders."

"Everyone is responsible for their actions," said Nil-Far.

"What will happen?" repeated Duggan.

"I am not sure," said Nil-Far after a pause. "You will be detained for a time. After that, I cannot say."

"Very well," said Duggan. He cut the connection to the battleship.

"He didn't give much away," said Chainer.

"I wouldn't read too much into it," said Duggan. "Keep your fingers crossed that Admiral Teron is as good as his word."

Chainer was too worried to attempt a wisecrack and he simply nodded in response.

"I wonder if we got enough data away to the Space Corps for them to learn something," said McGlashan. "It would be a shame if we were shut down before it could happen."

"At the very least, they'll know a bit more about the Ghast home world. Whether it'll do them any good is another matter," said Duggan. An idea came to him. "Lieutenant Chainer, can we still access the data we gathered?"

"There doesn't appear to be anything stopping us looking," he said. "In fact, we're still gathering. It's like we've been put in a position where we can't escape or do any harm, but are permitted to observe."

Duggan checked their speed again – the *Dretisear* was taking them to their destination at a much-reduced velocity. "I don't know how long until we get to where we're going, so we should make good use of our time. Why don't we analyse what we gathered and see if we can unearth what we came for? Once the Ghasts take this ship from us, there'll be no way to access the data again."

Chainer's expression changed until it showed something akin to eagerness. "I'll give everyone an equal section of the data to view. I usually rely on the AI to flag up points of interest, but sometimes there's no replacement for watching something with your own eyes."

"Let's do it," said Duggan. A series of files appeared on his main screen – they were colossal in size, being a raw capture of everything the warship's sensors had gathered. He didn't hesitate and opened the first one.

# CHAPTER THIRTY-THREE

DUGGAN HAD no idea how long remained until they were marched off the *Ransor-D*. He'd spent the last ten minutes studying video streams of Vempor's surface, whilst trying to identify signs of a Dreamer presence on the planet. Several of his files showed nothing apart from the blue-green of deep oceans and he was able to check through these ones quickly. Some contained high-resolution videos of lush countryside and farmlands. He learned little from these and was left with the impression much of the planet was used exclusively for growing an unknown type of grain. At another time, he'd have permitted himself a minute or two studying it closer.

When ocean and countryside ended, there were cities – vast, neatly-ordered metropolises, which must have been home for tens of millions of Ghasts. The architecture in these cities bore little resemblance to anywhere found within the Confederation – the alien species eschewed concrete and nearly everything was built from metal.

"Domes everywhere," said Breeze. "Some of them are huge."

"I've seen one or two which could house a million people," said McGlashan.

"There's lot of heavy industry," said Chainer. "They're throwing all sorts of crap into the sky. It's no wonder they've got no windows."

Chainer was the man to spot these details and Duggan hadn't even noticed the high levels of pollutants in the air. The Confederation planets had tightly-controlled guidelines on industry and you could go more or less anywhere without fear of having your lungs clogged up with airborne toxins. One or two of the military labs operated under looser rules, though they were required to be many kilometres from populated areas.

"Lots of soot, not much else," said McGlashan. "There's nothing here which suggests the Ghasts are in alliance with the Dreamers."

"They've got more planets than this one," said Chainer. "Each world might set its own rules. We know so little about their politics. So little about anything related to the Ghasts, come to think of it."

"This is the world they first came from," said Duggan. "The data which the Space Corps pulled from the *Ransor-D*'s memory arrays referenced this world as their seat of power. If there's something to find, it's most likely to be here."

"Not definite, though," said Breeze.

"This is where we've come, Lieutenant," said Duggan, dismissing any further talk on the matter.

"We're slowing," said Chainer. "Coming in to land soon."

"What's our destination?" asked Duggan, his eyes not moving from the rolling images on his screen.

"There's a landing area dead ahead. We passed near it when we first arrived."

"We don't have long," said Duggan. "Keep searching."

A few minutes later, the *Ransor-D*'s automatic landing systems kicked in. The warship descended vertically for a thousand kilometres. Below, the Ghast base beckoned. Duggan spared himself a moment to look – it was as though the land had been clad in metal. Dozens of square kilometres of dull silver-grey lay beneath them, completely flat in places and with dome-shaped buildings in others. There were more than a dozen Kraven light cruisers, lined up neatly. A few kilometres away, there were two Cadaverons – they looked subtly different to the others Duggan had seen.

"New models," he said.

"There's no need for them to stop building," said McGlashan. "The Confederation has imposed nothing upon them yet."

"They need to, and soon," said Duggan. "Even if the Ghasts aren't allied to the Dreamers and even if we need them to fight with us, we can't permit them to outgun us again. Not after last time."

The lower they came, the more details were visible. Aside from the spaceships, there were smaller objects moving across the open spaces. Some of these objects gathered around the docked ships and Duggan guessed them to be maintenance vehicles. He was right – there were many cranes, along with other vehicles he didn't recognize. They were of different shapes and sizes, moving about with purpose.

"We could be back on Pioneer," said Chainer. "They aren't far removed from us."

"I never thought they would be," said McGlashan. "If you examined the minutiae, I bet everything would look strange and different. When you pull away and look at the broad picture, the similarities are striking."

"I don't know if that makes me happy or sad," said Breeze.

"It doesn't make me either," said Duggan. "Except to say that it'll be easier to deal with a species which is similar to us than one which is vastly different."

The *Ransor-D* landed, away from the other warships berthed here. There was no perceptible sensation of setting down – the Cadaveron was too heavy to land at anything other than a snail's pace. The outside view was one of activity – vehicles closed in, several of them quite obviously troop transports.

"Here they come," said Breeze.

"The centre boarding ramp is opening, sir," said Chainer.

Ghasts climbed from the transport vehicles. There were dozens of them, dressed in grey uniforms that blended in with their skin. They were armed with heavy gauss rifles and they ran beneath the *Ransor-D*. Duggan wasn't sure if they'd be carrying interpretation modules and he didn't want to be shot because of an early misunderstanding. He opened the bridge locker and pulled out two of the helmets, meaning to activate their translation facilities.

"Sir, you've got to see this!" said McGlashan.

There was something in her voice which made him set the helmets down with a clatter on the floor. He ran past his console to stand next to her. Chainer and Breeze joined him.

"What've you got?" Duggan asked.

McGlashan said nothing and simply pointed at her display.

"Shit," said Chainer. "Is that what I think it is?"

"It can't be anything else," said McGlashan. She called up further details on what she'd discovered. "It's too dense for the sensors to provide an exact reading from the height we crossed over it. The estimate is that it's several hundred years old."

"How long ago did we capture these images?" asked Duggan.

"Not long after the *Dretisear* showed up, sir."

Duggan put a hand on top of his head, rubbing his short-cut hair. "Did we get it away to Monitoring Station Beta?"

"I don't know, sir, I'm sorry."

"I'll find out," said Chainer.

He sprang away and threw himself into his seat. Before he could settle, the door to the bridge opened and Ghast soldiers came inside with rifles levelled. Their grey uniforms rustled and swished as they spread out to either side. Fifteen or twenty of them entered, the shortest of them towering over Duggan. Their expressions were not friendly and there was little mistaking the message behind the gestures they made. Through the bridge door, others were visible, lined up against the corridor walls.

"Stop what you're doing and act friendly," said Duggan to the others.

They did so, taking their hands away from their consoles and remaining in place. The Ghasts didn't relax and kept their rifles steadily aimed. Minutes passed and nothing happened. Duggan asked questions, without getting a response. He pointed towards the spacesuit helmets on the floor and made a careful step towards them. The reaction from their captors made him stop in his tracks.

After another ten minutes, there was movement outside the bridge and another Ghast came through. This one was dressed in the same stiff cloth uniform as the others – just as he had been when Duggan first met with him. The Ghast spoke in short, harsh phrases. When his words ended, they were replicated in the Confederation tongue by a small amplifier badge he wore on his chest.

"You have caused much trouble, John Duggan," said Nil-Far. "Your actions have brought us anger and uncertainty."

"I have fought too long to desire anything other than peace," said Duggan. "I came here to discover if your species is planning an alliance with our enemies. I have acted of my own free will and without sanction from the Confederation. I was asked to hand over the *Ransor-D* in neutral space and I chose to come here."

"You've risked much in your cause," said Nil-Far. There was no reproach in the words. "Tell me – have you found signs of deception?"

Duggan shook his head, not sure exactly what to say. "I don't think so."

"You are not certain?"

"You took over our ship before we had enough time to finish," said Duggan with a half-smile.

"You will have to come with us."

Duggan had already asked what the Ghasts planned for his crew, without receiving any assurances. There seemed no reason to ask again. "We'll come," he said.

The crew were led away from the bridge one-by-one. Each had two Ghast soldiers in front and two behind. Not once did their escorts speak, nor did they drop their guard for a moment. There was no point in resistance and Duggan allowed himself to be taken from the bridge, keeping his eyes fastened on the broad shoulders of the soldier in front.

The four of them were taken to the top of the boarding ramp. Heavy, warm air filled the airlock. It was brighter outside than it seemed from the sensor data and much hotter than Duggan had expected. He idly wondered if Vempor was as hot as this across much of its surface. Heat and pollution would explain why the Ghasts chose to live in sealed domes.

Outside, the feet of humans and Ghasts made little noise on the thick metal ground. Duggan looked around him. He was familiar with the feeling of insignificance that came from standing amongst the gargantuan spaceships of the Space Corps fleet. Here, the feeling was exacerbated somehow, though the Ghast machinery didn't look any larger than its human equivalent. A figure loomed at his side.

"We are taking you there," said Nil-Far, lifting an arm to point at a distant building. It was another dome, over a kilometre away.

"What will happen to us?"

Nil-Far shrugged, a startlingly human gesture. "We'll see, John Duggan."

Duggan was herded towards an opening in the rear of a fifteen-metre-long transport vehicle. It made the Space Corps' designs seem like an indulgence of frivolous bells and whistles, since it was little more than a hollow metal box with a gravity engine. He climbed the high steps and one of the soldiers indicated a nearby metal seat. Duggan sat, breathing the warm air in through his nostrils. Sweat was already running down his spine. The others were in front of him, though none turned to catch his eye.

As the transport headed off, carrying the four of them into the unknown, Duggan's mind spun in turmoil as it searched for an answer to what McGlashan had found on the *Ransor-D*'s sensor feed. There had been a pyramid of black metal, with a base measuring fifteen hundred metres to each side. Buildings surrounded it – enormous industrial complexes with unclear purposes.

The transport came to a halt. In the journey's short time, Duggan had only been able to reach a single conclusion and was unsure if it was even remotely correct. The presence of the pyramid suggested that far from being allied to the Dreamers, the Ghasts and Dreamers were, in fact, one and the same. What this meant, Duggan couldn't begin to imagine, but it had become imperative that he get back to the Space Corps and tell them what he and his crew had discovered on Vempor. One thing was certain – nothing would be straightforward in the months to come.

———

The Survival Wars series continues in Book 4, Fires of Oblivion!

Follow Anthony James on Facebook at
facebook.com/anthonyjamesauthor

## THE SURVIVAL WARS SERIES

1. Crimson Tempest
2. Bane of Worlds
3. Chains of Duty
4. Fires of Oblivion
5. Terminus Gate

29365602R00153

Printed in Great Britain
by Amazon